Hello Love

OTHER TITLES BY KAREN MCQUESTION

For Adults:
A Scattered Life
Easily Amused
The Long Way Home

For Young Adults:
Favorite
Life on Hold
Edgewood (Book One of the Edgewood Series)
Wanderlust (Book Two of the Edgewood Series)
Absolution (Book Three of the Edgewood Series)

For Children:
Celia and the Fairies
Secrets of the Magic Ring

Hello Love

A Novel

Karen McQuestion

LAKE UNION
PUBLISHING

To my beautiful niece, Michelle, who always brings the levity

ONE

The little dog waited, ears rising expectantly with the passing of every car, her eyes never leaving the door. Dan stood and watched her for a second before whistling to break the spell, but she still didn't move. "Come over here, girl," he urged. "No point in waiting."

Anni heard him; he was sure of it. He even suspected she understood every word. She was one smart dog, more intuitive than a lot of people. Anni was a mixed breed, with the floppy ears and nose of a beagle, and the short coat and tan coloring of a dachshund. A mutt by design, but a champion at heart. If Anni knew the futility of waiting by the door, she just didn't want to believe it.

Dan crouched down and rubbed behind her ears, and when she looked up at him with her big, compelling liquid eyes, there was understanding between them. "It's okay, girl," he said. "It's okay."

But it wasn't okay. The idea that Christine was never coming back just wasn't right. His wife had been the hub of their lives; the house had been ingrained with her footsteps, the walls still held echoes of her laughter. And there had been a lot of laughter. But that was before.

Proof of her existence was everywhere: the grocery list stuck to the front of the refrigerator; her jacket on the hook by the back door; the book she'd been reading still askew on the end table, a tasseled bookmark holding her place. He'd flip the kitchen calendar and see appointments written in her handwriting and reminders to visit her former boss Nadine, a difficult woman who'd had a series of strokes and now lived full-time in a medical care facility. Christine was good that way, loyal, always thinking about others. "It's no big deal," she'd say when Dan would call her a saint. But he knew it was a big deal. Most people couldn't be bothered, but Christine wasn't most people.

The funeral had been unreal, a nightmare he hadn't been able to wake up from. Life wasn't supposed to go like this. He'd always envisioned that he'd be the first to die, and with that in mind had made sure there was enough life insurance for Christine and their daughter, Lindsay, to be financially secure. But of course, he'd also imagined that would be far in the future, when they were old. Very old with hearing aids and walkers—not while they were still young, or youngish anyway, Christine only thirty-nine and he a year older.

She would always be thirty-nine now, while he would grow older every day, always alone, every passing year a little further from when they'd been together. The grief came in waves: sometimes so intense it almost kept him from functioning; other times lurking in the background, like a dull headache.

A year. More than a year, really, since she'd been gone. Unthinkable that time kept passing without her. In the evening, Anni still waited by the front door for Christine's return, and whenever Anni was outside, she would wander to the end of the driveway to look down the road. The sight of the dog sitting patiently, watching for the sight of Christine's car, was a real heartbreaker.

Dan understood what Anni was waiting for because he wanted the same thing. If life were fair, any minute they'd hear Christine's key in the lock, and she'd come through the door, just the way she used to. It would turn out that she hadn't really died at all, that there'd been a mix-up at the hospital. Some other patient, one who looked a lot like her, had died, while Christine had made a miraculous recovery. *You thought I was dead?* Christine would say incredulously, dropping her purse to the floor. They'd laugh and then cry and finally feel terrible for the other family, the one who'd been on the other end of the mix-up—those poor people who'd really lost a mother and wife, but didn't know it yet. Dan knew the pain those people would feel when they found out the truth.

The day after Christine had died the seasons changed, like nature itself had acknowledged her passing. Summer was over. The autumn air was brisk, the leaves changing color before dropping to the ground. Winter loomed ahead.

There was a time when dinner on the table at six o'clock was a given. Now he couldn't remember if he'd eaten that evening. He wasn't hungry, though, so it didn't matter. Lindsay was at a friend's house working on a group project for her psychology class. The house felt empty, the air heavy. His arms hung uselessly at his sides. What did he used to do on weekday evenings back before the funeral? He couldn't remember.

It wasn't really cold enough to light a fire in the fireplace, but it was something to do, so he set to work painstakingly arranging the logs and putting kindling beneath the grate. He crumpled some newspaper and shoved it underneath. Lighting a match, he held the flame to the paper and watched as the fire flickered and spread. Once he was sure it wouldn't burn out, he closed the glass doors. Still facing the door, Anni whined and lowered her body, her nose over her front paws. The sight was like his own grief displayed in front of him.

"Anni!" he called. "Get away from there." It came out harsher than he'd intended, but it got results. Anni got up and wandered out of the front hall. She looked like someone who'd suddenly become homeless and wasn't sure where to go.

Watching her, he felt flooded with regret. "Anni, come here," he said, speaking softly this time. When the dog reached his side, he dropped to his knees and hugged her neck. "I'm sorry, Anni. I didn't mean to yell at you." He closed his eyes and rested his forehead against her side, tears sliding down his cheeks.

———

After his wife's death, time went at a different pace. Dan and Lindsay went to grief counseling sessions to learn a new normal. Life without her still felt wrong, but it was all he had. Eventually he was able to find joy in small things, like seeing Lindsay perform in the high school play or having a productive day at work. He was lonely, though. The worst part was when Lindsay was gone in the evenings. As a senior she had a lot going on—a boyfriend, plans for college, drama club, a part-time job at the local Walgreens. Some days he only saw her in passing.

Without Anni, the hours would have been unbearable. The dog had been a better therapist than the psychiatrist they'd seen. Dan found himself talking to Anni, confiding all his woes and telling her about his day. The dog had a habit of tilting her head when he spoke, as if she were really listening. And at the moments he felt his worst, when he felt so depressed that life seemed pointless, she invariably brought her leash, nagging him to take her for a walk. Something about being outdoors, putting one foot in front of the other, the fresh air all around, always lifted his mood. He and Anni had covered a lot of miles that way, walking the country lane in front of his house before wandering into the woods and fields beyond. He always felt more joyful on the walk home than he did when they first ventured out the door.

Yes, he loved his daughter, appreciated his friends and relatives, and respected the grief counselor, but Anni had done more to heal his sorrow than all of them put together.

TWO

Andrea wanted to believe today was the day life would change for the better, but she was afraid to get her hopes up. She stared out the passenger-side window and watched as the suburbs melted into farm fields and woods. They'd gone by fields of meadow grass and cow pastures, all of them ringed by thick clusters of trees. Even if the day came to nothing, it was a pretty drive anyway, the leaves in full autumn glory, red and gold and yellow. "It's beautiful out here," Andrea said, turning to her friend Jade. "Peaceful."

"Yeah, if you like being in the middle of nowhere," Jade said, tapping her fingers on the steering wheel.

"I like it. I'd love to live out here," Andrea said, admiring the houses with their clapboard siding and covered porches. Most of these places were five or ten acres, enough for the residents to play at farming, but not enough to do it for a living. Some of them just liked country life, fresh air, peace and quiet. When she'd been married, before they built their house, she'd wanted to look at houses out here, but her husband, Marco, wouldn't consider it. It would be a half-hour commute, maybe more in winter, he'd pointed out. Besides, the people were probably hicks.

While the radio played a catchy pop tune, Jade flipped on the turn signal with a dramatic flourish and veered onto a side road.

Jade did everything with flair. She gestured with gusto when telling a story and greeted everyone she met with a dazzling smile. Her speech was littered with hyperboles. Everything was "awesome" or "amazing" or "life-changing." From the top of her curly red hair to the tips of her sequined shoes, everything about her was extreme. She was a rare thing in America, a large girl who thought she looked perfect. Jade enjoyed good food, good drinks, and a hearty laugh. Her default mood was happy. Yet she could be completely sympathetic when the need arose. When Andrea's marriage had fallen apart, she'd had to tell Jade, "You were right about Marco."

Anyone else might have been smug. Anyone else might have said, "I told you so," but not Jade. "I didn't want to be right," she'd said, and the sorrow in her voice exactly matched how Andrea felt.

After that, Jade had given Andrea a pep talk to boost her self-esteem. "It's his loss," she had said, and went on to list all of Andrea's virtues: her quick wit (something Marco had never appreciated); her straight brown hair with natural highlights; her intelligence, dimples, great laugh, and perfect skin. "And you do that shy smile thing that men love," Jade added, dipping her head to one side and slightly lifting the corners of her mouth to illustrate. Andrea appreciated the compliments, but still felt unworthy.

And now they were driving out into the boonies to attend some weird ceremony for the kind of people who believed in druids and fairies and whatnot. If anyone else had suggested going to this woo-woo event, she wouldn't have agreed to do it. But Jade had been persuasive. She'd gone to this very ceremony the previous year and swore that it changed her life, putting everything in perspective. It had, she said, made her life purpose crystal clear. Her eyes sparkled when she told Andrea, "You will be blown away. I promise you. It just confirms what I've always thought about how interconnected the universe is." That was one of Jade's big things. She was always looking for signs that things were meant to be. Every coincidence was proof of the way the universe was interconnected. Andrea listened, but wasn't entirely convinced. Sometimes coincidences were just coincidental.

Andrea watched as the road became asphalt, lined on either side by deep drainage ditches. "What's the name of this thing again?" she asked, turning away from the window.

"It's called the Create Your Own Future Workshop."

"Hmmm."

"I know what you're thinking," Jade said. "You think it sounds like a load of crap."

This was exactly what Andrea had been thinking. It was uncanny how Jade picked up on these things. There was no point in lying. She might as well agree. Andrea laughed and said, "Something like that. But I'm here, right? Present, accounted for, and prepared to be blown away."

"Atta girl!" Jade said. "Way to keep an open mind."

That was another thing about Jade. She always had an open mind. She'd gone to this workshop last year and swore her new boyfriend and job promotion had been a direct result. Andrea wasn't so sure, but she was willing to give it a shot. "How long is this thing going to last?"

"Not too long. No more than two hours, anyway."

They pulled off the road onto what looked like a gravel parking lot just off a barren field. The car bumped as it went over ruts, and Jade pulled into a space next to a Mercedes. Ahead of them a group of middle-aged women clustered together. Off to one side, a covered park pavilion sheltered several picnic tables.

"This is it?" Andrea asked, surveying the crowd. She and Jade were clearly the youngest ones there. All these middle-aged women looking for a quick fix for their lives. Gullible, that's what they were.

"Yep. We're here." Jade turned off the engine and gathered up her bag. She got out of the car and Andrea followed, confused.

"Where's the building?"

"There's no building. It's all outdoors. We're communing with Mother Nature." She gave Andrea a good-natured jab. "Relax, it's going to be fun."

Jade made her way around clusters of women with Andrea on her heels. When they got to the front, they found the organizer, Martina Dearhart, holding a clipboard. "Name?" Martina asked, smiling benevolently. Andrea had checked out Martina Dearhart online. In person she looked exactly like her photo, right down to the flowing silvery-gray hair and the loosely belted purple dress, its fabric draped around her arms and floating to the ground. The multiple silver bracelets adorning each wrist jangled when she lifted her hands.

"Jade Belson and Andrea Keller," Jade said, speaking for both of them. Behind them, small groups of women chatted quietly.

Martina checked off their names and then looked up at Jade, her brow furrowed. "You were here last year, weren't you?"

"Yes," Jade said, smiling.

"And things have worked out well for you." It was a statement, not a question. Martina looked pleased.

Jade nodded, her curly hair bouncing. "Like a charm! I know it's going to help Andrea too. I had to drag her here, but I told her you were the real deal and that this workshop would change her life. Believe me, she's a skeptic."

"Welcome, Andrea," Martina said. "I'm glad you're here."

They were the last to check in, as Andrea discovered when Martina pulled a mouth organ out of her pocket and blew into it, making one sweet, loud note. After she'd gotten everyone's attention, Martina said, "Since we're all here now, we can begin." She ushered them to a space farther back from the road and all twenty women followed, tramping down tall grass as they went. When they reached a clearing, Andrea saw a fire pit surrounded by a large log circle. The pit wasn't currently burning, but the darkened remains and smell of burnt wood indicated that it had been used recently. "Sit, everyone, sit!" Martina urged, gesturing to the logs, and the group followed orders, sitting on the rough logs, their legs awkwardly positioned, their designer handbags balanced on their laps or set down on the ground. "I'm Martina Dearhart, your workshop leader today. I'm a licensed therapist, working mostly with women in crisis. Let's go around the circle, shall we, and introduce ourselves."

One by one, they each gave their names and their reason for being there. Many of the women were getting over the death of a loved one, but Andrea was relieved to see she wasn't the only one getting over a divorce.

"Let's start with a prayer, shall we?" Martina motioned for the women to join hands. "We'll form a mystical circle. Together we're a force to be reckoned with. Now bow your heads and we'll begin."

Out of the corner of her mouth Andrea sputtered to Jade, "You didn't say anything about a prayer."

Jade shushed her. "Hang in there."

Even though they were supposed to have their heads bowed, Andrea snuck a peek and saw that Martina's face was lifted heavenward. Her expression was serene. "I'm gathered here today with a collection of fabulously lovely women, all of them wanting to fill a void in their lives. All of them longing to achieve what it takes to be their best, most authentic self. On their behalf, I ask that their requests be considered and granted, and that the changes within lead to external changes in their lives. Oh Heavenly Father, goddess mother, spirits of the universe, let our vibrations be positive and our actions harmonious. We will watch for your signs and proceed confident in the knowledge that everything happens for a reason." She raised her arms, and around the circle the women followed suit, grasping hands until they'd made the points of a crown. "Amen!"

"Amen!"

"Amen!"

"Hallelujah!"

Arms dropping, hands releasing, the women lost their physical connection, but the energy in the group had heightened. Andrea shot another look at Jade and raised an eyebrow questioningly. *Oh Heavenly Father, goddess mother, spirits of the universe, let our vibrations be positive and our actions harmonious*? Jade frowned and flashed her a just-go-with-it look.

Once Andrea gave in to the woo-woo-ness of the occasion, she found herself melting into it. There was singing, complete with tambourines, and an opportunity for them to take a turn to tell their story, if they so desired. Andrea did not desire a turn of her own. Who wanted to hear another sad story about a defective wife whose husband had left her for a younger, prettier woman? It was nobody's business, frankly. And besides, she didn't think she could talk about it without crying, and she hated crying, the way her face got so blotchy and red and her nose began to run. Not happening.

It occurred to her, as she listened to each story in turn, though, that there were a lot of brave, strong women in this group, and she felt a flush of shame recalling how she'd judged them when they'd first arrived, thinking they were middle-aged, middle-class sub-urbanites looking for magical solutions to their almost certainly insignificant problems. She'd been so wrong. One by one, the women revealed tales of tragedy that would have kept Shakespeare busy. Problems so seemingly insurmountable that Andrea wondered how some of these ladies got out of bed in the morning.

There was depression and divorce and cancer and disaster. One woman's house had burned down three years earlier. "It was horrible, so horrible. But this is the lucky thing," the woman said, twisting her hands. "We all got out safely. It was a miracle, truly." She nodded her head. "But I still smell the smoke at random times. It's only my imagination, but it makes me crazy. That's why I'm here today. I want to not smell it anymore. I want it *gone*. I want to be able to move on." She looked down at her shoes, her voice cracking. "I know it seems silly."

But it didn't seem silly to any of them.

When the last participant had spoken, Martina cued a round of applause for everyone there. "And now," she said, when the clapping had died down, "for the most important part of today's session. Letting the universe know what we want. Making our wishes known." She approached the lady whose house had burned down and said, "I don't want to cause you any pain, but usually we write out our wishes, make a bonfire, and burn them, but if that's a problem, we can think of some other way to release them into the universe."

"Oh no. I'll be okay." The woman's face broke into a sly grin. "A fire here wouldn't bother me. You can't do it anywhere near my house, though," she added, which brought a few laughs from the group.

Martina handed out large index cards, two apiece. As she distributed them, she called out, "For now, just hang on to these. I'll be giving you directions in a minute. This is a simple exercise, but it can be life-changing if done right, so I'll need your complete attention."

THREE

Down the road, Dan saw the squad car in front of his house and felt his heart thump against his chest. This couldn't be good. All he could think of was his daughter, Lindsay. He'd just made a quick trip to the grocery store to pick up a few items. What could have happened in that short a time? Different possibilities ran through his mind as he pulled his truck into the driveway and raced toward the house. Through the open doorway he saw an officer in the front hall, his daughter right behind him, and he exhaled in relief. She was still alive, so everything was okay. Whatever it was, it couldn't be too bad.

"Dad!" Lindsay's face was tear-stained. "I've been trying to call you!" Frustration, that's what he heard in her voice.

"I'm sorry. I didn't have my phone on." He addressed the cop, a young guy who didn't look entirely at ease in his grown-up uniform. "What happened?" The guy didn't look like he could enforce much of anything, much less the law.

"It's Anni. She's gone," Lindsay blurted out.

Dan ran his hand through his close-cropped brown hair. "What do you mean, she's gone?"

"It was only for a few minutes. I just let her out to pee and I was texting Brandon, so I didn't check on her right away and she wandered off and went down to the end of the driveway, you know how she does that." Dan knew. Even now, more than a year later, Anni still watched for Christine. "I saw a car stop right by her and I opened the door to yell for her to come back." Her breathing was ragged; she could barely get the words out. "I'm so, so sorry, Dad. I saw it happen, but I couldn't stop it." Lindsay gulped. Tears poured down her face, and the sick feeling Dan had when he'd first seen the police car was back.

He was afraid to ask, but he had to know. Part of him thought he already knew. It had to be that Anni had been hit by the car and was dead. "What happened?"

"Your dog has been stolen, sir," the young officer said.

"Stolen?" Dan looked at Lindsay, who nodded in confirmation. He held his arms out and his daughter walked in, burying her head in his chest. She was too far gone to talk, her chest heaving with sobs. "Who would steal my dog?"

The cop read off his notes. "Apparently at two thirty p.m., a dark-colored, four-door sedan stopped, blocking the entrance to your driveway. A young male dressed in a dark jacket or sweat-shirt, either black or navy blue, and wearing a baseball cap, got out of the vehicle, grabbed your dog, placed it in the backseat, and drove off."

"Her," Dan said, feeling the blood run from his face.

"What?"

"Anni. She's a *her*, not an *it*."

"Oh, I'm sorry. And I'm sorry about your dog. I'm new at all this," he said. He did sound new, and unsure too, like he wanted to help but was clueless how to go from here. Poor guy didn't seem up to the task. It didn't seem right that he was working solo. Didn't police officers always come in pairs? Where was his older, more experienced partner?

"But why would someone take Anni?" Dan said. "She's not a purebred. Could it be kids playing a prank? Maybe someone from your school?" He addressed the question to the top of Lindsay's head.

She pushed away from him, rubbed her eyes, and swallowed. "No, this guy was older, I think. He had another guy in the car and they were playing really loud music. Some heavy metal. I didn't recognize the song." She pointed outside. "The bastard," she said bitterly. "He didn't just put her in the backseat, he threw her in really hard and hurt her. She made that yelping noise like she was in pain. I ran after them screaming my head off, but they were all the way down the road by the time I got to the mailbox. I saw them throw a bottle out the driver's side, and I saw Anni's little face looking out the back window. I'm so sorry, Dad. I know I should have watched her better."

"It's not your fault, Lindsay. You didn't do anything wrong." Dan spoke to the officer. "Does this happen sometimes? Dogs get taken and turn up again soon? Like kids taking a car for a joyride?"

He shook his head. "I guess it's possible, but I've never heard of it happening, at least not around here."

"But it could be a prank, right?"

"Sure, it could be." He shuffled his feet uncomfortably. "I'll ask the other neighbors on this road and see if anyone else has heard anything."

"What about the bottle?" Dan asked. "You could check it for fingerprints."

"It was an empty bottle of Jim Beam," Lindsay said. "I found it in the ditch and picked it up with a plastic bag so they could take it to the lab."

"Your daughter gave me the bottle, sir. I will be turning it in with the paperwork." The look on the cop's face told Dan there was no lab, and even if there had been, a stolen dog wasn't a top priority. He referred back to his notes. "The description your daughter gave me is that Anni is about thirty pounds, with a reddish-orange coat. Mostly one color with a light-colored streak on her nose and underside. Mixed breed, some beagle. She's wearing a collar and identifying tags. She said she doesn't bark much, and is eight years old. Do you have anything to add to that?"

Dan thought. "Her collar is red and her name, Anni, is stitched right into the collar. She's well behaved and knows her name."

The police officer dutifully added these details. "Very good, sir."

"When she does bark, it sounds really cute," Lindsay said, sniffing. "Not yappy, just sort of short and crisp, like she's talking."

"Okay." The officer nodded, but he didn't write it down.

Dan asked, "So what's your plan to recover Anni?"

The cop shifted his stance and closed the notebook. "I'll ask around and we'll have our eyes and ears open."

"That's it?" Dan couldn't hide his frustration.

"Pretty much. Without a license plate number or more identifying information, there's not a lot we can do," he said apologetically. "I'll leave it up to you to file a missing pet report with the Humane Society. It's too bad your dog wasn't microchipped. That would help if she's found far from home."

Dan had wanted to get her microchipped, but Christine didn't like the idea. Now he wished they'd done it anyway. "Thanks, Officer," he said. "If you hear anything, anytime, day or night, please let us know."

Dan and Lindsay stood in the doorway and watched as the squad car drove away. She said, "Daddy, I'm really sorry." The despair in her voice was heartbreaking enough, but the fact that she'd called him "Daddy" made it even worse. She hadn't called him that in years.

"Get your jacket," he said. "I want to drive around and look for her."

FOUR

Andrea stared down at the two large index cards in her hand. So many narrow lines on each one. She was supposed to fill these with words? All around her, women were digging into their purses, fishing for pens. Jade found two of them and handed one to Andrea without saying a word.

When everyone had their cards, Martina said, "I'd like each one of you to think about what you really want in the foreseeable future. What will enrich your life? A better job, help around the house, a new relationship? Think about where you'd like to be a year from now and use every bit of your imagination to visualize it. You'll need to do this with a serious intent if you want to make your wishes your reality."

She continued, "What we're going to be doing today is placing an order. Let me give you a real-world example. Say you're at home and you want something, like a book, so you go online and order it from Amazon. Two days later, the book you ordered is in a box on your front porch. What if you'd just thought, 'I *wish* I had that book,' but you didn't do anything else? Would it be on your porch two days later?" A few ladies shook their heads. "No, it would not. Because you didn't put in an order. Think of all the times you've said, 'Why isn't this happening for me?' or 'I want this,' and nothing ever changes. Without placing your order, you're just saying words that circle in the air. You need to let the universe know your wants, your wishes, your intentions. I'm not talking about something materialistic like a Lamborghini. Just what you need to be a happy, fully realized person."

The words poured out of Martina faster and faster, her enthusiasm spilling out as she talked. "Who knows? Maybe the very thing you've been wanting has been circling around you the entire time, just waiting for you to call its name. So it's time to say 'hello, love!' or 'hello, new job!' or 'hello, energy' or whatever it is you need to become fulfilled. Someone is going to get it. Why not you?"

"So this is like that attractions book?" one woman called out. "Because I've been trying that, but it didn't work."

Martina pursed her lips. "I think I know the book you're talking about, but this is different in that it isn't dependent on a belief or an attitude. You can secretly think this is all hogwash and it will still bring results, as long as you put it out there in a positive way." She went on to explain that this was based on scientific principle—physics and the study of small particles. Every cell in your body, she said, was a quark, a sort of vibrating string. And through their thoughts and intentions, human beings had an almost magnetic power to attract similar strings out in the universe. As the number and intensity of these attracted strings build, a critical mass is reached and the want, whatever that may be, comes into being. "Most of us are more powerful than we know. We are each in charge of our own vibrating energy."

Andrea looked around to see how the others were reacting to this pseudoscience. Most of the group was nodding along. Only one other participant had a dubious expression on her face. A different woman raised her hand. "So are these vibrating energies the reason why people say we're all connected?"

Martina nodded. "Exactly. And we can use that connection to make our wishes a reality. The key is to be specific, but still open to different possibilities. Sometimes you'll find that you'll get what you need, but it doesn't come in the way you'd hoped. For instance, you might want a new job because you hate your boss and your work is tedious. If the mean boss leaves the company and you get a promotion to a position you like better, you'll have achieved your goal without changing jobs. Not what you asked for, but exactly what you needed. When life goes the way it's supposed to, everything falls into alignment."

A woman on the opposite side of the circle raised her hand and asked, "So what exactly do we write?"

"You're placing an order," Martina said. "Start off by writing, 'I am ordering . . .' at the top and then go on from there. Be specific."

Jade nudged Andrea and said, "Get writing. Time to write down what you want in a man. And you might want to ask for a new job too, while you're at it."

"I don't mind my job," Andrea said quickly. Losing a husband and a house was bad enough; she didn't think she could cope with more change in her life.

"Really?" Jade said. "Because working for Tommy McGuire would make me crazy. You sit alone in that office day after day. I'd go insane."

"Well, I don't mind it."

"Okay, then. Just order a new man."

That's what Jade had done the year before, and only a month later, she'd met Matt, who Andrea had to grudgingly admit seemed perfect for her. Both of them had boundless energy and goofy personalities. They made each other laugh. Matt was handy around the house, liked to cook, and had good manners. He wasn't career oriented and didn't seem good with money, but neither aspect troubled Jade. When Andrea was around, Matt always included her and didn't make her feel like a third wheel. Jade credited this workshop for leading Matt right to her. "I don't know how it works," she'd said. "It just does."

Andrea sat down on the log and stretched her legs out in front of her. In the middle of the circle, Martina Dearhart arranged logs in the fire pit, wedging brown paper in between each one, and dousing the whole thing with starter fluid. All around, women furiously scratched out words onto the cards. She overheard one woman say, "I'm glad I don't have to believe in this for it to work, because I have my doubts."

Andrea felt the same way, but she was willing to give it a try. She'd sat here for this long; she might as well see it through. She tapped the pen against her lower lip and thought about everything she'd like in a man. Surprising that she was even thinking this way. Even after Marco had left her for a flashy blonde named Desiree, she would have forgiven everything to have him back. And then, when she didn't want him back anymore, she didn't want anyone else. The pain was too new, too raw. The rejection had shredded her heart and self-esteem. Within a few months she was feeling better about herself, but was still guarding her heart. She wasn't eager to date again, but if the perfect guy showed up in her life, well, who knew what she might do? Feeling foolish for even participating in this crazy exercise she wrote, *I am ordering*, and then stopped. What was it that she really wanted? Next to her, Jade was scribbling quickly, probably ordering the perfect wedding and, after that, the perfect baby.

"Remember," Martina called out in her best cheerleading voice, "we're all the stars of our own lives. Let's make it the best production we can!"

Andrea sat for a few minutes, flexing the card in her hand. This whole exercise was ridiculous, magical thinking at its best, she thought, but if nothing else it would force her to set specific goals and that was valuable all by itself. She'd done way too much floundering in her life. Getting on some sort of track might be helpful. And what if it did work? On the off chance that this was the case, she should choose her words carefully. The old adage "be careful what you wish for" rang in her head. Marco was a good example of that. She'd always been the quiet type and found herself attracted to bold, confident people—Jade being one of them. Marco had seemed like just what she needed, with his boisterous, charming ways; a perfect counterpart, she'd thought. What a disaster that had turned out to be. Marco was a selfish man. A selfish, charming, boisterous man. But mostly selfish. Everything was always about Marco.

Martina lit a match and a big whoosh rang out as the flames devoured the paper and began licking the wood. "Time to finish up. Just a few minutes more," she called out. "Remember to be specific in your request, but open to what you'll receive. And feel free to write whatever you want. No one will see it but you."

Most everyone was busy reading over what they'd written. Some of them were putting away their pens, clearly finished. Andrea took the plunge and quickly wrote everything that came to mind. When she was done, she read it to herself: *I'm ordering a man who is kind, considerate, and caring. A real man, not a boy. He has to be taller than me, not interested in playing video games or going to the bar to play pool or darts. He has to want to spend time with me, find me desirable, and really listen when I talk. Please let him be smart, but not in an intellectually superior way.* She scrunched her forehead and gave it some thought, then jotted down one more sentence. *I would like it if he'd get it when I'm joking.*

"It looks like everyone is nearly finished," Martina said. "Am I right?" She smoothed the front of her flowing purple frock and raised both arms. The gesture, accompanied by the light of the fire illuminating her from behind, gave her an otherworldly appearance.

"Yes."

"Finished."

"All done."

"All right then," Martina said. "One by one, I'd like you to step toward the fire, read your card to yourself, and drop it into the flames. Envision your order going straight to the order taker, whoever that may be. Depending on your belief system, it may be God, or the angels, or the universe, or the great beyond. It doesn't matter. Just choose what works best for you, and imagine the order arriving and being put in the queue. I can't guarantee a two-day turnaround with a package on your porch, but I know that all of you will be heard."

When it was Andrea's turn, she decided to get into the spirit of the thing. She shook off her doubts and stepped forward resolutely, read her card to herself, and threw it into the crackling flames. It floated down into the fire, which flared slightly before consuming her words and turning them to ashes. She watched the smoke rise and tried to imagine her order being delivered into capable, caring hands. Maybe next year at this time she would be like Jade, happily connected to a man she loved. She tried to picture her wished-for man, but the image in her head was fuzzy, only an outline, and a second later even that was gone.

FIVE

Lindsay hung out the passenger-side window of the truck screaming Anni's name. She didn't have her seat belt on, something that
would have given Christine fits. Dan too, under regular circumstances. But they were driving slowly enough, fifteen miles per
hour, which felt like a crawl. Dan's reasoning was this: if the guys
that took Anni wanted to flee the area, they could be fifty miles
away by now. More likely, they took the dog as a lark and let her
out somewhere nearby. If that were the case, she might be injured,
lost, or afraid, but she'd come forward if she heard Lindsay's voice.

There were plenty of spots for a wounded or frightened dog
to hide. Drainage ditches, thickets of trees, clusters of shrubbery.
They lived on a country road, in what Christine affectionately
called "the sticks." The long commute to Christine's job in the
city was the only downside, but ultimately she had decided it was
worth it. Dan worked as a plant manager at a microbrewery only
fifteen minutes from the new house, so the move to the country
had actually shortened his drive time.

He and Christine had loved being so close to nature—
cross-country skiing in the winter, long walks in the woods the rest
of the year. Christine had been a gardener and he liked to putter
around with projects, building a deck one year, a gazebo the next.

Their own little patch of paradise. The two of them, plus Lindsay, had been enough. It had all been so perfect.

And Anni had been part of that perfection. Dan had grown up with dogs, but Christine was a cat person who thought a dog would be too much work. She worried about muddy paws and shedding hair, having to give heartworm pills and taking the dog for walks. No, a cat was the best pet, in her mind. Low maintenance, able to stay alone in the house for long stretches of time. So Dan didn't get his dog. The first part of the marriage they'd had a tabby named Whiskers, a big bruiser of a cat who came bounding out of her spot by the window whenever she heard Christine opening the kitty treat packet. "See?" Christine had said teasingly. "She comes when you call her, just like a dog." When the death of Whiskers (old age, but still so sad) coincided with buying this house, he'd started campaigning for a dog. Christine had an argument to counter every one of his reasons, so he thought he didn't have a chance, but on their twelfth wedding anniversary, she'd told him his present was out in the garage.

"Surprise!" Christine had said, indicating a small brown dog lying on a carpet remnant next to the lawn mower. The dog, a medium-size short hair with floppy ears, got up from the carpet square and regarded him with deep-pooled eyes.

He squatted down to pet the dog's head, then looked up at Christine. "This is my dog? To keep?"

Christine grinned. "Yep. She's all yours, if you want her." She clasped her hands together, delighted that she'd pulled off the surprise.

From the second he saw her, he wanted her. He named her Anni because she'd been an anniversary present. The name seemed to fit her sweet disposition. Every dog owner thought their dog was the smartest and cutest, but with Anni it was true.

Initially they'd pretended Anni was his dog, but after a few weeks it became clear that the dog's heart belonged to Christine.

Dan understood this completely because he felt the same way. When Christine died, Dan and Lindsay and Anni had mourned together. And now Anni was gone and Dan couldn't bear to lose her too.

So he drove slowly, scanning each side of the road, while Lindsay cupped her hands around her mouth and yelled out the window. They had to find her. They just had to.

SIX

Andrea was quiet as they drove away from the Create Your Own Future Workshop. She'd only gone to the workshop to humor Jade. It was supposed to be for kicks, but the whole thing had turned out to be completely unsettling. People had so many problems. Houses burning down. Drug-addicted daughters. Mental illness. Financial issues. Cancer. And every day these women got up and did what they had to do because they were caregivers, wives, friends, mothers. There was no curling up in a ball when other people depended on you. These ladies were everyday heroes just doing what they had to do. Andrea couldn't even imagine having to cope with what they did on a daily basis. Life could be overwhelming if you thought about it for too long.

As if hearing her thoughts, Jade said, "When I went last year, it wasn't quite so depressing." Her tone was apologetic. "That group was a lot more fun. We got into a big talk about men and relationships and our jobs. One woman was hilarious. She could have been a comedian. Seriously, it was a laugh fest." She turned onto a country highway. "I'm sorry if this brought you down."

"No, it was okay," Andrea said, giving Jade a small smile. "Not a laugh fest, but interesting. It really puts life into perspective." That was an understatement. Here she was asking for a man who got her sense of humor while another woman was hoping her MRI would show the tumor hadn't grown. "I guess I don't have it so bad after all."

Jade said, "Don't discount what you're going through. Marco was a jerk and you're better off without him, but that doesn't lessen the pain."

"He wasn't always a jerk," Andrea protested mildly. "There were some good times."

"Oh, Andrea." Jade sighed and fiddled with the radio, flipping from station to station. When she found a song by Adele, she stopped searching. Jade was fond of women singers with strong voices and would sometimes belt out a tune along with the radio. Her voice was appallingly bad. If Andrea didn't know better, she'd think Jade was trying to sing out of tune, but that wasn't the case. It made it easy to join in and sing along, because no matter how Andrea sounded, it couldn't be any worse. Today, though, Jade just tapped on the steering wheel in time to the music and Andrea watched the landscape go by.

"What have we here?" Jade asked, stepping on the brake until they were nearly stopped.

Andrea shifted her attention to the road ahead and saw a red pickup truck in their lane. The brake lights weren't on, but the truck was crawling along at a very slow pace. A teenage girl hung out the passenger-side window, yelling something over and over again. It sounded like she was saying, "Annie."

"Someone's kid didn't come home on time," Jade mused. "Little Annie is going to be in a big load of trouble when they finally track her down."

They crept behind the truck another minute before the driver noticed them and waved his arm for them to go by. Jade swung out onto the oncoming lane and swerved around him. As they drove alongside the truck, Andrea caught a glimpse of the driver—a good-looking man no older than forty, high forehead, wavy dark-brown hair. Something about his expression tugged at her. He must have felt her stare because he turned his head; but just before their eyes could meet, they'd already driven past. Andrea swiveled around, but there was too much distance between them to get a good look.

"What?" Jade asked.

"Do you think we should have stopped and offered to help?" Andrea asked, still looking back. Maybe the women's stories from the workshop were still on her mind, but something about the man in the truck and the yelling girl struck her as tragic.

"They looked like they had it under control."

Andrea turned around and sighed. "I guess. She just sounded so frantic. And the man looked . . ."

"Looked what?"

She'd only seen his face in profile and it was just for a moment, but there was anguish there. "He looked sad. Like his whole world was falling apart."

"You got all that in the split second going by?" Jade asked.

Putting it that way, it did sound ridiculous. It was really more of an impression than anything else. Surely she was projecting. "Yeah, it was just something about his expression."

"We could stop and help," Jade said, talking through the problem, "but they'd probably say no, thanks, anyway. I mean, it's not like a lost child would come running to a couple of strangers, am I right?"

Andrea knew the answer Jade wanted to hear. "You are right as usual, my friend."

"Good. Glad to hear it." Jade's lips curved in approval. "You want to get something to eat? I'm kind of hungry."

SEVEN

Dan had trouble falling asleep that night. After driving around for hours, they'd stopped at the Humane Society in the city and reported Anni missing, then picked up Chinese carryout to take home. He and Lindsay had silently eaten dinner at their kitchen table, picking at their egg rolls and sweet-and-sour chicken, both of them hoping to hear the scratch at the door that never came. Finally Lindsay said, "I'm so mad at myself. I can't believe they just took her. I was here and I couldn't stop them." She dabbed her eyes with one of the cheap paper napkins that came with the order. "Those guys were evil. Who would hurt Anni? She's just the sweetest girl ever."

Anger surged up in Dan's throat at the sight of his daughter in pain. He didn't even want to think about what those men had done with Anni. A raw fury, the kind that caused men to kill other men, rose up in him, and he had to force himself to stay steady. "It's not your fault, Lindsay. You did everything right. I'm very proud of how you handled it, calling the police, getting a description of the car."

"No license plate, though," she said, still frustrated. "And I don't know cars at all. I didn't even know what kind it was or how old or anything. The cop kept asking me questions and I had to keep saying, 'I don't know. I don't know.' I felt like such an idiot."

"You did fine," Dan said. "Tomorrow we'll print up posters and look again."

Lindsay smirked. "Really, Dad?"

"What?"

"You want to put up posters? What is this, 1956? Don't you think it would be more effective to put something on Craigslist and Facebook, and call the local media?"

"That was what I was going to say next."

"Right."

But at least he got a smile out of her. Lindsay had told her boyfriend she didn't want to go out that night because she was too upset, so Brandon had come over instead. They'd posted information about Anni online and then turned on the TV, some reality show with competing tattoo artists. The tattoos were secondary to the snarky comments and contestant drama. Periodically Lindsay checked her phone to see if anyone had spotted Anni, but there was nothing but sympathetic comments and promises from friends to watch out for her.

Brandon sat with one unmovable arm around Lindsay's shoulder, and they probably would have stayed on the couch like that all night, but at eleven Dan told Brandon to go home. They'd had a hell of a day and Lindsay needed to get some rest.

Now Dan lay in bed, staring up at the ceiling. He'd left a water bowl on the back porch, just in case Anni came back and he didn't hear her. He'd considered leaving food too, but decided against it, thinking it might attract rodents or raccoons. Dan always slept with his hands folded over his stomach. Christine said if she stuck a lily in his hands, he'd be ready for a funeral home viewing. That was back when they joked about death, when it seemed like something that happened to other people. He couldn't believe he ever thought it was funny.

It took so long to fall asleep that when he had a dream and it took place in his bedroom, it felt more real than usual. He was in bed, hands folded, his eyes fixed on the ceiling, when he became aware of Christine standing in the doorway. His first thought was that she'd gotten up to go to the bathroom or get a drink of water, but then he remembered that she'd died. "Christine?" he said, sitting up.

The dream had woken him. Or was he still sleeping? He rubbed his eyes, and now he was truly awake. Christine wasn't in the doorway. He sat up for another minute or so, confused. He'd been so certain she was there, but of course she wasn't. Wishful thinking had intruded into his dreams.

When he woke up the next morning, his eyes flicked to the doorway, half expecting to see Christine there, and then he remembered that it had been a figment of his imagination. The funeral director had given him a booklet about grief, and one of the things mentioned was how common it was to dream about a deceased loved one. Some believed it was a message from the beyond, while others thought it was one's own psyche doing some self-soothing. Dan had waited for over a year for a dream of Christine and this was the first time he'd even come close.

He was the first one up that morning, which wasn't a surprise. He drank coffee and toasted a bagel for himself. When he heard Lindsay hit the shower, he remembered the Saturday morning tradition they'd had when she was a little girl, and he got out the waffle iron. By the time she came down to breakfast in her bathrobe and slippers, he had a plateful of waffles and a pile of crispy bacon ready and waiting. With Anni gone, she'd been a wreck. Maybe this would help.

"Unbelievable," she said, her eyes wide, taking in the breakfast scene.

"I know," he said, pleased. "I haven't done this in years."

"This is really freaky. Whoa." Her hand raked through her damp hair. "I can't believe it." She pulled a kitchen chair away from the table and sat down with a thud. "I mean, I smelled the bacon, but the waffles too . . ."

Something in her voice worried him. "Are you okay?"

"Dad, you're going to think I'm losing it, but I had this dream last night." Lindsay looked up at him, her palms flat against the table like she was trying to hold on. "And Mom was in it. And she said you would make waffles and bacon for breakfast."

"Really." Dan felt his heartbeat pick up, but he tried to keep his voice steady. He sat next to his daughter and looked her in the eye. "Tell me about it. What else did she say?"

Lindsay gave him a small smile. "In the dream I was in my math class and my teacher, Mr. Freiberg, said I should collect my things and go to the office, that my mom was there. I went down the hall and she was standing by the front entrance of the school, and I was so confused because I thought she was dead. When I asked her why she was there, she said she missed me and just wanted to see me. She looked just like she always did. Before, you know?"

Dan nodded. He knew.

Lindsay continued, "And then I remembered to tell her about Anni and how I messed up, and she said not to worry about it, that we'd get Anni back and that it wasn't my fault."

"What else did she say?"

"Not too much." Lindsay shrugged. "I asked her if this was real, and she said yes. Then she hugged me and said that Dad would be making waffles and bacon for breakfast. There might have been more, but that's all I remember." She blinked back tears. "Do you think it was really Mom talking to me in my dream?"

He nodded. "I'd like to think so." Even if it were only a dream, he envied Lindsay the experience of speaking to Christine, but he didn't begrudge her that. In fact, he wouldn't have had it any other way. "What do you think?"

"I think it was Mom," Lindsay said firmly. "She said you'd make waffles and bacon, and look—here they are." She reached for the syrup. "I think it was her. I think she watches over us and knows what we're doing. And she said we're going to get Anni back too, so that's good." She let out a long breath. "I hope it happens soon."

EIGHT

Weeks had passed since the Create Your Own Future Workshop and Andrea hadn't met any new men at all, unless you counted Cliff Johnson, an old guy who'd moved into the condo across the street a few weeks earlier. The Sunday after Thanksgiving he'd stopped her on the front walkway to introduce himself and chat her up. He explained that trading in his house for a condo made sense after his wife died. "The yard was too hard to keep up and it was kind of lonely all by myself. What do people do for fun around here?" He gave her a toothy grin, his blue eyes peering through thick wire-rimmed glasses.

Andrea stood holding her bag of groceries and inwardly winced. This guy was looking for friends. "The library has a lot of great programs," she said. "Different clubs meet there; they have speakers, discussions." She extricated a finger from under the handle of the bag and pointed. "It's just a few blocks away. Brand-new building, really nice. You should check it out."

"I will," he said, nodding approvingly. "Gotta love a good library. The hub of the community."

Their condo complex was set up like a small village with winding streets lit by old-fashioned lampposts. Each unit was two stories tall, with a small covered porch, and a cobblestone walkway.

They each had a garage, as well as a private patio off the back. She'd bought the condo with the settlement from her divorce. Marco had kept the house, buying out her half with an inheritance from his grandfather. Originally she was going to rent and hang on to the money. A nest egg for a rainy day. But Jade had talked her into buying this condo. Her back patio overlooked a marsh that could never be built on because it was a conservancy, classified as wetlands. "You deserve to have something of your own," Jade had said, admiring the view. "Just think, you can look out here every morning when you have your coffee. What a way to start the day." So Andrea had bought the condo and Jade had been right. The view was magnificent, almost as good as living in the country. Private too. The neighbors generally kept to themselves, but Cliff, it seemed, hadn't gotten the memo.

"It was nice meeting you," Andrea said politely.

Cliff still stood there, wanting to prolong the conversation. "I'm usually pretty quiet," he said. "Let me know if I'm not. I'd hate to disturb you."

"I'm sure you'll be fine," she said.

"Well, I thank you for your time. You're a very kind young lady." He gave her a little salute and headed back across the street to his own place.

It was the closest thing to a compliment from a man she'd gotten lately. Her boss, Tommy McGuire, liked to toss out a "Well done, as usual, Ms. Keller," but with him it was automatic, like someone saying "gesundheit" after a sneeze.

It wasn't always like that. When she'd first started working for him years earlier, he'd plied her with compliments on a daily basis. His last assistant had been so inept that he couldn't believe his good fortune in finding Andrea. Her organizational skills blew him away. Her people skills were unbelievable, he'd said. Her ability to handle things when he was out of the office was unprecedented. She'd overheard him bragging about her on the phone to his cronies.

She quickly found out that if you start to do more than the boss expects, pretty soon he expects you to do more. Eventually she was running the whole office, taking over a lot of Tommy's work.

Tommy had been divorced when she first began working for him, but soon married a gorgeous younger woman. Now, most days he stopped in for an hour or two to check in with Andrea and get the mail. He and the new Mrs. McGuire went on a lot of trips and did a lot of golfing. He'd never looked happier or tanner.

Jade met Tommy when she stopped in at the office one day and they were introduced. He'd plied her with his Tommy McGuire charm, but for some reason she took an immediate dislike to him. "How can you work for that slumlord?" she asked. "And doesn't it bug you that you're the one doing all the work?"

Andrea shrugged, not able to deny any of it. Slumlord? Maybe. It was true that Tommy owned and managed more than a hundred properties around the city, many of them in subpar shape, but he also charged less rent than his competition. "The disadvantaged need a place to live too," he'd explained when she was first hired. "If they want to paint or make improvements, I'm open to reimbursing them for materials, but McGuire Properties is not a charity. We're a business that is all about maximizing profit. And pouring money into old buildings in sketchy neighborhoods is not good business." It wasn't exactly a charitable philosophy, but she could see that it made a certain amount of sense, at least from his point of view. Besides, he paid her significantly more than she'd make elsewhere and when they went out for lunch, he always picked up the tab and tipped well. When the waitstaff saw him coming, they vied to get him seated in their section. Andrea also knew that he gave generously to charities and paid for his niece and nephew's university tuition. He was an enigma—sometimes cheap, sometimes generous. Like most people, Tommy was a mixture of good and bad. She liked the good and could live with the bad.

On this particular Monday afternoon, Tommy had stopped in on his way to the airport. He and the glamorous Mrs. McGuire (she'd opted to wait in the car) were on their way to spending ten days on an island in the Caribbean. While he leaned on one corner of her desk, rifling through the mail, Andrea entered data into the computer. "Anything else I need to know about before I go?" he asked, setting the stack of envelopes down next to the keyboard.

"Well." She paused from her work. "Just one thing. We have a reported 42 at the Berkshire property. The frat boys. I've gotten calls from two different tenants about a barking dog." A 42 was Tommy's code for "unauthorized pet." Some of his buildings allowed pets, and some didn't, but even the ones that did charged extra each month. There was always someone trying to sneak in a pet, usually a cat.

With so many properties, Tommy and Andrea didn't know the names of all the tenants, but the frat boys stood out. First of all, they weren't really boys. They were grown men in their midtwenties, but apparently no one had told them they'd crossed the line into adulthood because they still lived a fraternity lifestyle. Tommy had called them the "frat boys" once to be funny and, in the office, it had stuck. McGuire Properties tolerated them because they were good tenants. They'd lived in the apartment for three years and always paid their rent on time. And since they were in a building filled with other young people, their loud parties weren't usually a problem. But a 42 was something different altogether. A dog that barked when people were trying to sleep made even the most forgiving tenants cranky.

"You know the drill," he said, putting on his sunglasses. "Call them one more time and tell 'em the usual. If they're not compliant, send Stan down with a letter." Stan was the only other employee on the McGuire Properties payroll. His job title was building manager, but he did far more than that, dealing with delinquent tenants, showing available units, making repairs. The only time

Andrea saw him at the office was when he was picking up keys or dropping something off. He was pleasant, but perpetually nervous. He never made eye contact with Andrea and darted out of the office as soon as he had what he needed. Whenever someone violated a rule, Stan delivered official-looking letters that made it sound like legal action would be taken if they didn't comply. Just the threat was usually enough.

Tommy jangled his car keys. "Anything else?"

"No. Just have a good trip."

"Oh, I will, Ms. Keller," he said, twirling the keys around his finger. "Believe me, I will."

Andrea watched through the window as Tommy went out to the car. His wife looked up and smiled as he fastened his seat belt. They laughed as he backed out of the space. Tommy was in his late fifties and the new missus in her midthirties. Originally Andrea had wondered if this was a real love match, or if the new wife was a gold digger, but she'd come to the conclusion that it was true love. Would the McGuire marriage stand the test of time? Who knew? She'd given up trying to predict such things. At one time she'd have bet her life that she and Marco would grow old together, that's how certain she was of their commitment and love. Clearly, her take on such things was questionable.

She looked up the number for the frat boys and decided to try the first number, the guy who'd told her weeks ago that they only had the dog for a weekend. They were watching it for a friend, he'd said. Before she dialed the number, Andrea entered a code so that "McGuire Properties" wouldn't show up on their caller ID. When she got voice mail, she hung up and tried his roommate. This time someone picked up.

"Yello," he answered, his voice booming. In the background she heard sounds of other men talking, and the clanking of machines.

"Hello, this is Andrea from McGuire Properties."

"Yeah?" His tone turned antagonistic. Even though they were on the phone, she reflexively shrank back. There was a good reason she never used her last name when talking to tenants. Everyone wanted to shoot the messenger.

"We've had reports that you and your roommate have an unauthorized pet . . . a dog?"

"Oh *jeez*." He spat out the word. "Who's been saying that? Is it the stoner downstairs? Because I'm telling you, we smell weed in the hall every single day. Every. Single. Freakin'. Day. If anyone should be complaining, it should be us. Secondhand smoke kills, ya know."

Andrea had made hundreds of these calls over the years. She knew the drill. Tenants often played offense, thinking it would throw her off course, but she was too good to let that happen. "I'm calling to let you know you have twenty-four hours to comply with the rules of the building. Your lease specifically—"

"Just a minute." She heard him talking to someone else, his voice faint like he'd pressed the phone against his side. When he came back, he said, "Look, lady, I'm at work right now and I don't have time for this. You tell that stoner if he's going to be making up crap about us, I'm going to beat him so hard his eyeballs will shoot out the back of his head."

"Threatening other tenants is not—" she started, but the phone went click, leaving her stunned. What a jerk. Seriously, what a jerk. Usually tenants begged for a little more time, and pleaded innocent to the terms of the lease. "I don't remember seeing that!" they'd cry. "Please, couldn't you make an exception, just this once?" Oftentimes she had to steel herself against such pleas because it would be so easy to just give in. She wasn't heartless after all. But this jerk? He'd ignored her, threatened another tenant, and hung up on her. Granted, judging from past experiences with the frat boys, the threat was all bluster, but it still was a nasty thing to say.

She wasn't going to let this go.

NINE

Dan pulled his truck into a parking space close to the front of the veterinary clinic. It was the beginning of December and the vinyl-sided building was covered with red and green lights. A wreath festooned with sparkly dog bones hung on the door. Dan glanced over at Lindsay. "Are you ready? Or do you need a minute?"

She'd been quiet the entire trip. Thirty minutes of car silence. No music. No texting. Nothing. He didn't feel like talking either, but they both knew this had to be done.

Lindsay blew out a puff of air. "No. Let's do this."

They'd been home for the evening after a long day of school and work—Dan cooking, Lindsay doing homework at the kitchen table—when Lindsay's phone rang. Dan saw her answer it and watched as her face crumpled at the news. When she silently handed the phone to him, he expected the worst. It was the mother of a friend of Lindsay's, a woman who worked as a tech in a vet clinic. Someone had brought in a stray dog that had been hit by a car. The injuries were so extensive the vet had wound up euthanizing the poor thing. All the while the woman was talking, explaining about the car accident and the old lady who'd brought the dog in, Dan wondered what this had to do with him. It never occurred to him that it might be Anni. "The thing is," the woman said, "the dog looks a lot like yours." She said she had seen the posters he'd posted in the small businesses around town, and when they brought the dog in after the accident, she immediately noticed the resemblance.

There was dead silence while Dan tried to process the idea. "Oh," he finally said, leaning back against the kitchen counter.

"I mean," she backtracked quickly, "it's probably not your dog, but I know if it were me, I'd want to know either way."

She'd gone on to say that if they wanted to view the body, her boss had given permission for them to come that evening. After Dan agreed it was a good idea, they set a time to meet after dinner, and now they were at the vet clinic. After Dan shut off the truck's engine, he asked, "What's the woman's name? The one we're meeting?"

"It's Patrick Dunne's mom." She shook her head. "I don't remember her name."

Luckily, the woman reintroduced herself right away. "Hi, thanks for coming," she said, swinging open the front door as they approached. The clinic had closed for the evening, so they were the only ones there. "I'm Julia Dunne. I'm the one who called."

"Thanks for doing this," Dan said. "We appreciate it." He glanced at Lindsay, who didn't look like she appreciated it at all. The blood had drained from her face, and she was shaking slightly, like she was about to come apart. "Are you okay, honey?"

"I think I need to sit down."

Julia Dunne gestured to the chairs in the waiting area. "I'll get you some water." She left them alone, and Dan guided Lindsay to a seat. When Julia returned, she had a plastic cup of water, which Lindsay took with both hands.

Dan said, "Why don't you just stay here, Lindsay? I can do this." He waited for Lindsay to object, but she just nodded mutely and sipped again from the cup.

Following Julia to the back room, Dan felt the need to explain. "Lindsay's mom died a little more than a year ago and it's been hard on her. She's really been a trooper, but after all that we've been through, losing Anni was devastating for both of us."

"I understand," Julia said, "and I'm sorry to put you through this, but I thought it might bring closure, if it is Anni."

"No, you did the right thing. I'm glad you called."

Julia opened a door at the end of the hall and Dan got a whiff of something antiseptic as she flipped on the fluorescent lights. Open shelves on two sides of the room held bottles of medications and other medical supplies, and in the center, a metal table held what had to be the dog's body, covered by a dark cloth. "Her head was not struck in the accident, so she just looks like she's sleeping." She pulled the cloth back slowly, revealing the top of the head, the floppy, dainty ears, and the sloped snout. The eyes were closed. Julia was right; she looked like she was sleeping.

Dan took in a sharp breath and felt the tears come to his eyes. He hadn't realized how emotional this would be.

"Can you tell, or should I show you more?"

"You don't need to show me any more. I can tell."

When he went back to the waiting area, Lindsay stood up to meet him. "Well?"

"It's not her."

The tension melted from Lindsay's face, and she let out an audible sigh of relief. Her hands clasped together, she looked up at the ceiling and said, "Oh, thank you, God."

TEN

Only a minute after talking to frat boy number two, Andrea had made a decision. She picked up the phone and dialed Stan. After it rang five times, he finally picked up. She said, "Hi, this is Andrea. I was hoping you could deliver a letter tonight to some tenants who work first shift."

But Stan could barely talk and was, he told her, taking a sick day. "Maybe tomorrow?" he croaked. "If my feber goes down."

She could tell by his voice that he'd been sleeping. "Did I wake you up?"

"Yeth." Even listening to him was painful. "I'm really out of it. I took a lot of NyQuil." He let out a raspy laugh that morphed into a hacking cough.

Andrea said, "Go back to sleep and don't worry about it. I'll give you a call in a day or two." After they said their good-byes, Andrea wondered if he'd even remember their conversation. She went back to the computer and found the form for a 42, inserted the date and the frat boys' names, and printed the letter. She stamped it at the bottom with Tommy's signature and tucked it into an envelope. The guy's sneering words still rung in her head: *Look, lady, I'm at work right now and I don't have time for this. You tell that stoner if he's going to be making up crap about us, I'm going to beat him so hard his eyeballs will shoot out the back of his head.*

Who talked like that? Andrea hadn't denied it was the stoner downstairs, and maybe she should have, because it hadn't been him at all. The two girls across the hall had been the first ones to call. Simone, the one who actually talked to Andrea, begged her not to reveal their identity. "We've partied with those guys and they're cool and all," she said. "But why should they get to keep a dog if no one else can? They said she was a stray they picked up by the side of the road, and that was nice of them and all, but dogs aren't allowed in this building. They've had her for weeks and weeks and at first it was kind of cool, but now they don't even take care of Anni and she barks all the time. It's totally against the rules." The whine in her voice reminded Andrea of a girl in middle school. Why should someone else get something if I can't? And then Simone added, "And one time my roommate saw one of them kick her."

"He *kicked* her?" Andrea couldn't keep the horror out of her voice. "And no one reported this?"

Simone must have realized she'd crossed a line, because she said, almost defensively, "Well, it was more like he shoved Anni really hard with his boot. But she made that crying noise dogs make sometimes. I just don't think they should have a dog."

Andrea took a deep breath and started taking notes. "So it's a female dog. Anni? How big is she?"

"I don't know," Simone said. "Not too big." She covered the phone and conferred with her roommate before coming back to say, "Gretchen says the dog is medium-size. Kind of orange-ish like a dachshund, but she doesn't look anything like a dachshund. She's got floppy ears kind of like a beagle, and they keep yelling at her because she craps in the kitchen." She let out a sigh of exasperation. "But you didn't hear any of this from us, okay? Because I don't want those guys mad. They get kind of crazy sometimes. You never know what they might do."

"I would never divulge the names of those who make a complaint," Andrea assured her. "Don't worry, this will be handled in a timely manner. I will use complete discretion."

"Well, okay," Simone said. "As long as you don't tell."

"I won't be telling," Andrea said. "Trust me. It will be taken care of."

If she was determined then, she was even more determined now. There was no way she was going to let this thing go. She usually tried to avoid conflict, but something about this guy really aggravated her and she didn't want to wait until Stan was available. It occurred to her that the frat boys didn't know what she looked like. If Stan couldn't deliver the letter, she could do it herself. She'd say she was legally representing McGuire Properties. It gave the impression she was with a law firm without technically lying.

She finished out the rest of the workday before grabbing the letter and the keys for the Berkshire property and heading out the door. Doing this felt right, and the sooner the better. They would learn not to screw with McGuire Properties. Or Andrea Keller.

Twenty minutes later she'd arrived at the apartment building on Berkshire Drive. Parking in the university area was always difficult, so she didn't even bother looking for a space on the street. Instead she pulled around to the small lot in back. This building was one of Tommy's smaller rentals with only two apartments on each floor. The units were nearly identical except that the upstairs apartments had balconies with a picturesque view of the parking lot. Ironically, except for the frat boys, all of the tenants were college students. There were only six parking spaces in the back lot and Tommy charged extra for the honor of using one. None of them were assigned, so the tenants just pulled into any available spot. Today, three of the spaces were empty. Two, after Andrea parked her car in the space closest to the building.

As she walked up to the door, a small flurry of snow drifted downward. The first of the season. Maybe they'd have snow for

Christmas after all. The back door was safety glass, the kind stores used, and it was locked for security reasons. The door opened into the downstairs hallway, a straight shot to the front door, also glass and also locked. From where she stood, she could see all the way to the front door and the street beyond. She held the key ring under the light fixture, trying to find the one for the back door, when she heard a scrabbling noise on the balcony to her left. The frat boys' balcony, situated right above her parked car.

Andrea took a step back to look and blinked while her eyes adjusted to the dim light and the drifting snow. She held a hand over her eyes and could only make out a charcoal grill, the cover askew. The door that led to the balcony had a glass pane on the upper half and it was dark, like no one was home. She was about to turn back to her keys when she heard a small whimper. "Hello?" she called out, taking yet another step back into the parking lot. More scrabbling. Someone was on that balcony, but they weren't sitting or standing or they'd be in view. No one would be lying outside in this cold if they could help it, so whoever it was had to have gone out on the balcony and then collapsed. But from what? The frat boys were too young for a heart attack. A drug overdose, maybe? Or else, drunk. That was more likely.

She took off her gloves and fumbled in her purse until she located a small flashlight. "Hello?" she called out, shining the spotlight upward. What she saw made her gasp. Two sad, dark eyes peered down at her. "Anni?" she said. "Is that you?" The dog whined in response. In the light of the flashlight beam she saw that the dog was chained to one of the balcony posts. She couldn't believe what she was seeing. Who would leave a dog chained up outside in the cold?

Andrea snapped off the light and located the back door key. Once inside, she walked down the hallway, passing the doorways of the downstairs tenants. The frat boy had been right about the smell of weed coming from the lower apartment, not that she cared all that much. She passed the mailboxes embedded in the wall near the front door and turned to go up the stairs. Her heart pounded as she climbed the steps.

One of the stair treads was broken, the board actually missing, which could only mean that someone had removed it. Under normal circumstances, Andrea would have made a note to have Stan come out to fix it, but she was too angry for that. A broken stair was fine for animal abusers. Too good for them, actually. That poor dog. With her big sad eyes and beaten-down demeanor, the dog looked like one of the pets in the commercial to raise money for an animal rights group. Someone should chain the frat boys to the balcony out in the cold. Then they'd know how it felt.

Andrea rapped on the door three times, waited a few seconds, then pounded with the side of her fist. "Hello!" she shouted. "Anyone there?" No answer. She expected others in the building to come see what was going on, or at the very least, open their doors to listen, but there was no movement in the building as far as she could tell. She tried again, knocking and yelling, "Open up." But still nothing.

Disappointed, she realized they must not be home. And just when she was ready to tell them off too. Andrea glanced down at the letter. The envelope looked official. She'd made sure of that. She could prop it up against the door or leave it in the mailbox, then contact the authorities to report an abused dog at this address. How long would it take for the crime to be investigated? Soon enough to get Anni out of the cold? It was after office hours: Would that make a difference? Probably, she decided, although she really didn't know for sure. She looked down again and realized that right in her hand, along with the envelope, was a key ring holding a key for every apartment in the building, each of them labeled in Andrea's own neat handwriting. Unit number four happened to be right on top. Without making a conscious decision, she inserted the key into the lock and turned it. When she heard a click, she turned the knob and the door swung open. A sign. If she really wasn't meant to open the door, the frat boys would have installed a dead bolt, and she wouldn't have been able to get in.

She flipped on the light switch and the living room came into view: sagging couch with a dark-green blanket draped across the top, a coffee table littered with beer cans and assorted snack bags, dirty linoleum floor covered with clothing and what looked like crushed potato chips. Yuck. And the place smelled too, like cigarette smoke and poop. Looking oddly out of place was a whopping big-screen TV, one of the largest Andrea had ever seen. "Hello?" she called out, closing the door behind her.

Being in someone's apartment without permission felt all kinds of wrong—but it was exhilarating too. What was she doing here? With her back flat against the door, she felt her heart pounding. What would she say if one of them came out of the bedroom right now? She could run, and if they didn't catch her, they'd have no way of tracing her. Unless they looked out the window and took down her license plate number.

Another possibility—telling them Mr. McGuire had told her to enter the premises to check on the unit. If she were lucky, they wouldn't know this was illegal and they wouldn't check with Tommy to confirm her story. They seemed like the kind of guys who wouldn't know their rights. At least that's what she hoped. People had a way of surprising her, and sometimes not in a good way.

Her best bet, she decided, was to not get caught.

She crossed through the living room and went into the small kitchen where the smell of feces was even stronger. Now that she had an explanation ready in case she got caught, she felt a little better, but she still moved quietly and quickly. She tucked the letter and key ring into her purse and went to the balcony door on the far wall of the room. The door had a hook-and-eye closure that wasn't lined up perfectly, so it took a bit of tugging to free the hook. She turned on the outside light and stepped outside. The air was filled with swirling flakes of snow and the dog was covered with a layer of white.

"Anni?" Andrea knelt down next to her, and the dog shrank back, shaking. Poor little thing was either shivering from the cold or terrified. The dog's red collar was attached to a short, bulky chain wrapped around a balcony spindle. Andrea followed the chain to where it was connected, relieved to see it had a simple thumb-push fastener rather than a lock. It only took a second for the chain to come free. "Come on, girl," she crooned. "Time to get out of the cold." She pulled gently on the chain and immediately regretted it. Anni cringed like she expected to be hit. "It's okay, Anni. It's okay." She wished she had more experience with dogs. Was there some reassuring phrase that all dog owners knew? A secret code that would put Anni at ease? She was ill equipped for the situation, but doing the best she knew how. She ran a hand over Anni's back and made what she hoped sounded like soothing noises. "You're a good girl; yes, you are, Anni." Anni's ears perked up hopefully when she heard her name. Within a minute or so Andrea felt the dog's body relax under her hand, and she knew what she was going to do. She was going to steal a dog.

Andrea disconnected the chain from the collar. It wasn't the right kind of chain to be a dog leash, way too heavy and much too short. She stood up, patting her thighs. "Come on, girl," she said, but Anni, even as her eyes pleaded, didn't move. Andrea opened the door, and waved a hand toward the inside. "Let's go!" She said the words with a faked enthusiasm. Although Anni lifted her head and looked longingly through the doorway, she didn't get up. Andrea reached down and scooped the dog into her arms. Good grief, she was heavy for such a small dog, but at least she didn't struggle. Andrea got the overpowering odor of wet dog; it was clear Anni needed a bath. She'd been afraid Anni would fight being carried, but the dog settled against her chest like she knew she was in good hands.

Andrea struggled through the balcony doorway, then closed the door with her back end, not bothering to latch it with the hook and eye. She crossed the room, shifting Anni's body so that she could grab the knob. Once she was out in the hallway, she breathed a sigh of relief. She hadn't left anything incriminating behind. They'd just be less one neglected dog—a dog they weren't supposed to have in the first place. First, though, she had to get away from here. Far away from here.

As she made her way down the stairs with Anni in her arms, making sure to avoid the missing step, she prayed she wouldn't run into any of the other tenants. The first rule of any crime: no witnesses. All she had to do was get to her car and she'd be home free. As she got to the bottom of the stairs, she got a whiff of marijuana mingled with the wet dog smell. So be it. Hopefully the stoner tenant would be too mellow to wonder who was coming down the stairs. She got to the bottom and Anni squirmed and made a sharp bark. Andrea shushed her, and Anni settled down as if she understood.

She passed the two doors leading into the downstairs apartments, one on either side of the hallway, and she was almost to the glass door when she saw the glare of headlights as a car pulled into the parking lot. She froze, watching as the frat boys got out of their car. One of them gestured up to their balcony, and she heard him yell, "*What the hell?*" Oh no. She panicked as she remembered leaving the balcony light on. All instinct and fear, she whipped around to go out the front door, knowing that they were heading this way.

Halfway there, a door opened in the hallway, and a young man stuck his head out like a curious gopher. Andrea pushed past him right into his apartment and he stepped aside to let her in like they'd planned this. She hissed, "Shhh. Close the door."

He didn't look the least bit surprised, just shrugged and followed her directions. She whispered, "We have to be very quiet."

He was about nineteen or twenty with a full-blown bushy beard, the kind young guys grow just because they can. Besides the beard he was clean-cut with short hair and neat clothes: dark jeans and a navy button-down shirt. A bong sat on the kitchen counter next to a bag of chips, but otherwise the apartment was orderly. He hooked his thumbs in his belt loops and leaned in conspiratorially. "Why do we have to be quiet?"

"Shhh," Andrea said, hearing the back door open and the thumping of the frat boys' steps as they ran past. Anni was getting heavy, but still Andrea cradled her against her chest, glad to see the dog looked content. Hopefully Anni would remain quiet and not give them away.

When she heard the two men's footsteps up the stairs, she noticed a thump as each one jumped over the missing step. Clearly something they were used to doing. When they reached the top landing, she knew it was time to go. "Thanks," she whispered. "I have to go. Can you get the door?"

"Sure thing."

She made a quick decision to go out the front and he followed her to open and hold the door. Participating in this getaway was risky with the frat boys right at the top of the stairs, likely to charge down at any moment, but he did it with gentlemanly ease, no sign of stress on his part. He said, "Take care now."

"Thanks." Andrea walked quickly along the side of the building to the back, staying in the shadows as much as possible. Thankfully Anni stayed quiet even as Andrea opened the car door and set her on the front passenger seat. By now her chest was pounding, her heart beating with such force that she wondered if she was having a heart attack, but there was no time to think about herself. As terrifying as it was, it was also thrilling in a spy movie kind of way. Now she knew what people were talking about when they mentioned the adrenaline rush that came with doing something dangerous.

As she backed out of her space, she glanced up. If either of the frat boys had been looking down, they could have clearly seen her car pulling out from under their balcony. Luckily for her, the balcony was empty.

What would they do, she wondered, stepping on the gas. Call the police? Question the other neighbors? She hoped the college student who'd let her take refuge in his apartment wouldn't be blamed for her crime. She glanced down at Anni curled on the seat, her head resting on her paws. The dog yawned and closed her eyes, looking curiously relaxed. Obviously, she wasn't aware they were on the lam.

All the way home Andrea darted looks at her rearview mirror, half expecting to see flashing lights accompanied by a police siren. By the time she'd turned down the side street to her condo, her guilt had abated. Anni was neglected and, judging by the length of chain and the fact that she was outside in the cold, a case could be made for abuse. Those two bozos didn't deserve to have a dog. And technically, she hadn't broken in. She'd knocked first, and let herself in with a key. Plus, it wasn't like they were completely blameless in all this. They'd mistreated a dog, violated their lease, and hung up on her when she was just doing her job. She imagined that there wasn't a jury in the world who could find her at fault.

ELEVEN

That night after Lindsay went to bed, Dan gathered up all of Anni's things: the dog bed next to the fireplace, the squeaky toy on the top shelf of the bookcase, and the leashes hanging on the hook by the door. All of them went into a large plastic storage container, which he carried down to the laundry room in the basement. After that he went to work in the pantry closet, culling the dog food, heartworm pills, and dog treats. The opened containers were tossed in the garbage, the rest set aside to drop off at the food pantry on his way in to work the next day.

As relieved as he'd been to see that Anni wasn't the dog under the sheet at the veterinary clinic, it had also given him a moment of clarity. It was time to face the truth: Anni probably wasn't coming back. It was a horrible thought and nothing he'd say out loud to anyone, much less his daughter. Lindsay still held out a childlike hope that Anni would magically show up at their doorstep one morning.

Outside it was beginning to snow and the wind had picked up as well, howling outside their snug house. The dream with Christine came to mind and Dan directed a thought her way: *Please, Christine, if Anni is still alive and we can't get her back, at* least let someone else find her. Someone who will take good care of her. Someone who will be kind to her.

In the morning as he drank coffee and mentally planned his day, Lindsay came down for breakfast. Of course the missing dog bed was the first thing she noticed. "So now you're just giving up on her?" Her finger jabbed angrily in the direction of the empty space. "Like she was never here?"

Even though he was prepared for her reaction, the vehemence of her accusation hit him hard. "I didn't throw anything out," he said quietly. "Just packed things away for now."

"Because you think she's gone for good." Lindsay pouted and he got a glimpse of a younger version of his daughter. Lindsay, age eight, angry at having to come home from a friend's house when she wanted to stay longer; again at age eleven, upset at not being invited to another girl's birthday party; and at age thirteen, mad at not getting a good grade on a social studies project she'd slaved over for hours. Lindsay's moods were mercurial and her ire easily raised. When she got upset, she made what Christine had called her "rain cloud face" because you just knew a storm was brewing.

"No, because it makes me sad to look at them." He gestured for her to pull up a chair, but she held firm, standing with her arms crossed. He tried again. "Look, I hope Anni comes home, I really do. I just don't need constant reminders that she's not here. It doesn't help find her and it's upsetting to both of us."

"It's not upsetting to me."

Dan sighed. "Well, it is to me. It's painful to have to keep looking at her things and not know where she is."

She tapped her foot. "Talk about ironic."

"What?"

"That you can't stand to see Anni's bed on the floor, but don't seem to mind that there are reminders of Mom everywhere."

Dan's stomach dropped. "Do you *want* me to get rid of Mom's things?" He glanced around the room. Everything here held memories of Christine. She'd picked out the furniture, the paint color, the flooring. She'd chosen which photos to frame and had arranged the furniture, more than once. He'd have to strip the house down to the studs to remove her influence.

Lindsay's face softened. "Well, that sounds horrible when you say it like that. No, I don't want you to get rid of Mom's things. But you know, Aunt Doreen did offer to go through the closets and pack up her clothes to donate to Goodwill." She shook her head. "I couldn't do it myself, but you know that Mom would like that. You know how big she was on helping people."

Aunt Doreen was really Lindsay's great-aunt—Dan's aunt. She'd been to their house many times since the funeral—dropping off meals, staying with Lindsay when she had her wisdom teeth removed, and another time, waiting for the plumber when Dan had to work. Aunt Doreen had buried a son and a husband, the fun-loving Bruno. She knew firsthand about death and the grieving process and the value of time to heal, but the last time she'd been at the house, she had been appalled by how many of Christine's personal possessions were still around more than a year after her death. Aunt Doreen had just come out of the bathroom that still held Christine's toothbrush and cosmetics. All of it there because Dan didn't have the heart to dispose of anything. "You know," Aunt Doreen had said, "after Bruno died, it helped me to pack up his shaving things and donate his clothing. It didn't take away from my memories and I was glad to think of someone getting a warm winter coat and everything else." That was when she'd offered to do the same for Lindsay and Dan.

"Thanks, but I'm not there yet," Dan had said.

Aunt Doreen had nodded. "I understand. The offer stands if you change your mind." She gave his arm a maternal squeeze. "It really does help."

He'd forgotten the conversation, but it all came back to him now. Rewinding the memory, he spotted Lindsay in the scene, sitting on the couch looking at her phone. Even when he thought she wasn't paying attention, she was there, taking it all in. "You're right," he said with a sigh. "Your mother would like that. I'll give Aunt Doreen a call and see if she can come out this weekend and help us go through some things."

TWELVE

Andrea pulled into her garage, a feeling of relief washing over her. She'd made it home without being followed or arrested. And Anni hadn't freaked out, which was good. If the dog had started barking or moving around in the car, she didn't know what she would have done. Anni's peaceful acceptance of the situation made it all seem right.

She shut off the engine and pushed the remote to close the garage door behind her. The jolt of the car coming to a halt had roused Anni, who opened her eyes and looked around. Andrea reached over and rubbed Anni's head, scratching behind her ears. "We're here, girl. We're home." Andrea had never stolen anything before, not even gum from the drugstore when she was young and the other kids were doing it. And now she'd stolen a dog, a living, breathing animal, who had been someone's pet. So unlike her. So daring, so despicable.

She sat in the dark car sorting out her feelings while petting the dog, who pushed her head against Andrea's hand. On the one hand, it was wrong to steal, no doubt about that. It was one of the top ten worst things to do, right there in the Bible. And on the legal side, there were laws against taking someone else's property and awful penalties. Jail time. And in this case, it might be even worse because Anni wasn't just property, she was a pet. Even though Andrea had never had a dog, she knew how people felt about them. People loved their dogs. They were their children, their companions, sometimes even their soul mates. Some people swore that their dog had an almost psychic connection with them, sensing when they were sad and bringing them comfort. If Andrea had thought she was taking that away from the frat boys, she would have started up the car and taken Anni right back, right then and there.

But in her heart, she knew that wasn't the case. Simone had said the frat boys had picked Anni up; that she was a stray. So she hadn't had a good home to begin with and the frat boys were no better. In fact, they were abusive.

Anni tilted her head, luxuriating in being petted. "Did they kick you?" Andrea crooned. "How could they do that to you, sweetheart?" Such an innocent being, this small creature with the big, dark trusting eyes. Kicking her would be like kicking a baby. And who could leave such a sweet dog chained up out in the snow and the cold? Assholes. No, she wouldn't be returning the dog, and she wasn't going to get into trouble either. She would be careful, so careful that no one would ever know what she had done. Anni was with her now, and there was no turning back. She would keep Anni and give her the love she deserved.

THIRTEEN

Aunt Doreen came over that Saturday, and set to work emptying closets and drawers, sorting through Christine's clothing and other personal items. Working quickly and efficiently was her usual way of doing things. Doreen was one of the busy retirees; a trim, gray-haired lady on the move. No rocking chair and remote for her. She volunteered and walked two miles a day and took interest in everyone and everything. And today, she acted as if she were honored to help sort through Christine's possessions.

She made Dan and Lindsay part of the process, coaching them through the sorting and asking their opinion, while clearly steering them toward parting with most of the items. "Some poor soul is going to love getting these blouses," she said, neatly folding the jewel-toned tops and placing them in a box labeled "Donation." "Some young woman going back into the workplace who needs professional clothes. Maybe a young mom who took a break and doesn't have the budget to buy a new wardrobe." The same young woman was going to love Christine's blazers and dress pants. Doreen tilted her head to the side as if picturing what the recipient would look like. "Christine would love knowing you're doing this, Dan," Doreen said. "She was all about paying it forward."

Together Lindsay and Doreen sorted through Christine's jewelry, keeping the few nice pieces for Lindsay and setting aside the rest to donate. According to Doreen, the costume jewelry would be the perfect accessory for the fictitious young woman's new look as she headed into the office her first day.

After a few hours they were done. At first it had been painful, but Dan had been surprised at how cathartic the whole thing had turned out to be. Doreen was right: donating the clothes was a way of honoring Christine's memory. They didn't benefit anyone hanging in the closet. "And look," she said with glee, moving the empty hangers in the front hall closet aside. "You have so much more space for your coats now. Everything's not crammed in there anymore."

By the time they were finished, it was nearly dinnertime and somehow Dan got wrangled into going out for dinner at a Mexican restaurant with Doreen. She'd offered to take both of them, but Lindsay had to take a shower and meet up with Brandon.

"I guess it's just us then," Doreen said brightly, hoisting a box to carry out to the car. Following her lead, Dan grabbed another box, which they would, Doreen said, drop off on the way to dinner.

An hour later they were munching on chips and drinking margaritas at La Fiesta. "I've never eaten here," Dan said, looking around at the murals on the brightly painted walls. "What's good?"

"Everything," Doreen said, her finger jabbing the menu in front of her. "Every single thing. You can't go wrong, really. I think I've had everything on the menu. Bruno and I used to eat here a few times a month." Bruno had been dead for several years. Even though he'd been in his late seventies, it was a shock when Dan and Christine got the call about his fatal heart attack. He was a stocky man full of love and enthusiasm, seemingly in good health. At the funeral, hundreds of people had shown up, most of whom only knew him as the local pharmacist. It was amazing how one person could touch so many lives.

"You miss coming here?" Dan asked, guessing.

"Oh no, I come here all the time. I miss Bruno, though. That never changes." She dipped a chip into the salsa. "But we were lucky to have all the years we had. You and Christine were lucky too. It should have been longer, but at least you had true love. Some people never get that." Her eyes were fixed on him, waiting for a response.

This was not the conversation Dan wanted to have with Aunt Doreen, or anyone else for that matter. Even at home he and Lindsay avoided lengthy conversations about Christine, afraid they might make each other cry. It was easier to keep busy and hold in the pain. Maybe easier wasn't the right word. It was never easy. Just a way of coping. "You're right," he said, and changed the subject, telling her the latest news of his parents, who had retired to Tucson several years earlier.

"They're the smart ones," Doreen said. "Fleeing the frozen tundra and following the sun."

Over dinner they discussed movies, and the book she'd read recently for her book club. Then she asked, "How come I never see you at church anymore?"

He hadn't gone to church since the funeral. "I sit in back. You must not see me."

"Ha-ha," she said. "You need to start coming. It might do your soul some good. If nothing else, you'll get to see me."

"I'll think about it," he said, then gave her an update on his job at the brewery. Anything to change the subject.

"Tell me," she said over dessert (fried ice cream for him, flan for her), "have you thought about getting a new dog?"

"No." A knee-jerk response, said more vehemently than necessary. He didn't mean to be rude; it just came out that way.

"Well, that was quick." She laughed. "You wouldn't consider it at all? Not even for Lindsay's sake?"

He shook his head. "Never. There's no replacing Anni. She was one of a kind. Christine said she was a person disguised as a dog." He smiled at the memory. "And Lindsay will be going off to college soon, so it would be pointless to do it just for her."

"I see," Doreen said, her lips pursed. "I only mentioned it because a dog can bring such joy. Bruno always said there was nothing like the unconditional love of a dog. We had many over the years and none of them replaced the other. They each had their own unique place in our family."

"I understand. I just don't think it would be right for the dog or for Lindsay at this point."

"And what about you?"

"What about me?"

"Do you get out at all?"

He grinned. "All the time. I'm here with you tonight, aren't I?" Truthfully his social life had ground to a halt after Christine died. For the first few weeks after the funeral, he'd gotten a few pity dinner invitations, but after a while, even that dried up. The world seemed made for couples, and he was now the odd man out. "I'm fine, Doreen."

But she wasn't going to be deterred. "Lindsay says you never go out. You work and come home and that's it. You're still a young man, Dan. You can't be a shut-in."

"I'm forty and I'm hardly a shut-in."

"But Lindsay says—"

Like most teenagers, Lindsay didn't know the half of what he did to keep their lives running. "Yes, I know. She said I go to work and then I'm home. But I also go to the grocery store and get my hair cut and do yard work. Snow blow the driveway. And I watch the Packers games with Peter." That had happened only once, but still, it counted. Peter was his brother, and Doreen's nephew. The familial reference had to carry some weight. "You don't need to worry about me, Doreen. I live a full life."

"So you don't have any problem with socializing? Maybe going out to dinner once in a while, seeing a movie?"

"Certainly not." Then he added, "When I have the time."

"Well, that's a relief," she said, "because I did something I was afraid would anger you, but now it seems like you'll be okay with it. There's this lovely woman, the daughter of a friend—" He felt his jaw drop and she must have seen it too because she held up a hand to keep him from saying a word. "Just hear me out. She's really a lovely person. You would like her, really you would. Early thirties, pretty, smart. She had a bad breakup recently. The guy is a real rat. She's been so down on herself lately, it breaks my heart to see."

"And?"

"I told her all about you, and she's not interested in dating either, so don't get ahead of me here," Doreen said hurriedly. "But it's nice to have someone to see a movie or go out to eat with. You have to admit that would be nice."

Dan cleared his throat. "I appreciate the thought, but I don't think—"

"She's the loveliest person. A little chatty, which might be nice because it makes it easy to talk to her. You would like her; really, you would."

"So you said."

"I gave her your number and told her she simply must make the call because you're such a quiet, shy man."

"You didn't."

"I did." She leaned back, took the napkin off her lap, and set it on the table. "You can always say no, but why not give her a chance? She already knows this won't be a romance, so there's no pressure that way. Just a companion, someone new to talk to."

"I really don't need anyone new."

"Ha! That's where you're wrong." Doreen patted his arm. "Staying stuck at home is dishonoring Christine. She'd want you to be out in the world interacting with other people. Doing things. Going places."

"I don't really think it's right to act as if you're speaking for Christine." Dan had said her name more this evening than he had in all the months since her funeral. "That's not playing fair."

"I see your point, but I still think it's true. Christine thought the world of you. She wouldn't want you moldering at home. And believe me, if the shoe had been on the other foot and you had been the one to die, I'd have encouraged Christine to get out there and socialize."

"Thanks," he said dryly.

"This world is made for the living, Dan. Death, and accepting death, is a part of life. You're only forty. You could live for a few more decades and you deserve some happiness along the way. Going out to eat with someone and making polite conversation doesn't take away from what you had with Christine."

He exhaled loudly. "I just don't think I can do it, Doreen. Making small talk with a strange woman sounds exhausting to me. Can you just tell your friend's daughter no for me?"

She gave his arm another pat. "Just think about it. One dinner, or maybe even just out for coffee. It won't kill you."

FOURTEEN

Andrea had been home all of ten minutes when she realized she didn't have any dog supplies. As a new guest, Anni had shown good manners, following her from the garage into the kitchen and taking ladylike slurps from a cereal bowl Andrea had filled with water. When the dog glanced upward, Andrea read it in her eyes. "Are you hungry, girl?" She rummaged through her cabinets, moving boxes and cans aside, as if dog food would magically appear there. She wasn't normally well stocked with food. It was just her living in the condo, after all, but now she clearly saw how pathetic her pantry really was. Crackers, energy bars, canned chicken noodle soup, and dry pasta. The only thing that could possibly work was a can of tuna (and even that was iffy), but after she dusted off the top and saw that the expiration date had come and gone, it was no longer a contender.

Clearly, she was going to have to buy dog food, but how? Leaving Anni alone in the house seemed risky. Despite the dog's sweet disposition, it was possible she had a destructive streak and Andrea didn't want to chance it. The second thought, taking the dog with her to the grocery store, wouldn't work either. That left PetShop, a place she knew allowed animals. Anni followed her to the bedroom and watched curiously as Andrea pulled a plastic storage container out from under the bed. Her wrapping paper bin. She found some red velveteen ribbon, cut off a length, and looped it through Anni's collar. It was as good a leash as she was going to come up with on short notice.

The drive to PetShop was uneventful, with Andrea driving very carefully, and Anni scrunching down in the front seat like a fugitive. When they arrived at the store, and Andrea opened the car door, Anni leapt out of the front seat with a joyful exuberance, almost as if she knew where they were. Andrea looked down at her in wonder. How trusting she was. She thought again about the frat boy shoving her really hard with his boot, making her cry out in pain. Even the thought made her shake her head in anger. What was wrong with people?

The idea that the frat boys or someone who knew them might be in the store and recognize Anni crossed her mind, but she was less afraid than she'd been before. They didn't strike her as the type of people to shop at PetShop. There hadn't been any dog toys in the apartment, and the chain they used to keep her tied to the balcony was industrial strength, clearly not intended for a dog. No, it was fairly safe to shop here.

Inside the store, Anni walked alongside her. They passed cages filled with squawking birds, but Anni expressed only a mild interest. Going past the gerbil and hamster cages, the dog kept her nose forward as if she couldn't be bothered with such things. Anni acted as if shopping at PetShop was routine for her, while Andrea felt a little overwhelmed.

Going down one aisle, Andrea noticed a white-haired lady pushing a small terrier in a cart, and like proud mothers they exchanged nods in passing. Andrea chose a leash, and weighed several dog toy options, finally throwing a variety into the cart. From there she picked out some treats, dog shampoo, and an oval bed, putting it on the floor and pressing on it to see how comfortable it would be. She urged Anni to step inside the bed and said,

"Lie down," then beamed with delight when the dog did just that. "Good girl!" Anni had to be the smartest dog ever. Andrea couldn't believe how quickly they were getting everything done.

Anni looked so comfortable in the bed on the floor of the PetShop, it seemed a shame to disturb her, but Andrea was on a mission, so she tugged on the ribbon and Anni reluctantly got out. After putting the bed into the cart, they headed to the back corner of the store to pick up a bag of dog food. When they got to the food aisle, the actual thing they'd come for, the number of choices stopped her cold.

The wall of food went from the floor to over her head. Not only were there different brands, but they also were categorized by the size of the bag and the type of dog. There was food for puppies and for senior dogs, bags labeled with words like "longevity" and "all natural." Some promised superior ingredients and no artificial flavors or colors. Andrea looked down at Anni as if the dog might indicate a preference. "What do you think, girl?" She smiled at how quickly she'd become one of those crazy dog ladies, the kind who spoke to their pet like they were human.

Anni sat at her feet and leaned against her leg while Andrea read the labels, trying to make sense of it all. She got out her phone to Google brand names and was so engrossed in her search that she didn't even see the older gentleman approach. "Can I help you, miss?" he asked, startling her.

"Oh! I . . ." She shut down the phone and put it back in her purse. "I'm trying to figure out what to buy."

"What a cutie!" He leaned over to pet Anni, giving Andrea a view of the top of his shiny pink scalp. When he stood up, he clasped his hands together. He was a portly man, at least seventy or so, not much taller than she was. The hair he did have formed a fringe around his ears and circled around the back of his head. He wore a white lab coat. Most of the other employees were teenagers.

This man had to be the manager. "And what might this beautiful dog's name be?"

"Anni."

"Very good. Am I right in guessing that you just got her recently?"

Was it that obvious? Andrea nodded. "Yes."

"Aha, I knew it. The makeshift leash gave it away."

Oh, the leash! "Yes, I had to improvise," she said.

"Well done." His wide smile made her feel at ease. "She was a rescue, I take it."

He sure nailed that one on the head, Andrea thought. If only he knew what lengths she'd gone through to bring Anni to safety. "Yes, a rescue."

"I thought so." He nodded. "I'm very good at reading animals, and I can tell that you and Anni were meant to be together." He reached down to pat Anni's head. "Isn't that right, Anni? Oh yes, it is. You are a very sweet girl."

"Maybe you can help me pick out some dog food?" Andrea said, looking at the wall of choices. "I don't mind spending the money. I just want to get her the best. She's been through a rough time."

"Once you take her to the vet, you can ask what they think, but for now I would suggest starting out with this," he said, indicating a blue bag that promised superior nutrition and a lack of chemical additives.

"Thank you. I don't think I caught your name?" She hoisted the bag off the shelf and put it in the cart.

"Just call me Bruno."

She rubbed her hands together. "Well, thank you, Bruno. I appreciate the help. I could have stood here for hours trying to decide."

"My pleasure. You know there is something . . ." He hesitated, like someone about to give bad news.

"What?" Andrea took in a sharp breath. She had a sudden sense that she'd done something wrong, made some kind of blunder that had given away the fact that Anni wasn't legally hers.

"I don't want to overstep my bounds, but I want to tell you that you need to keep Anni with you whenever possible. Let her be your little shadow. I think you'll find she's going to be a life changer for you."

What an odd little man, but how sweet too. "I think she's already been a life changer." Andrea reached down to pet Anni's head. "I wouldn't be at PetShop today otherwise."

Bruno leaned in to say, "And there's a coffee shop called Café Mocha that allows people to bring in their dogs. You and Anni should check it out sometime. It's over on Pleasant Street."

"Okay, I will."

"Can I help you with anything else?"

Andrea glanced down at her full cart. "I think I have everything for now."

"Very good." He bent down at the waist and gave Anni one last pet. "Well, good-bye then, Anni. I'm glad to see you landed in a good place with someone who will love you." When he straightened up, he gave Andrea a two-fingered salute and headed to the end of the aisle.

"Thank you," she replied, giving Anni a little tug on the ribbon and following behind. When she turned the corner, though, Bruno was nowhere in sight. She stopped, puzzled. She was only three seconds behind him. Where could he have gone? Anni led the way up the aisle, and Andrea's eyes darted down each side row, thinking he might have somehow dodged them. But there was no sign of the white-jacketed man anywhere. To get out of view that quickly he had to have broken into a run as soon as he turned the corner. Very curious. Andrea looked down at Anni, who walked ever so ladylike, not seeming to have noticed anything out of the ordinary.

Andrea shrugged to herself before making her way to the cash register. When it was her turn at the front of the line, the teenage cashier, a beautiful young girl with jet-black hair and a tattoo of a gravestone on her arm, greeted her with, "Did you find everything okay?"

Andrea began piling items on the conveyer. "Yeah, I did. I was a little overwhelmed in the dog food aisle, but then—"

But apparently it had been a rhetorical question, because the girl was already scanning the items and didn't appear to be listening. Andrea kept an eye on Anni even as she watched the cashier ring up her purchases. The dog was fine, sniffing her feet and the floor in general, unperturbed by being abducted and getting a new owner all in the space of the last hour or so.

As they left the store, Andrea took one more look around, but Bruno was nowhere in sight. He'd been super helpful and she'd wanted to thank him again, but it wasn't worth dwelling on. He'd given her the tip about Café Mocha too, a place she passed all the time going to work, but had never visited. Good to know they allowed dogs there. Still, it was weird how he'd completely disappeared seconds after going around the corner.

FIFTEEN

When his cell phone rang while he was walking out to his truck after work, Dan didn't recognize the number, but he answered it anyway. That was his first mistake.

The wind was howling and he'd fumbled to answer the phone while simultaneously taking off a glove so that he could root around in his coat pocket for his car key. "Hello?"

A woman's voice on the line said something about her mother knowing Doreen. At first he couldn't quite follow what she was talking about, and then he had a memory flash and, oh man, his heart sank as he realized what this was all about. This was the fix-up that Doreen swore wasn't a fix-up. The disembodied voice on the phone was the "lovely woman" who'd just experienced a traumatic breakup. "Oh, hi!" he said, probably a little louder and more upbeat than he'd intended. He wrestled the key fob out of his pocket and unlocked the door. "Just a second. Can you hang on? I . . . just a second."

Once inside the cab of the truck, he was cocooned from the wind. Pulling the door shut turned his vehicle into the equivalent of a sound booth. "Sorry about that. I was outside and couldn't hear." Complete silence on the line. "Hello?" Outside, confetti snow drifted and blew, swirling so randomly that it was hard to tell if it was still coming down or just rearranging itself.

"Hey, I'm back!" She sounded cheery. "I got distracted and the phone slipped off my shoulder. Anyway . . ."

And then she stopped talking, as if Dan should take it from there. He cleared his throat, the preface to telling her that Doreen had spoken out of turn, that he had too many projects at work and a teenage daughter and repairs to do at the house. Anyone could see that this particular combination of responsibilities would keep him from expanding his social circle. But in that split second of hesitation, in the instant that he used to rehearse the words in his mind, the woman jumped in and sucked away his free will. She was quicker and more decisive and that gave her an edge.

It all came out in a rush, her words stacked one on top of another. She said, "Now I know you're not up to dating. Doreen made that very clear, so I especially appreciate that you're willing to hang out with me occasionally. I've been so depressed since, well, we have plenty of time to talk about that when we meet in person. Doreen talked you up, by the way, like you wouldn't believe. I said I didn't think there were any good guys left and she was adamant that meeting you would restore my faith in humanity. So I was thinking maybe lunch on Saturday? This coming Saturday—in two days. Somewhere casual? How about Bodecker's on Main at noon? Is there some reason that won't work for you?"

And just like that, his excuses drifted off like the snow. She'd catapulted so many words at him, his own mind went blank. He barely knew his name or what day it was. He couldn't think of a single reason he couldn't be at Bodecker's on Main at noon on Saturday.

"No, I can make it," he said. And that was his second mistake. He found himself thanking her for the invitation.

"I'll be wearing a black leather jacket and a Hermès scarf," she said.

"Got it," he said. "Black leather jacket."

"And a Hermès scarf."

"Okay." Already, he regretted this, but the wheels had lifted off the runway and there was no getting off the plane now.

She said, "Oh, this is going to be so much fun!" which was the complete opposite of what he'd been thinking. After they'd said their good-byes, he hung up, silently cursing Doreen, even though he knew she had the best intentions.

SIXTEEN

Jade was already there, a cup of coffee in front of her, when Andrea arrived at the restaurant that Saturday. She told the hostess, "I see my friend," and breezed past, sliding into the empty side of the booth with a smile.

"Someone's in a good mood," Jade said, adding two sugars to her cup and stirred briskly. She tapped the spoon against the rim before setting it down on the saucer.

Andrea unwound the scarf from her neck and shrugged her arms out of her jacket. "Yeah, life is definitely looking up," she said. She'd only been a dog owner for a few days, and Bruno had been right: Anni was a life changer. Since her visit to PetShop, she'd taken Anni to a veterinarian who checked for a microchip, but didn't find one. The dog had already been spayed, so obviously someone had cared for her at some time. Unlikely to be the frat boys. They'd acquired her too recently. Besides, Andrea couldn't imagine them being that responsible.

The vet proclaimed Anni to be underweight but otherwise in good shape and said that the food Bruno suggested at PetShop was fine. After giving Anni a heartworm test plus some necessary vaccinations and Andrea a brochure on canine health, the vet sent them on their way. Andrea's biggest fear, that someone at the vet's office would question her ownership, was never an issue. In fact, when she'd said that Anni was a rescue, Andrea had gotten a high five from the receptionist. And now that the dog was listed as "Anni Keller" in their patients' file, it seemed official.

The first full workday as a dog owner, Andrea had tried to leave Anni at home while she went to the office, but after checking on her at lunchtime, she found the dog a stressed-out wreck. The poor thing's ears were tucked back, and her tail hung low. She paced nervously, sniffing the floor and avoiding eye contact with Andrea. The most telling (and pungent) sign that all was not right in Anni's world was the pile of poop in the corner of the kitchen. Andrea had worried that this would be an ongoing problem, but after that she took Anni with her to work and there hadn't been any more accidents.

Taking the dog out for a walk, they'd come across her neighbor, old-guy Cliff, who was out getting his newspaper. Surprisingly enough he took a liking to Anni almost immediately and Anni took to him, bouncing on her back legs to meet his extended hand. He'd always had dogs, Cliff said, but now those days were over. "I sure do miss having a pup around," he said, rubbing behind Anni's ears. "If you ever need someone to watch this little muffin for you, I'm your man." That's where Anni was now, parked next to Cliff's recliner, the old man's arm trailing down to stroke her side. It was a sweet and unexpected scene.

"See that guy over there," Jade said, jerking her chin toward a man at a booth behind Andrea. "I've been watching him. He's meeting someone here and he doesn't know what she looks like."

Andrea turned her head to see a single guy sitting with his back to them. He had wavy dark-brown hair and good posture. She must have passed him on the way in, but she hadn't noticed him. "Why do you say that?"

Jade grinned. "He's all nervous, checking the time on his phone every two minutes. It's so cute. The waitress came over and he couldn't decide if he should order a drink until she came or not. All of which is very telling. But the main reason I know? When I walked in, he checked me out, like he thought it might be me. I think it's one of those online dating things. I can't wait to watch how this goes." She craned her neck to get a better look.

"Ahem," Andrea said, snapping her fingers. "All eyes on me." She pointed to her nose like doing a sobriety test. "Don't you want to hear my news?"

"Yes!" Jade said. "I almost forgot. Let me guess." She tapped her lower lip with her index finger. "The workshop worked and you met someone."

"Yes and no," she said, enjoying the look on Jade's face.

"Tell me everything. I am dying here. Absolutely dying."

But she had to wait a little longer because the waitress chose just that moment to stop at their table. Andrea and Jade had eaten at Bodecker's on Main many times and always ordered the cashew chicken salad with the dressing on the side, so the exchange went quickly. The second the teenage waitress scooped up the menus, Jade's eyes widened. "Still dying here. Tell. Me. Now."

"You are not going to believe it," Andrea said. "I have a dog."

"You have a dog," Jade repeated, clearly not getting the significance of it.

"Yes, a dog, and she's the cutest thing you ever saw. You will never guess how I got her. I'm only telling you and no one else. You have to swear to keep it a secret or I could go to prison." It was a bit of an exaggeration, but Jade loved a good story, and the mention of prison really amped things up.

When Andrea was finished telling the story, she sat back with a satisfied grin. Jade had hung on every word, her eyes fairly bugging out when Andrea got to the part about entering the apartment.

"Really," Jade said, her mouth dropping open. "I can't believe you did that. Breaking and entering. And stealing a dog! That's so"—she paused to think—"ballsy. Not like you. I mean, that's really not like you at all. I'm not even sure *I* would do that and, frankly, I always thought that, between the two of us, *I* was the bigger badass."

"You would have done it," Andrea said confidently. "If you had seen Anni up on the balcony, you would have gone right up there and saved her too. *Anyone* with half a heart would have done it."

"But," Jade said, sputtering, "what if those guys find out? If they know it's you, things could get really nasty. What if they saw your license plate as you drove off?" She jabbed a finger on the place mat. "Or what if the stoner dude tells them it was you? You just called and talked to them about the dog earlier in the day. They might make the connection."

Andrea had thought of all these things. They'd haunted her the first day she'd had Anni, causing her to lose an entire night's sleep. The next morning she'd anonymously called the downstairs tenant, identifying herself as the girl with the dog who'd taken refuge in his apartment. "Hey!" he'd said, as happy to hear from her as if they were long-lost friends. "Too funny that you called 'cause I was just wishing I could let you know what happened after you left."

"What happened after I left?" Andrea felt the color drain from her face.

"It was totally hilarious. Those two morons came pounding on everyone's door in the building asking if anyone had seen who took their dog."

Now her heart stopped. "What did you say?"

"I said I knew exactly who took their dog. That it was the police and that the cops knocked on my door and were asking all kinds of questions about where the dog came from and how long they had it and whatnot. Then Zak was all like, 'You didn't tell them anything, did you?' and he's got his hands on my shirt and I just pushed him away and said, 'No, I didn't tell the cops anything.' Zak was totally shaking and Justin looked like he was gonna puke. I've never seen them that way. I totally had them worried."

Andrea had exhaled with relief. "Thank you. I really appreciate it."

"My pleasure, really. They totally bought it." He'd cackled with glee. "It was hilarious, believe me."

"That was some fast thinking on your part," she'd said. "Coming up with a story like that. Thank you."

"Maybe you could thank me in person sometime?" he'd said, his voice changing from cocky to hopeful. "Buy me a drink and we'll call it even. I mean, if you want to."

Andrea heard the vulnerability behind the words and didn't want to crush his spirit, but there was no way they were meeting for a drink. She was pretty sure he wasn't even old enough to drink. "I'm sorry, but no, I don't think so."

"Yeah, I pretty much figured that a classy woman like you wouldn't be interested in a guy like me. But I thought it was worth a shot."

"Under different circumstances, I'd buy you that drink," she'd said. "Really, I would. I just think it best to stay anonymous given the circumstances."

"Yeah, I get it. Thanks for letting me down easy."

"I didn't just say it to let you down easy. I meant it. Really, under different circumstances . . ." And then she said a hurried good-bye and ended the call. Talking to him had lifted an anvil off her chest. The frat boys wouldn't come looking for Anni and, in fact, they were afraid they were in trouble with the law. No, they wouldn't be pursuing this. And maybe they wouldn't mistreat other animals in the future. It was a sign, she thought, a sign that even though she'd technically broken the law, she had done the right thing. Martina Dearhart was right. When life was going the way it was supposed to, everything fell into alignment.

Across the table, Jade marveled over what Andrea had done. "I mean, what if those guys call the police and they dust for finger-prints? You weren't wearing gloves, were you?"

"First of all, my fingerprints aren't on file anywhere, so they couldn't trace them to me." Andrea had never been in trouble with the law. The one time she'd gotten stopped for speeding, she'd involuntarily begun to cry and the officer had let her off with a warning. "And secondly, they won't call the police. The stoner guy downstairs told them the police were the ones who took Anni."

"And you know this how?"

"I called him the next day." To counter the surprised look on Jade's face, she said, "Don't worry, I didn't tell him my name. I just told him I wanted to follow up and see if I'd caused him any trouble. Turns out he had totally covered for me. He told the frat boys the police were there asking questions and then they took Anni. They completely believed him, he said, and they were scared out of their minds."

"Your knight in shining armor," Jade said approvingly. "I guess chivalry is not dead."

"He's a hero," Andrea agreed.

By the time the server arrived with the salads, Andrea had already shown Jade multiple photos of Anni on her phone. "Isn't she cute?" She scrolled to one in particular. "This one kills me. It's her making her guilty face." She turned the screen so that Jade could see.

"Cute."

"Oh wait, you have to see this one." Andrea scrolled through a few photos before thrusting the phone in front of Jade's face. "Anni in the bathtub, the first night I got her. By the end of it I was as wet as she was. And even after I toweled her off, she rolled around on the carpeting, which was . . ." A look on Jade's face made her stop. "What?"

"Obsessive, much?"

"What do you mean?"

"I mean you're a little bit fixated on this dog. If you ask me, the workshop signals got crossed. When you said 'hello, love' the universe thought you wanted a dog instead of a man."

"Well, at least Anni won't ever break my heart."

Jade smirked. "So are you going to turn into one of those crazy dog people who buys birthday cakes for their dogs and dresses them in sweaters?"

"Maybe," Andrea said, spearing a piece of chicken with her fork. "Why not?"

They sat and ate quietly for a few minutes, until Jade dropped her fork onto her plate. "Oh my God. You are not going to believe this." Her gaze shot up and locked on a spot somewhere over Andrea's shoulder, toward the front of the restaurant. Andrea started to turn and look, but Jade hissed, "Do not look. It would be too obvious."

"What? What is it?"

"It's Desiree."

"Desiree? Marco's Desiree?"

"Yep, one and the same. She's sitting with the guy who was waiting."

"But . . ." Andrea was at a loss for words. Desiree, the woman who broke up her marriage, was on a blind date? "Are you sure it's her?"

"One hundred percent sure."

Andrea didn't care how obvious it looked—she had to see for herself. She turned and stared in disbelief. Without a doubt, it was Desiree. She was, as Jade had said, sitting across from the dark-haired man, talking a mile a minute while simultaneously fluffing her hair. Unbelievable. Desiree's hair was a brighter blond than the last time she'd seen her and her eyebrows darker and more dramatic. She wore a shiny red top with a deep V neckline. Dangly chandelier earrings dropped down to her shoulders. To Andrea, she looked exactly like the type of person who would steal another woman's husband.

The waitress stopped by to ask how the salads were, and Andrea reluctantly turned her attention away from Desiree. "Fine, thank you," she said.

"Best salad I ever had," Jade said. "Give my compliments to the chef."

The waitress, a fresh-faced teenager with a thick ponytail said, "I would, but there's not really a chef. The prep station girl makes the salads."

"Very good," Jade said with a flourish of her fork. "Tell her she deserves a raise. And a promotion. Best salad I ever had. Really."

"Okay," she said, looking unsure. "I'll tell her."

After she'd wandered away, Andrea said, "I can't believe Desiree is here. I just can't get over it." What she really couldn't believe was that Desiree was there with another man. The last she knew, Desiree had been living with Marco in the house he'd built with Andrea. It had truly been her house, custom built to her specifications. Marco had requirements when it came to the garage and the countertops, but otherwise he'd left it all up to her. She'd selected everything from the light switches to the brick exterior. Her dream house. They'd lived there just a few months when he'd told her he wasn't in love with her anymore. The man she loved most in the world had treated her like she was nothing to him. As cold as can be. He'd stood there with his arms crossed and said, "I don't love you anymore."

From there he'd gone on to say he wasn't sure he'd *ever* been in love with her. That getting married after dating three years just seemed like what everyone assumed they'd do and that he'd gotten swept up in other people's expectation. She'd looked down at her wedding ring, the one he'd placed on her finger in church, in front of God and everyone, while promising to love, honor, and cherish her forever, and the only thing that made sense to Andrea was that this had to be some kind of a cruel joke. In a second he'd say he was only kidding and she'd tell him it wasn't funny. But that moment never came and each word out of his mouth had been an assault to her heart. Stunned, she'd barely processed what he was saying before he'd moved on to talking about the logistics of the divorce—a divorce she never saw coming. And that was it. The beginning of the end. The demolition of her happy ending.

Andrea had tried to reconcile, offering to go to counseling and saying she would give up on the idea of having a baby. When she hadn't gotten pregnant after a year of trying, she'd wanted to follow up with testing to see which of them was at fault, but he'd refused. It became a sticking point between them, and she had to believe this was the cause of Marco wanting a divorce. She would have done anything to make it work, but he would have none of it. She still had hope right up until the day she came home from work to find he'd packed up her things. He wanted her out. If that weren't bad enough, around the same time, her grandmother's engagement ring had disappeared. Gram had given it to her for safekeeping right before moving into a nursing home and it was Andrea's most prized possession. Marco claimed he had no idea where it was, but with all the lies he'd been spewing, his word meant nothing. They'd had a big screaming match over the ring, and Andrea had said some ugly things she didn't even want to think about later on.

Eventually Marco had used the money he inherited from his grandfather to buy out her half of the house and she'd moved out. Right after that, Desiree had moved in. It was such a cliché that her replacement was a perky, big-busted blonde, the type of woman who favored sparkly jewelry and bright-colored clothing. She looked like the kind of stereotypical home wrecker one saw in movies and on TV. It was like he'd held an audition and picked the most obvious choice. Marco had no imagination at all.

So many times since then Andrea had pictured Desiree luxuriating with a glass of wine in *her* spa tub, surrounded by lit candles (something she'd meant to do but never got around to), or sitting in front of the fireplace with Marco, his arm around her shoulder, sharing the day's events. He'd done that a few times with Andrea, but it wasn't as romantic as she'd anticipated. His arm was unbelievably heavy, like having a concrete boa constrictor around her neck; the weight caused her shoulder muscles to cramp. Plus, he barely listened when she talked about her workday; clearly he was just waiting until she was done so that he could talk. And, whoa, could he talk. On and on and on. She tried to be interested, but between her shoulders tensing and the nonstop bragging, she found herself losing interest. Honestly, in retrospect, they weren't a good fit as a couple. But that didn't mean she wanted to get booted out of her own house.

"Maybe it's not a date. Maybe it's a job interview or something?" Andrea suggested.

Jade wrinkled her nose. "If it's a job interview, she's being awfully flirtatious. Right now she's rubbing his arm."

"Maybe he's a relative? A cousin she hasn't seen in years?"

"Or, more likely, she's a slut, sleeping around on Marco." Jade's eyes widened. "Oh, that would make me so happy. Proof that there is some justice in the world."

"Well, I don't really care," Andrea said, and she meant it. As painful as the divorce had been, she was tired of dredging up all the negative emotions. Tired of being sad and angry and regretful. In the early days of the divorce, feeling like a victim had seemed to come with the territory. But she was beyond all that now. Desiree and Marco were going to do what they were going to do. Honestly she didn't want Marco back. And the house hadn't been her house in a long time. The condo felt like home now. And the truth of the matter was that Marco was a man who needed a woman. If he weren't with Desiree, he'd be with someone else. A few weeks ago this scenario would have aroused all kinds of emotions, but not anymore. She was just tired of it all and ready to move on. Besides being a little curious, she just didn't care.

"Well, I care," Jade said. "I'm going to say hi to her when we walk past. I want to see her reaction."

"You can if you want." Andrea pushed her empty salad plate to the edge of the table. "But I'm not going to give her the satisfaction. I don't even want to acknowledge her existence."

SEVENTEEN

Thirty minutes earlier, Dan had pulled into the restaurant parking lot. He looked at his watch and rolled his eyes. A family curse, always getting to places too early. His parents had instilled in him a fear of arriving late. They constantly drilled into him the need to allow extra time for train crossings and heavy traffic. Showing up late was a sign of disrespect, they'd said. Teachers would fail you. Prospective employers would write you off. Dates would think you were irresponsible. Dates. How did his mind wander over to that? He was a forty-year-old widower with a nearly grown daughter. He shouldn't be dating. Even though he'd told himself this wasn't a date, it felt like one and it also felt wrong. He should have been done with dating a long time ago. Everything was out of order. His life should not have played out this way.

He considered his options and decided to go inside instead of sitting out in his car. It was too cold and, who knew, maybe she'd be early and they could get this thing started and then over with. Bodecker's on Main was welcoming—warm and cozy without being too formal. Dark wood with brass accents. Hanging light fixtures that looked like bulbs inside glass canning jars. The framed Art Nouveau prints gave it the look of an upscale pub. The waitress was a young girl with a bouncy walk and a big smile. About

Lindsay's age, if he had to guess. She asked if he wanted a drink while he waited, and he vacillated. On the one hand, it would be a start. On the other, what if the mystery woman never arrived? Would he feel obligated to order a meal and eat all alone? Finally, after hemming and hawing, he said he'd take a lemonade with very little ice. When the drink arrived, he saw that the waitress had erred on the side of caution with a very full glass and no ice at all. He took the straw out and sipped carefully.

Focusing on the drink kept him occupied for a bit, but as it got later and later, he became fidgety. Every woman who entered the restaurant was a possibility. A lush redhead who flashed him a smile seemed like a candidate, but she walked right on by. He'd actually hoped that the next woman would be his date because there was something about her that seemed warm and appealing. She was slim and pretty, wearing a camel-colored cloth coat, tied at the waist. The coat was long, coming all the way to the top of her boots. She looked about thirty, so the age matched, but she didn't acknowledge him at all, and he remembered that she didn't fit the description. He was looking for a woman wearing a black leather jacket. And a Hermès scarf.

Each time a potential woman went past, he felt a rising hope and then had to reset his expectations and wait some more. Twenty minutes after the expected time, with no sign of his date and no phone call, Dan decided he'd had enough. He was getting ready to leave when a blond woman arrived in a tizzy, dropping into the seat opposite him. "Dan?" she said, and when he nodded, she began talking a mile a minute about the traffic and something about her car being a mess. She explained that she'd stopped to fill up with gas and then got sidetracked washing her windows and scooping out all the trash that was in the backseat. "You know how that happens," she said, as if of course he'd know. Dan wasn't sure if she meant that he'd know about stopping for gas and getting side-tracked, or if somehow he was supposed to know about the trash in her backseat. Why would there be garbage in her backseat any-way? And why didn't she allow extra time if she knew her car was low on gas? It was all so confusing, and trying to sort it out was too much work, so he nodded and agreed, just letting her talk.

He allowed himself to look at her when she ordered the meal. She was a bleached blonde with black eyebrows and dark-red lips. Her shiny top hugged her pushed-up rack. The whole effect reminded him of a film star from the fifties. Doreen had said she was chatty, which he now saw as a euphemism for "will not shut up." She seemed unable to help herself. Even as the waitress was telling them the specials, she made commentary. "Braised beef tips? Oh ho!" she exclaimed, and reached over to squeeze Dan's forearm. "Do I have a story about beef tips. I will definitely tell you later, don't worry about that," she added, as if he'd been begging to hear it right away. Besides the constant talking, it took her forever to order because she had to know the ingredients in several items and then questioned how everything was prepared.

"Maybe they'll let you go back and watch the cook make it," Dan said.

His suggestion drove her to stunned silence. But not for long. A second later she realized he'd been facetious and a smile stretched across her face. "You're kidding! Oh, you." She slapped his arm playfully.

After the waitress abandoned Dan, and he was left alone with her, he tried to steer the conversation in a way that would enable him to figure out this woman's name. He hadn't caught it during the phone call and was embarrassed to ask at this point. He'd Googled her cell number, but didn't come up with anything. He'd consid-ered calling Aunt Doreen and asking before heading out to the restaurant, but he didn't want to reopen the whole conversation. She might take it as encouragement and start fixing him up with every woman who came across her path. No, he figured she'd just say her name when she arrived, the way a normal person would, but she hadn't and now he really couldn't ask. So very awkward.

Dan had the feeling someone had once told this woman she was the cutest thing ever and she took it to heart. Maybe when she was a little girl, her cutesy antics and bright smile got her so much attention that every year she amped it up until she was the human equivalent of a neon billboard. She threw her head back when she laughed and widened her eyes for emphasis like a cartoon character. How could Doreen have thought he'd enjoy her company?

The woman's hands fluttered as she talked, and Dan found himself watching the slim manicured fingers rising and falling in a sweeping motion. It was mesmerizing. Not once did she ask him anything about himself, which was a relief, frankly, but still annoying. How could someone be so self-absorbed? She leaned across the table when making points and touched his hand or arm. The motion gave him a good view of her cleavage and the lacy bra beneath her top. He wasn't interested in her, but he wasn't dead either. She didn't come off as overly bright, but she had to know the effect this kind of thing had on men. She was definitely cunning.

"So," he finally said after the food was served. "Were you named after someone? A relative maybe?"

"No."

He waited for her to elaborate, but she had run out of verbal momentum for the moment and was concentrating on her club sandwich. He tried again. "I've never met anyone else with your name. It's really . . . interesting."

"Thanks," she said, lifting the bread off the sandwich and checking to make sure her request of no tomatoes had been honored. "But your name, not so unusual. I've known a couple of guys named Dan. Mostly older than me. Some go by Danny or Daniel. They're all over the place. Two guys at the oil change place are named Dan. One of my teachers in high school was a Daniel. Daniel Tuttle was his name. There are lots of you guys."

"Yes." Dan nodded. Before she could ramble on about nothing again, he steered the conversation in another direction. "Doreen said you were having some relationship problems?" He hoped his tone was more kindly uncle than prospective boyfriend. He had a reason for asking this. A plan. Once she finished venting, he'd have an opportunity to work in how little free time he himself had for socializing. He'd apologize for his pushy aunt and explain how he wasn't ready to get together after this one time. Having a deceased wife was a horrible but handy excuse to get out of meeting up with this woman again. Time to draw a circle around himself and declare the space inside a dating-free zone.

"I wouldn't really call them relationship problems," she said in disgust, like she didn't want to talk about it, but clearly she did because she kept going. "More like finding out a man's true colors. Talk about someone turning out to be *not as advertised*." Odd, the way she worded things, as if they'd just been talking about people turning out to be not as advertised when that wasn't the case at all. "Marco is his name. *Was* his name. Ancient history, or at least he will be when I find my own place." As it turned out, they were still living together, but it was completely platonic, she'd hurriedly told him. Dan wondered if Aunt Doreen was aware of this. Probably not, he decided. She wouldn't have approved.

The woman said that this boyfriend, the horrible Marco, had told her that she was the kind of woman who could drive a man to drink. "Can you imagine that?" she said, her eyes widening. "What a mean thing to say. And I'm telling you that this came out of nowhere. I kept the house super perfect, cooked his meals, did his laundry, and everything else." She winked at the "everything else." "There was no reason for him to turn on me like he did. My sister said she thinks he's a sociopath and I Googled it and guess what?" Before Dan could answer, she answered her own question. "I read the description of a sociopath and he fits it perfectly." She ticked off on her fingers. "Charming, manipulative, lack of empathy for other people, inability to truly love. I'm telling you, I dodged a bullet with that one."

"Sounds like it," Dan said.

"So if you know someone with a place to rent, I'm definitely in the market. It wouldn't have to be a whole apartment at this point. Just a room would be okay. I really have to get out of there."

He shook his head. "I don't know of anything offhand. If something comes up, I'll have Doreen let you know."

After that he kept the conversation on an even keel, talking about his work in between bites. The food kept her somewhat occupied, but she still managed to interrupt him a few times. She'd never heard of a microbrewery. "Let me guess! It's a teeny, tiny brewery!" she said, throwing her head back and laughing like it was hilarious. Dan had never seen anyone so entertained by their own words. "I would love working at a place where I could drink beer all day," she said, making a show of tipping an imaginary bottle to her mouth. "Way cool."

"A lot of people think that we get to drink beer all day," he said, "but that's not how it really works. We wouldn't get anything done if we were drinking on the job." Truthfully they were entitled to one glass a week. Many of the guys saved it for lunchtime on Friday. Besides the allotted amount, Dan occasionally did some taste testing when they were developing a new beer or ale. It wasn't his area, but sometimes they asked his opinion. But he almost never mentioned that perk of the job.

She winked. "But I bet you can kick one back when no one's looking, right? Especially being the boss and all."

That was exactly why he never mentioned it. Everyone assumed his job was a forty-hour-a-week kegger, and it just wasn't true. "I could, but I don't."

"Aw, come on, I won't tell anyone! Fess up. Every once in a while when you're having a bad day, it has to be a temptation, am I right?" She reached over and patted his wrist in a familiar way.

"Actually, no . . ." He paused, aware of a woman who'd stopped at their table. He glanced up to see the voluptuous redhead who'd arrived at the restaurant just after him. Her friend, the familiar-looking brunette, kept going, her boots clicking their way toward the front door.

The redhead smacked her palm against the table and leaned toward his eating companion. "Hello there, Desiree."

Oh, Desiree! Mystery solved. Dan now had a name to use when he let her down gently at the end of this lunch.

Desiree said, "Hi?"

"Are you enjoying your lunch date?"

Desiree glanced from Dan to the red-haired woman, clearly confused, then down at her nearly empty plate. "Yeah everything was good, thanks."

Dan said, "It's not a date." But before he could say anything else, the woman strode away, flipping her knit scarf over her shoulder. "Do you know her?" he asked, watching until she disappeared around the corner.

Desiree shrugged. "She looked sort of familiar. Maybe she's the manager here?"

Dan shook his head. "She's not the manager. She was eating lunch right over there the whole time we've been here. Plus, she knew your name."

"Oh yeah." Desiree looked uninterested. "I get that a lot. I don't want to sound conceited, but people always remember me, but I don't always remember them." She tucked her hair behind her ear. "I mean, I remember the important people. I'll certainly remember you, don't worry about that."

Again she grasped his wrist, but this was one time too many for him. He felt his skin crawl at the intimacy of the gesture, and made a sudden decision. It was okay to be a little bit rude, just this once. "I hate to do this," he said, pulling out his wallet and peeling off a couple of twenties, which he left in the middle of the table, "but I can't stay any longer. I really have to go, so I'll leave this here. If you'd take care of the bill, I'd really appreciate it. It was nice meeting you, Desiree." He returned the wallet to his back pocket and got out the keys to his truck.

She watched, confused, as he slid out of the booth. "Well, maybe next time we can—"

"I'm sorry, but there won't be a next time. Enjoy the rest of your day." Leaving the restaurant, Dan felt his mood lift and as the cold outdoor air hit his face, it struck him as invigorating. The sun was high in the sky now too, the light a welcome sight after sitting for so long in the dim restaurant. During the whole meal he'd dreaded coming up with an excuse when all it took was telling her that there wouldn't be a next time. Huh. Who knew how easy it could be? He felt the words still lingering on his tongue. *Sorry, but there won't be a next time.* Simple, direct, nothing to argue about. He wasn't trying to hurt her feelings, but there was no sense in prolonging the inevitable. And after all, he'd promised he'd have lunch with her and he'd fulfilled that obligation.

EIGHTEEN

Andrea waited to meet up with Jade in the restaurant parking lot. "So?" Andrea asked, when she saw her friend come out with a big smile on her face. "What did you say to her?"

Jade grinned and reenacted it, bending at the waist to rest her hand on an imaginary table. "I said 'Helllllooo, Desireee. Are you enjoying your lunch date?'" She shook her head. "When I looked down I could totally see her black lace bra down the front of her shirt. So sleazy. She's like her own peep show."

"What did she do?"

"She's such a ditz. I don't think she recognized me at all. She's all, 'My lunch was good, thanks,' like I was the waitress or something. The guy, though, he was quick to jump in and say it wasn't a date."

Good for him not wanting to be associated with Desiree, Andrea thought. At least there was one man in the world with some common sense. "And that was it?"

"Pretty much. I just walked away after that. I can't believe she didn't remember me from that day I helped move your stuff out of the house." Jade frowned. "Everyone remembers me. I mean, *everyone*. It's the red hair." She twirled a lock around her finger. "I'm distinctive."

"Yes, you are distinctive." Andrea grinned.

"Anyway, I've got to run. I'll stop by after work one night to see your new love interest," Jade said, giving her a hug before climbing into her car. "See you later, you crazy dog stealer," she called out, driving away.

Andrea waved and then fished her keys out of her purse. A slight gust of snow drifted down, almost in slow motion, and she took a deep breath of the bracing air. She wondered what Desiree would have done if she had been the one to stop at the table. What if she had very snarkily asked how Marco was doing? A barrage of scenarios ran through her head, things she could say to embarrass Desiree or messages she could send back to Marco, but none of it was appealing. She just didn't care. If she were going to say anything to the blonde home wrecker, it would be that she was welcome to Marco, that in the long run she'd done Andrea a favor. But even that seemed too much. Just let them live their lives and she'd live hers.

Just as Andrea was about to get into her car, the restaurant door burst open and Desiree's date (the one who had told Jade it wasn't a date) sprinted out like a man fleeing the scene of a crime. He had a wicked grin on his face as he came her way. Presumably headed to his getaway car.

Andrea had never been one to chat up strangers, especially strange men, but as he got closer something made her call out, "You seem to be in a hurry."

He clearly had been lost in thought and hadn't noticed her standing next to her car, because her comment startled him into slowing. He ran a hand over his wavy brown hair, and gave her a smile. "Not in a hurry. Just heading home."

"The way you rushed out, I thought maybe you'd robbed the place," she said, her car keys looped around her fingers. "Or maybe you were skipping out on your date?"

"Oh, that wasn't a date. Believe me, not a date." He shot a glance back at the restaurant and then said, almost apologetically, "That was a . . . well, I don't know what it was. Just lunch, I guess."

"Just lunch," Andrea said and then flinched at her own stupidity. She couldn't come up with anything better to say than that? He had stopped now, five feet away, and he was still looking at her with a smile. He was really cute, she thought. Distinguished, but not in an old-guy way. Older than her, though. Maybe late thirties. Hard to judge, but certainly no older than forty. His navy jacket was open, casually left unzipped like he didn't even feel the cold. The breeze kicked up and snow drifted around them like they were characters at a skating rink in a movie. "Well," she said, "I guess I better go home and feed my dog." Again, she flinched and inwardly groaned. Go home and feed my dog? She needed a better scriptwriter because that was the worst line ever. Jade would have had his name, address, and social security number by now, but that was Jade. She was outgoing, bold, unafraid. Andrea wanted to be all those things, but she never seemed able to summon it at the time.

He nodded approvingly. "Okay. It was nice talking to you . . . ?"

"Andrea."

Again, his head bobbed up and down, like her name met with his approval. "Andrea. Nice talking to you, Andrea. Maybe we'll cross paths again sometime."

"Yes, maybe we will." Andrea watched as he went over to a red truck, and she heard the beep as he unlocked the door. "That's it?" she murmured to herself, disappointed. She took one daring step in his direction and blurted out, "Hey! I don't think I got your name."

"My name?" He paused, his hand on the open door. "It's Dan."

"Nice to meet you, Dan." She raised her hand and gave him a fluttery wave.

Again, he gave her that adorable little boy grin, like he was getting away with something. "Nice to meet you too, Andrea." And then he got into his truck and started the engine.

As Andrea saw the brake lights of the truck at the edge of the parking lot, all she could think was she should have kept the conversation going. It might have even led to her suggesting they get together sometime. Why had she held back? Women had been asking men out for ages now; it wasn't a new concept. Clearly, there'd been some attraction there and she could have handled it in a smart way, not disclosing her last name or where she lived. It would have been easy to exchange cell phone numbers, or make plans to meet at this same restaurant on another day. But she knew what it was. Besides the fact he was a complete stranger, the fear of rejection had held her back. And he'd been there with Desiree. It seemed like he didn't want to be with Desiree, but still he somehow had wound up sitting opposite her at a restaurant and that alone reflected poorly on his character.

She sighed. Well, it didn't make a difference either way. She would probably never see him again, and besides, Anni waited for her at home.

NINETEEN

The next Sunday found Dan sitting in the back row of the church by himself. He hadn't been inside the building in over a year, and with Lindsay scheduled to work that morning, he was flying solo. Back when they came as a family, their usual spot was toward the front on the right-hand side. Often Aunt Doreen or one of the other relatives would join them, and most often they'd go to brunch afterward. Nothing formal, just the place on the lake that did made-to-order omelets.

He purposely avoided sitting with Doreen, who he saw was already seated up front, but he knew if they met up on the way out, he'd have a thing or two to say to her. Namely: What had she been thinking matching him up with that nightmare Desiree? He shook his head at the memory of the tacky blonde woman blathering endlessly about herself while fussing with her hair and earrings. Could there be a woman more different than Christine?

He'd thought that being here without his wife would feel like a betrayal, but instead it was fine. Just lonely, seeing all the couples and families troop in, greeting others as they proceeded to their seats. The only other singles seemed to be gray-haired ladies with thick glasses, clutching large handbags to their side.

The service began and he went along with the singing and praying and everything else, but it felt like rote. None of it came from the heart, the way it had in the past. His faith, once shiny and solid, was dinged up and rusty. Attending church, and everything that came with it, was part of his old life. Back when things made sense and God didn't strike down a healthy woman—a wife, a mother—long before her time, taking her away from everyone who loved her. There was no reason for her suffering and death, and, to add insult to injury, Anni was gone, stolen by some drunken cretins looking for sadistic fun. While everyone else recited a prayer, Dan made a mental bargain. *God*, he prayed, *if Anni is returned to us, unharmed, I'll give you another shot.* Well, what were the chances of that happening? Sadly, it was slim to none. And really, if bargaining had worked, he'd have Christine with him now. Best to just forget about it.

Maybe he shouldn't have come to church today. Instead of being a balm for his soul, the service had become an irritant to his inner peace. When the hour was over, he made his way through the crowd, hat in hand.

Doreen spotted him in the lobby and called his name, then worked her way to where he stood. "Dan." She threw her arms around him. "I'm so glad you came." The top of her head only came up to his armpit, but still her hug was firm.

"I told you I would, didn't I?"

"Actually, I believe you said you'd think about it. Aren't you glad you came?"

"Not really," he said. "In fact, I've got a bone to pick with you. That woman you set me up with? Sheesh. An hour with her—pure torture."

"That bad?" Doreen said, unsuccessfully suppressing a smile. "Ah, I was afraid that might be the case."

"What?" Dan gave her his narrowed-eye gaze, the one he used on Lindsay when she stayed out past curfew. "You were afraid that might be the case? You knowingly put me in the line of fire?"

"Oh, it couldn't have been as bad as all that," Doreen said soothingly. "Come to brunch with me and we can talk."

"I'm not all that sure I want to talk to you." He tried to keep up the pretense of being miffed, but a smile broke through.

"Come out with me and I'll explain my thinking," she said. When he didn't respond right away, she added, "Come on! It'll be fun. With any luck, some of my book club ladies might see us and I can get the gals talking about my mystery man."

An hour later he and Doreen sat at a table overlooking the lake, their omelets in front of them, mimosas to the right of their plates. Doreen was fond of mimosas, always ordering them at half strength and then claiming they were still too strong, but drinking them anyway—then ordering another one.

"So," Dan said. "Making me meet this woman for lunch was, what? A practical joke? Your idea of fun?"

"Oh no, dear, I would never do that to you," Doreen said, patting his hand in a motherly way. "Was it really that dreadful?"

"It was really that dreadful."

"There was nothing good that came of it?"

Dan thought about the fifteen seconds in the parking lot, the brief exchange with the woman in the camel-colored coat. Andrea. The effect she'd had on him was puzzling. The attraction wasn't even romantic or sexual, either, just the feeling that he knew her somehow. He liked her voice. Even her smile seemed familiar. And she had a dog that she had to go home and feed. A dog was about as good of a recommendation as one could get. He met Doreen's eyes and realized she still needed an answer. "Having to talk to Desiree was excruciating. I had no idea time could go so slowly."

Doreen said, "I knew you wouldn't end up together, but, you know, I think you both needed this. And honestly, Dan, how painful could it have been? It was just one lunch. Desiree was really in a bad place what with that schmuck breaking her heart, and you, well, you've been in that sad rut you've dug for yourself for so long now. Don't get me wrong." She held up a hand to stop his objection. "I've been there myself. When Bruno died, I didn't feel like doing anything. Didn't even feel like getting out of bed. So I get it. Really, I do. But at some point, a person just needs to move forward, and for me it happened gradually. One step at a time. You do one small thing and you get through it so you know you can do that and more too. One small thing." She dabbed her mouth with her napkin. "But you have to do that one small thing and I didn't see it happening for you, so I set up the dominoes and gave it a push. At least you have to admit that Desiree is a very attractive woman."

Dan felt the kindness in her words and knew she meant well, but still. "I appreciate the thought, but please, do not do that again."

Doreen smiled. "Always the gentleman. Even as a little boy you had good manners, and I've always liked that about you, Dan. Most men would have told me off for being pushy and annoying."

"I'm serious, Doreen. Don't even think about doing this to me again."

"Oh, I know you're serious. But I won't have to do it again. You already did your one small thing, and so it has begun. Next time you go to lunch with a lady, it will be much easier."

He'd intended to stay angry with her, but found it impossible. There was so much love in her eyes, it disarmed him. "*If* I ever go to lunch with a lady again."

She laughed. "You will. Just wait and see. One day you will."

TWENTY

Andrea decided Anni was the smartest dog on the planet. And not only intelligent, but possibly psychic too. All Andrea had to do was think about *maybe* taking Anni for a walk and her girl would excitedly troop to the door, pawing at the leash that hung over the knob. Within a few weeks, Anni knew Andrea's morning schedule, nudging her awake moments before the alarm went off on weekdays, and letting her sleep in a bit later on the weekends.

Originally she'd set up Anni's bed downstairs in the kitchen, scattering a few toys nearby so she'd get the idea that this was her space. Agreeably the dog settled into bed, but when Andrea headed up the stairs to go to sleep, Anni followed. She just didn't get that the dog bed was her place to sleep. That first night Andrea had been wary of letting the dog sleep in her bed. She really didn't know this animal, and besides, Anni had been mistreated. What if she bit or scratched Andrea while she slept? Anni looked so sweet, but anything was possible. Andrea's solution, setting the dog bed up in the bathroom and shutting the door, did not go over well. Anni cried pitifully until the door opened and then she happily scampered out. Finally, exhausted and defeated, Andrea patted the bed, "All right, you can sleep here." Anni immediately jumped up and curled up next to her. There was no turning back after that.

Almost by accident she discovered that Anni could follow commands. "Sit," came out of her mouth at one point and Anni sat with almost military precision. After that Andrea ran through the gamut of dog tricks and found that Anni knew all the basics: sit, stay, come, roll over, and play dead. The last one she discovered, "beg," Anni had done on her own, begging when she saw Andrea bring out dog treats. Such a smart dog.

And she was affectionate too, snuggling up against Andrea when she watched TV, and keeping her feet warm in bed. Sometimes Andrea caught the dog looking up at her adoringly, and her heart swelled. So this was why dog people were so insane! It all made sense now.

At the office, Anni sensed when she needed to be absolutely silent and would rest quietly at her feet. During the lunch hour, Andrea had to abandon her former habit of eating at her desk and actually venture out into the world. A quick outing to let Anni do her business evolved into a daily walk through the downtown area. Anni always leapt with delight the minute Andrea got out the leash and it seemed mean not to keep going. The world looked different with a dog leading the way. People who might have walked on by, not making eye contact at all, stopped to pet Anni and make small talk. Soon enough Andrea had talked to more people coming and going from the office than she had in years.

The first day Tommy came in after his vacation, Andrea braced herself, expecting him to say she couldn't bring a dog to work. But, just like everyone else, he was charmed by Anni. "Who do we have here?" he asked, crouching down to rub behind her ears. Anni lifted her head, luxuriating in being the center of attention.

"This is Anni," Andrea said, glancing down nonchalantly as if this were business as usual.

But Tommy McGuire was nobody's fool. "Is Anni now a regular here at McGuire Properties?" he asked, rising.

"You could say that," Andrea admitted. "I think she adds a certain something to the place, don't you? A touch of class?"

"So this is your dog?"

"Yes."

"And you plan on bringing her every day." It was half statement, half question.

Andrea hesitated. "If I can. I mean, if it's okay with you."

Tommy had a thoughtful expression on his face. "If she's always like this, I don't have any objections to her being here. If she causes any problems, though, I reserve the right to change my mind."

"Fair enough," Andrea said. Looking at Anni resting with her nose on her paws, it was hard to believe she could ever cause problems.

Luckily, Anni was well behaved, and Tommy became quite fond of her, usually greeting the dog first when he came through the door. One day Andrea and Anni came in to find a large glass jar filled with dog treats on the top shelf of the office bookcase, a jar supplied and replenished by Tommy himself. Anni got excited any time either of them even walked in the direction of the jar, and Tommy reinforced her expectation by getting her a treat every time. "Aren't you a sweet thing," he'd say.

So that was good.

A wonderful bonus to all the walking was the discovery that her pants now hung loosely off her hips. Puzzled at first, she wondered if they'd become stretched out in the laundry, but after trying on multiple pairs of pants, it was confirmed: she was thinner. Andrea dug out a pair of designer jeans, the ones she'd foolishly spent $150 on. She had only worn them once. Even in her thinner days, they'd just barely fit. She'd bought them thinking the fabulous cut, the stitched back pocket, and the amount of money she'd spent would motivate her to lose weight. But she never did, and eventually the sight of them brought a flush of shame. She finally hid them in the back of her closet and almost threw them out when she'd moved out of the house she'd shared with Marco. They seemed emblematic of her failure as a wife. What kind of woman couldn't even lose ten pounds? No wonder her husband's head was turned by a thinner, younger, curvier woman.

Andrea held the jeans up and turned them, once again admiring the cut and stitching. If only. She took off her pants, and held her breath as she stepped into the legs of the designer jeans. Here went nothing. Up they went, over her calves, and then her thighs, and finally over her hips. She zipped them with ease and felt like cheering. How had this happened in just a few weeks? She turned to look at her backside in the mirror, pulled up her shirt, and noted a lack of muffin top, not even a small one. Huh.

She studied the reflection of her face and neck, turning her head from side to side. Her cheeks looked less rounded and more sculpted, she thought. Nights filled with solid, restful sleep were another bonus of their long walks. She was so tired at the end of the day that she drifted off as soon as her head hit the pillow. As a result, her dark under-eye circles were nearly gone now. And here she'd thought they were unavoidable, a mixture of age and genetics. It wasn't until she'd noticed that people no longer randomly asked her if she was tired that she'd made the connection. Apparently, even when she didn't feel tired, the under-eye circles had made her look weary. Who knew having a dog would improve your appearance? Once pudgy cheeked (and full hipped) and tired-looking, she was now somewhat svelte and well rested. She'd have weighed herself to see the actual difference, but she'd let Marco have the scale in the divorce and she'd made a deliberate decision not to purchase a new one, reasoning she was already depressed enough. But now she put it on her list of things to buy the next time she was at Target. A nice new scale with a bright LED display.

Andrea started eating lunch at Café Mocha, the coffee shop that allowed dogs. It was nearly a mile from the office, a walking distance that would have seemed daunting in the past, but after regularly walking Anni, she was now used to it. If no one stopped them to socialize, they could make it in fifteen minutes.

Today she walked into the coffee shop, stamping her feet on the mat inside the front door. The Café Mocha was a good-size space, with fifteen tables and an assortment of upholstered chairs around the perimeter. The décor was modern with some vintage touches—black-and-white checkerboard tiles on the floor, light fixtures with a 1960s' look. A redbrick fireplace graced one wall. During the winter months, a fire was always blazing and the warmth and beauty of the flames made the surrounding tables highly coveted. The owner of the place, Joan, knew everyone and had an incredible memory for names and customer preferences. And she loved Anni.

"There they are," she called out from behind the counter. Anni strained at the leash to get the dog biscuit she associated with Joan's voice. "Andrea and Anni. The daring duo. The cutest of cute. The ones to beat. Two of my favorites."

Andrea had a feeling that most of the customers were her favorites, but there was still something nice about being included in that group.

Joan reached over the counter with a dog biscuit and dropped it down to Anni, who caught it between her teeth. "Oh man!" Joan said with admiration. "Did you see how fast she did that? I think we set a record here. Anni, you are awesome." Andrea ordered her usual cup of soup, iced tea, and half sandwich, paid, and went to sit down. Anni followed amiably as she wove around the tables, scanning the room. When Andrea saw a young couple, college kids from the looks of them, vacating one of the tables by the fireplace, she tugged on the leash and moved in to take it. The guy had already made his way to the door, but the girl still stood next to the table, adjusting her scarf around her neck. "You can have the table. We're all done," she said, sweetly stating the obvious. "Oh, what an adorable dog." The girl bent down, a sheen of dark hair curtaining either side of her face. She gave Anni's head a quick pet before gathering up her backpack and gloves.

"Thanks," Andrea said. She was getting used to taking credit for Anni's cuteness.

After the girl hurried away, Andrea took a seat, looping the end of Anni's leash around her chair and scooting Anni's hindquarters close to her feet so that she didn't block the aisle. Joan or one of the other women who worked here usually delivered the food within a few minutes, so Andrea took the time to gaze at the fire and think about the rest of her week, particularly her weekend. She definitely had to fit in a visit to Gram at the nursing home on Saturday. Okay, technically they weren't called nursing homes anymore; they were rehab facilities. Gram's was called the Phoenix Health Care Center. Phoenix. As if someone would be rising from the ashes. Well, they could call it what they wanted, but in Gram's case it was a permanent placement. Her dementia had progressed to the point that she couldn't live independently and no one in the family was equipped to take care of her. Andrea had been guilty of not visiting for a few weeks. It was always so depressing now that Gram didn't always recognize her, but she'd called the center and gotten permission to bring a dog. "Anni is very small and well behaved," she'd campaigned over the phone. She'd expected some resistance, but the nurse she'd talked to sounded rushed and, frankly, not all that interested, saying she thought it was probably fine for the third floor. "Visiting pets must be up to date on their shots, well trained, and leashed to ensure everyone's safety," she said. "Additionally, you must sign in at the front desk when you enter the building." Knowing she could bring Anni along put a new slant on the whole thing and now Andrea looked forward to visiting Gram.

Andrea watched the fireplace flames dance and made a mental list of everything she had to do that afternoon. She was completely lost in thought when a man's voice interrupted.

"Is this seat taken?"

She looked up to see a gorgeous man standing next to her, gesturing to the empty chair on the other side of the table. Breathtakingly gorgeous. She mentally cataloged his looks for the purpose of storytelling to Jade later: Tall? Check. Dark? Check. Handsome? Yes, yes, and yes. The kind of good looks that could make a woman speechless. She stammered, "The seat? No. I mean, no, it's not taken. Feel free. Of course you can sit there."

He sat, making apologies as he went. "I'm sorry to intrude, but all the other tables seem to be occupied."

"No, it's fine." Now that he sat across from her, she could see his face more clearly. He could have been a model, with his flawless skin, chiseled features, and strong jaw. His clothing could have said college student, but he was older, maybe thirty-five or so? Definitely worth chatting up, if she had the nerve. Jade's philosophy about the interconnectedness of the universe came to mind. Even if it came to nothing, who knew if he had a friend, or a younger brother? How bizarre to even be thinking this way. A few months ago she thought she'd be alone for the rest of her life. Now the world seemed full of possibility.

"Nice dog," he said, before getting out his phone.

"Thanks." If Jade were here, she'd already have this conversation started, but Andrea had never been a master of small talk. Luckily, just then Joan approached with her tray of food. "Well, hello there, Philip," she said, greeting the man while setting down Andrea's food. "How did I miss you coming in?"

Ah, so his name was Philip. He looked like a Philip. Suave and debonair, yet rugged. Philip looked up from his phone to flash a smile at the coffee shop owner. "Hey, Joan. I snuck in when you weren't looking."

"Where's your better half today?" Joan asked.

"At work," he said, sighing. "She should be here already, but things got crazy at the office. She texted and said she'd get here as soon as she could."

"Too bad." Joan's head tilted sympathetically. "Hopefully you won't have to wait too long. Do you know Andrea?"

"I do now." He reached over and Andrea dutifully shook his hand.

"You two should get along," Joan said. "You both have beautiful dogs."

As Joan walked away, Philip said, "My wife and Joan are friends. They went to college together."

How had she missed the wedding ring? His beauty had blinded her and jangled her nerves. Knowing he was married, though, made it easier. Andrea said, "Oh, I love Joan. It's amazing the way she remembers everyone's name." Philip agreed and they began talking about the coffee shop and the college Joan and his wife (her name was Vanessa) had attended, and before she knew it, they were completely engrossed in conversation. He and his wife had a sheltie, and soon enough he and Andrea were trading anecdotes about their dogs. *Look at me*, Andrea thought, *acting all casual while eating with a perfect stranger.* A really perfect stranger. Of course, he talked about his wife like they were newlyweds, which they very nearly were. He told Andrea, "I never knew someone like her existed in the world until I met her, and now I can't imagine the world without her."

Andrea could not imagine Marco saying anything close to this about her, or anyone else for that matter. Philip and Vanessa were a couple to envy.

Vanessa hadn't arrived by the time Andrea had finished her lunch, but Philip had acquiesced and ordered a coffee. He took small sips, like trying to make it last until his wife arrived. "It was nice talking with you, Andrea," he said as she gathered up her things. A simple thing like leaving became so complicated in the wintertime. There were gloves to keep track of and a scarf to adjust. A zipper to take care of before she stepped outside into the brisk air. A cumbersome routine, but there was no getting around it.

"I enjoyed talking to you too," she said. "I hope your wife gets here soon."

"Me too." He sighed again, like a lovesick teenager.

Anni yawned and then rose, shuddering a little as she got to her feet. Andrea said, "Time to go, Anni," and the familiar phrase gave the dog a surge of energy. When they got to the door to leave, Andrea glanced back to see Philip watching them. He gave her a little wave and she raised her hand in return. What a nice man.

When they stepped outside onto the sidewalk, the snow crunching under Andrea's boots, Anni took the lead and turned in the direction of the office. The sudden cold air sweeping across Andrea's cheeks made her eyes water; she pulled out her sunglasses and stuck them on her face.

A large man stood blocking their path, his short shadow a blot on the sidewalk. Andrea's eyes were on Anni, so she didn't get a good look, but she said, "Excuse me," before stepping to one side.

"Andrea!" The familiar voice penetrated right to her spine, making her heart sink.

She glanced up to see Marco. Even though he looked exactly the way she remembered, the sight of him was a shock. Several times after they'd separated and once after they'd divorced, she'd driven past her old house hoping to see him coming or going. Obsessive behavior, she knew, and unhealthy too. She wasn't even sure what she'd hoped to see or what it would accomplish, but it didn't make a difference, because she'd never spotted him. Once she saw Desiree backing her car down the driveway, and she panicked, thinking Desiree would see her and tell Marco. But Desiree drove right past, oblivious, actually using the rearview mirror to put on lipstick, which Andrea did not approve of for safety purposes, but at least it meant Desiree didn't see her. A few times she and Jade had made a point to go to a bar that had been a favorite of Marco's, but although they saw his brother one time, Marco was never there. Jade made Andrea pretend to laugh loudly and talk to some college guys because she was sure Marco's brother would give him the full report. They had no way of knowing if that ever happened, though, which was very unsatisfying.

"Marco," she said, not able to keep the surprise out of her voice. Funny that she'd run into him now when she'd given up caring.

"I can't believe you almost walked right past me." He held out his hands in mock dismay. "You would have kept going if I hadn't stopped you."

"Right. Okay then, if you could step aside, I have to get going." A hundred times she'd thought of what she would say to Marco if she ever saw him again. "I have to get going" wasn't what she'd planned, but it fell out of her mouth in a calm, cool manner like she ran into her ex-husband every day.

"You have a dog now," he said, leaning over, but as his hand came close, Anni took a step backward and stiffened. Her tail hung flat on her back end. She made a low growl followed by a sharp yip, and he straightened up in alarm. "But not a friendly dog." He glared at Anni.

Andrea looked down at Anni in shock. She'd never seen her do that before. "She likes most people."

"Anyway." Marco always did have a tendency to change the subject to suit himself. He fixed his gaze on Andrea and suddenly she found herself immobile. The power he'd once exerted over her had come back. "That guy you were with?" He jabbed his thumb in the direction of the coffee shop.

"Philip?" Her mouth suddenly felt dry.

"Yeah, I guess. Philip." He said the name with disdain. "I'd be careful if I were you. I don't know what he's told you, but I've seen that guy out with another woman."

"I don't really think this is any of your concern. We're divorced, remember?" She took a deep breath before giving the leash a slight tug to direct Anni to walk around him.

His arm came out to stop her. "Yeah, I remember. Boy, do I remember. It was probably one of the biggest mistakes of my life. I miss you, Andrea." His expression softened to one that she remembered well. In the past, he could tease her out of any bad mood, get her to accept any lie, sweep suspicions away like they were nothing. And she'd always drifted along with whatever he wanted. A happy Marco made life easier, more fun. And he was good-looking. She'd forgotten how good-looking, with naturally broad shoulders and a strong jawline. The kind of manly physique cartoonists drew to depict the hot lifeguard at the beach, the one carrying the pretty young thing out of the water.

Marco gave her a smile, a smile just for her, the kind that used to make her melt. He missed her. He'd made a mistake. She paused for just a second, every possible response streaming through her head. Marco, her first love, stood before her, admitting he'd been wrong, saying he missed her. Just what she had once hoped to hear, back in the day when she wished they'd get back together. Their marriage hadn't been bad, not at all. When they were together, life had been easy, there'd been a pattern, a routine. She knew his family and he knew hers. They had history. He was charming and good-looking. Bold and confident. Just the man you'd want to give a toast or tell a joke. Yes, Marco had been her first big-time love. And now he stood before her wanting a second chance. Really. She blew out a puff of air, watching it turn into a mist of cold and, in that instant, it all became clear. He'd been her first real love, but he wasn't going to be her last. And she would never go back to him.

"I was hoping we could still be friends," he said, giving her his most charming smile, a sort of self-confident smirk.

"That's not going to happen," she said. "Because we never were friends." And she clicked her tongue and directed Anni around him.

"How about you think about it?" he shouted when she was halfway down the block. A gust of cold air carried the words so that she heard them as crisply as if he were by her side.

For a split second she thought she was going to be the bigger person and ignore him, but something got into her, and in a flash she'd pulled off her glove. "How about you think about this," she called out, her voice strong, turning in time to see his shocked expression as she flipped him the bird.

Clearly, that was not the response he'd expected.

TWENTY-ONE

On Saturday afternoon when Lindsay got home from working a shift at Walgreens, she burst through the door calling for him. "Dad!" she yelled. "Dad, where are you?"

At the sound of her voice he left the laundry and jogged up the basement steps, thinking there was some tragedy. "I'm here. What's wrong?"

His daughter stood in the entryway, her hair and jacket dusted with snow. She owned a hat but almost never wore it for fear of hat hair. "There's nothing wrong." She took off her gloves. "I just wanted to tell you something before I forgot. I wanted to tell you first thing this morning, but you were still asleep." She said it accusingly, like he wasn't supposed to be sleeping in on a weekend morning. Like it was unfair she had to leave the house at seven thirty while he stayed in bed.

"Okay, what is it?"

"I had a dream last night and Mom was in it . . ." She shook her arms out of her sleeves and hung her jacket on the hook by the door.

Oh, here she went again. Since that first time, Lindsay had had several dreams involving her mother. Each time she was convinced it was Christine talking to her from the other side. Dan didn't want to squash her beliefs, but the dreams had gotten kind of convoluted. Sometimes she only had a sense that her mother was there. Other times Christine was there but didn't say anything, just looked on, smiling happily as if she were glad to see Lindsay. Clearly, her mother was on her mind, which was understandable. Lindsay was going through so much with it being her last year of high school. The prom and graduation were coming up, both things Christine would have had a hand in. Certainly, the two of them would have gone shopping for dresses and everything else. He understood how much Lindsay missed her mother. Christine's absence loomed large in their household and their hearts.

"And—wait, you look like you're not going to believe me," Lindsay said, the corners of her mouth suddenly turning downward.

"I'm listening. I'm listening," Dan said. "How can I not believe you when you haven't said anything yet?" He leaned against the doorframe, giving her all his attention.

"Because the last time I mentioned Mom was in my dream, you asked if I wanted to see the grief counselor again."

She'd been irate at the suggestion. And it was just a suggestion. Being a parent was so hard now that he didn't have someone else to turn to when he wasn't sure of the answers. And this dream thing struck a nerve with him. So many times when falling asleep he willed himself to dream of Christine, but it never happened. Why would she visit Lindsay, but not him? "I know," he said. "But that was last time. Could you give me the benefit of the doubt?"

"Okay," she said begrudgingly. "Anyway, I dreamed about Mom again and this time she talked to me and gave me a message for you. I actually woke up and wrote it down so I wouldn't forget. The paper is next to my bed, but basically she said"—she looked up at the ceiling, remembering—"'I needed to tell you to visit Aunt Nadine.'"

"Really." Inwardly he groaned. Not Nadine.

Nadine wasn't really Lindsay's aunt. In fact, she wasn't related to them at all. Nadine had been Christine's boss and when Nadine had retired ten years earlier, Christine had kept in touch, taking over the daughter role because Nadine's sons weren't all that attentive. Nadine had limited mobility due to severe arthritis, and later in life she experienced a series of strokes; now she lived in an old folks' home. Officially it was a rehab center, but in Nadine's case, she was there for good. Christine had kept up with visiting about once a month after Nadine went to live at the Phoenix Health Care Center and even took Anni with her on occasion, but Dan hadn't even thought about Nadine at all since Christine's death. And if he had thought of the old woman, it would not have been good thoughts. Nadine was difficult. Sharp-tongued, critical, argumentative. Dan understood why her sons didn't come around much. "I have no idea what you see in that woman," he'd said to Christine. She didn't have a good answer, just that Nadine was in a lot of pain. She'd been a terrific boss, and had hired Christine when the job market was terrible. Christine had a strong sense of loyalty. She said, "Have some compassion, Dan."

Dan had compassion. What he lacked was patience. "So I'm supposed to visit Nadine?" He couldn't help rolling his eyes. Of all the things for Lindsay to dream.

"I know. Weird, huh?" Lindsay said, grinning. "But better you than me. Aunt Nadine is so annoying."

"So annoying."

"So, are you going to do it?"

"Visit Nadine?"

"Well, yeah. I mean, I know you think it's just a random dream, but what if it really is from Mom? It's the kinda thing she'd do, don't you think?"

"Yeah, your mom had a soft heart," Dan agreed. "I'll think about it. You know, for all we know, Nadine isn't even there anymore."

Lindsay regarded him blankly. "Where would she go?"

"Another facility. The hospital. Or she could have died, even."

"I'm *sure* she didn't die," Lindsay said, frowning.

"She might have. It's not like anyone would have told us."

Lindsay dug her phone out of her purse. "Well, I think you should go. I mean, big deal, it's just an hour of your time."

"Just an hour." She didn't seem to realize how long an hour could be under the worst circumstances.

"And it's a nice thing to do, right?" Now Lindsay sounded suspiciously like Christine. A good attribute, usually, but in this case it seemed like emotional ammunition.

"Right. Well, I'll think about it," Dan said, but already he knew there was nothing to think about. Nadine had been Christine's friend. What would they even talk about? Besides, he still had some reports to go over for work and he needed to make a trip to the hardware store for water softener salt. Even if he wanted to go visit Nadine (and, truthfully, he didn't), it wasn't feasible. He just couldn't fit it into his schedule.

TWENTY-TWO

Andrea grew to love the sound of a dog in the house. The squeak of a toy as Anni carried it across the room to her, the sound of canine nails against the tile, the whimpering of appreciation when she got her morning ear rubs. Again she thought of how Anni had been mistreated by the frat boys, and how close she had come to not having Anni in her life. Imagine if Stan had been well enough to deliver the letter? The frat boys would have pawned Anni off on someone else, or dropped her off at the pound. Then some other lucky person might have adopted her. Or maybe not. Maybe no one would have adopted her and she would have languished in some cage somewhere. That scenario was too horrible to even contemplate.

"You're my girl now, aren't you?" she asked, stroking Anni's smooth fur, fully aware that her behavior was now mirroring that of people she used to make fun of. Well, so be it. She'd been in the dark and now had seen the light. Crazy dog lady. They could put it on her tombstone.

Today they were heading out to see Gram at the Phoenix Health Care Center. Andrea timed their Saturday visit for just after lunch. She and Anni pulled into the parking lot at one o'clock exactly, and were through the glass doors a few minutes later. She hadn't called ahead. There was no reason to, since Gram's existence went from moment to moment and her memory of Andrea was sketchy, if at all. A sad truth.

Anni strained at the leash, her nails clicking lightly on the grooved linoleum. Past the double doors, they stopped at the front desk to sign in. The woman behind the counter, an older lady with a silver bouffant hairstyle, gushed over Anni in a sweet, high-pitched voice. "What a cutie. Our residents love it when dogs come to visit. She doesn't mind strangers petting her, does she?"

"No. She's as gentle as a lamb," Andrea said, and then, remembering Anni's reaction to Marco, almost amended her statement, but the woman was already giving directions to a man who had arrived just after them.

They took the elevator to the third floor. Once they were buzzed in to the locked ward, down the hall they went, Anni trotting amiably alongside Andrea. As they passed open doorways, Andrea heard the residents' comments.

"What a cute dog."

"Hey, puppy!"

"So precious."

"I hope that thing doesn't start barking."

Andrea had to grin. There was always one grouch in the crowd. When she got to Gram's room, number 312, she paused and knocked on the slightly open door before entering. The room was a double, each side containing a twin bed, dresser, chair, end table, and lamp (the lamp was bolted down, Andrea had discovered during an earlier visit). A TV was suspended at the end of each bed, and the privacy curtain pulled back so that she could see the entire room at a glance. Today the room was quiet, both TVs off, and the roommate's side empty. Gram sat in her recliner, head back, eyes closed.

"Hey, Gram," Andrea said, leaning over to kiss her papery cheek.

Gram's eyelids fluttered, and she yawned. When Andrea was younger, Gram had colored her hair light brown, but the last ten years had not been kind to her. Dementia left her unable to keep up with her usual beauty routine, and the staff was too busy to do much more than run a comb over her head and help her brush her teeth. Family members used to take her home for visits, but she got too confused and upset, so eventually those visits stopped.

"Gram?"

"Hi, honey." Her eyes held a glint of recognition.

Sometimes she couldn't remember Andrea's name, but knew she was her granddaughter. Other times, especially in the evening, even that bit of information was lost. Andrea never knew what to expect from one visit to the next, but knew it was best not to push it because she didn't want to upset her grandmother. She clasped her grandmother's hand, taking care to be gentle. "Hi, Gram. It's me, Andrea. Look, I brought a friend." She gestured down to the floor next to the recliner where Anni sat, her tail sweeping the floor.

Gram peered over the side and a pleased expression came over her face. "Would you look at that. A sweet little doggy."

Anni opened her mouth and a short, clipped bark came out, like she was responding to Gram. Andrea put her hand over Anni's nose to keep her from prolonging the conversation. "This is my dog, Anni."

Gram looked at Anni and then at Andrea, her face pensive. "I had a dog a long time ago."

"Yes, you did, but that was a different dog, not this one."

"Oh."

"Do you want to pet her? She's really sweet."

"I would like to pet her."

Andrea adjusted the recliner so Gram could sit up, then brought Anni closer. Gram ran her hand over Anni's back and head, and the dog sat still except for her thumping tail. "Such a sweetheart," Gram murmured. "Hello, love."

During earlier visits Andrea had tried to fill the silence with chatter about the weather, current events, and work, but she'd learned that the words flew by Gram like so many sparrows, and caused the older woman grief trying to make sense of the patterns. The visits were less stressful for both of them when she made a point to just be there, speaking only when needed. Anni's presence made the silence enough. Her happy tail wag and appreciative gaze filled the room with all it needed.

"Such a sweetie," Gram said, stroking Anni's head. "I used to have a dog." She'd reached far back into her mind and accessed the part that recalled being a dog owner. Gram had, in fact, grown up on a farm and had a childhood full of dogs. So many years ago, but still present, back in her memory.

Eventually Gram sat back, tired, and watched as Andrea had Anni do a few tricks. "Sit," she said, and without a moment's hesitation, the dog sat. "Beg." Up went her paws, and Andrea pulled a treat out of her purse to reward her. After that she had her play dead. "Smart doggy," Gram said, clapping lightly.

They sat there for a time in companionable silence. Noises drifted from the hallway, the squeak of a pushcart, the sounds of conversations, laughter. "Can I help you, Mrs. Hoffman?" floated a voice from across the hall, most likely an attendant speaking to a patient, Andrea guessed.

Gram folded her hands in her lap. "I'm sorry. I just need a little nap," she said, struggling to get the words out. Her eyelids closed.

"Do you want me to pull the lever so the chair goes back?"

"No, honey. I'm fine."

"Okay then, Gram. Anni and I are going to go, but we'll be back next week, okay?"

Gram's head leaned to one side and she took a deep breath, already drifting off to somewhere else. Andrea liked to think she'd heard her. She'd seen the light in her grandmother's eyes when they'd first arrived and knew their visit had made a difference. They would be back.

Leaving took twice as long as arriving. Several people in the hallway, staff and patients, stopped her and asked if they could pet her dog. One woman in a wheelchair parked outside her room said, "What's her name?"

"This is Anni," Andrea said, directing Anni to a spot alongside the chair so that the woman could reach her.

"So soft," she said, her fingers trailing down onto Anni's back. Her white hair was short and wispy. Her lavender sweatpants matched her sweatshirt, which had several birds appliquéd on the front, to make it fancy. Andrea had noticed that most of the residents wore this kind of thing. Clothes chosen for the ease of getting on and off. As comfortable as the scrubs the staff wore. "So pretty," the woman said.

After a few minutes Andrea said, "It was nice talking to you, but we have to go now."

They went down the corridor and through the security door. When one of the two elevators arrived at their floor, the doors opened and a tall elderly woman with a walker emerged, accompanied by a female attendant. As they came out, the attendant kept a steadying hand on the woman's arm. She walked in baby steps, her eyes on the floor. When her gaze landed on the dog, the old woman asked, "Is that Anni?" The incredulity in her voice made it sound like she'd never seen a dog before.

"Yep, this is Anni," Andrea said, thinking about how quickly the word had spread. Her first time out and already Anni was famous at the Phoenix Health Care Center. Andrea held a hand out to keep the elevator doors from closing. The attendant said, "Let's keep going. Just a little more," but the woman stood locked in place, her mouth agape at the sight of the dog. It seemed rude to leave without saying a little more, so as Andrea stepped into the elevator she said, "We have to go now, but we'll be back next week."

TWENTY-THREE

By the next day, Sunday, Dan had forgotten all about Lindsay's dream, but unfortunately his daughter had not. As she walked into the kitchen, the first thing she said was, "So you didn't have time yesterday. Do you think you can go today?" He'd been engrossed in reading the news and drinking his coffee. It took him a moment to realize she was speaking about visiting Nadine.

"Good morning to you too," he said. Technically it was still morning, although it was closer to lunchtime. They'd done a reversal from their usual routine in that he was still in his bathrobe while she'd come downstairs already showered and dressed.

"It's really important, Dad," Lindsay said, pulling a chair up to the table. "I had another dream last night. I don't really remember much, but I *think* it was the same exact one."

He raised his eyebrows. "You think you had another dream? Could it be you're just remembering the dream from the night before?"

"Dad." She put both elbows on the table and cradled her head in her hands. "Don't change the subject. You need to go see Aunt Nadine. I think it's really important. And I know what you're going to say—that we don't even know if she's there anymore, but she is. I called yesterday and got her room number." She pulled a piece of paper out of her pocket and slid it across the table. "Mom was very specific about this."

Dan sighed. This dream thing was getting out of hand. Yesterday afternoon he'd called the grief counselor, who said it wasn't that unusual and if it was giving Lindsay a sense of connection with her mother, it could even be beneficial, so he shouldn't be worried about his daughter's mental health. It was just hard to take directions from Lindsay's subconscious. He said, "You know I don't know Nadine very well at all. I only met her a few times." Nadine had been one of Christine's projects. His wife had always been drawn to underdogs, to difficult cases. She had the ability to see the good in people. He wasn't sure when she'd become "Aunt Nadine" to Lindsay. Most likely Nadine had started it when Lindsay was a little girl.

"One hour of your time. No big deal. Please?" When Lindsay gave him the puppy dog eyes, it was hard to say no.

He took a sip of his coffee. "I tell you what. I'll go if you'll go with me. We'll do it together, okay?"

She sat up straight. "I don't know that I need to be there. In the dream Mom just said for you to visit Nadine."

He parroted her words right back at her. "It's just one hour of your time. No big deal." Her face had a conflicted look, so he added, "Please?" and did his own attempt at puppy dog eyes.

"It's just," she said, "that Brandon and I were going to go to the mall today."

"Okay." He picked up the newspaper. "Not a good day. I understand. Well, maybe we can go another time."

"Okay, wait, not so fast."

He lowered the newspaper, waiting. "Yes?"

"I'll go with you, but can we leave pretty soon and get it over with? And then afterward, can you drop me off at Brandon's?"

He shrugged. "Sure. Just let me get in the shower first."

Forty minutes later, they stopped at the grocery store to get Nadine a box of candy. From there they headed for the Phoenix Health Care Center. And half an hour after that, Dan and Lindsay stood in the elevator as it rose to the third floor. "Are we supposed to tell Nadine about the dream?" he asked Lindsay.

"If you want, I guess."

"So Mom didn't say *why* we have to see her or what we're supposed to talk about?"

Lindsay stuffed her gloves into her pockets. "You know how most dreams are—really hazy and time jumps around? This one wasn't like that. In the dream I was in my room listening to music and Mom came in. I took my earbuds out and she said to listen up, that she didn't have much time and she had a message for Dad."

"Meaning me."

"Yeah, well, who else? Anyway," she continued, "I said okay, and then she said, 'Tell Dad he needs to visit Nadine. It's really important that he goes to see her.'"

Dan said, "And then what?"

"I think I told her I'd give you the message, and that was it. I don't remember any more than that. I woke up and it was like two thirty. I turned on the lamp next to my bed, and I was just going to put it in my phone, but at the last minute I thought I better write it down old school, so I got a pen and ripped out a piece of notebook paper and wrote it down."

"Hmmm."

"It's okay if you don't believe me," she said. "I know what I experienced was real." The elevator came to a halt and the doors slid open. "It felt different than a regular dream."

"I believe you, Lindsay." He believed that what she experienced was real enough, at least to her, but he hesitated to believe it was a message from Christine. Why didn't she come directly to him, if that were the case? Stepping off the elevator, they both stopped to read the sign posted on the opposite wall. "This floor reserved for patients with cognitive impairment," he read softly to himself. "Please be kind and agreeable." And below that, instructions for getting into the locked floor: "Visitors, press buzzer for admittance."

"What do they mean, cognitive impairment? Is that like Alzheimer's?" Lindsay asked.

"Yes, like Alzheimer's or dementia."

"So Aunt Nadine won't know us anymore?" She looked up at him, dismayed.

"Maybe. Maybe not. There are varying degrees." He patted her shoulder. "We'll see."

Now he was really glad he'd insisted Lindsay come along. Nadine could be outspoken, and not in a good way, to begin with. Who knew how she'd be now.

Dan pressed the button, and a voice came through the speaker. "Hello?"

"We're here to visit—" The buzzer went off and he grabbed the door handle just in time. They passed the nurses' station on the way to Nadine's room, where a lone man squinted at a computer monitor.

When they reached room number 326, Lindsay knocked and stuck her head through the doorway. "Aunt Nadine?"

"Come in." Dan recognized Nadine's gravelly voice, the product of years of smoking. Before they had a chance to respond, she repeated, "Come in!" They walked in to find her sitting in an armchair, a remote control in her hand. The TV was on, but there was no sound. A collapsed walker leaned against her bed. She glanced up as they walked in, her mouth set in a grim line. "Well, don't dillydally, child. Come on in." She patted the bed, which was neatly made with a chenille bedspread. "The other one is sleeping, so we have to be quiet." She pointed to a bed on the other side of a partial curtain. A lump underneath the covers moved slowly up and down.

Dan stood nearby, while Lindsay approached Nadine, holding out the candy. "We brought you a gift," she said. Nadine took the box without comment and put it on the end table next to her.

"I'm Lindsay, Christine's daughter."

"Well, of course you are," she said. "I can see that."

"My dad is here too." Lindsay looked miserably up at him with a save-me expression.

Dan extended his hand and Nadine clasped it with her own pale, well-padded hand. She inspected it like the knuckles and joints would give her clues. She'd aged since Dan had last seen her. How long had it been? Maybe two years or so. Then she'd stood almost as tall as he. Nadine had always been a large, imposing woman, but sitting hunched over, she seemed to have shrunk. He gave her hand a squeeze and then pulled it away, sitting next to Lindsay on the bed. "It's been too long," he said. "I should have come to see you before this, but with Christine gone, we've been just getting through the days."

Nadine nodded like she understood, but something in her eyes gave away a lack of awareness. She was entirely too agreeable for Nadine, who used to love a good debate. Playing devil's advocate had been her hobby.

Now that Dan had begun, Lindsay's shoulders softened and she jumped in to get Nadine caught up, showing her pictures of Brandon on her phone, and telling her about her job at Walgreens. Nadine made all the right comments. She said Brandon was very handsome and nodded as Lindsay talked about work. But she'd lost her spark, the very thing that had made her Nadine.

Suddenly Nadine sat up straight and indignantly said, "No one ever comes to see me."

"Well, we did," Lindsay said. "We're here."

"I know, but no one ever comes."

"That's too bad," Dan said. He hoped that Lindsay wouldn't want to make this a weekly pilgrimage to see Nadine. The place was depressing and he was certain Nadine had no idea who they were. He sat with his hands folded and listened as Lindsay continued telling stories about school and work, most of them things she'd never told him. She told Nadine a story about how she'd noticed a young guy acting suspiciously at work and alerted her manager. He turned out to have about a hundred dollars' worth of over-the-counter medication stashed underneath his zippered jacket. "So stupid of him," she said, "because they have cameras everywhere." At school, she went on to say, they were having a talent show and one of Lindsay's friends, a girl named Nicole, was going to be singing. She was incredibly shy and had never sung in public before. "But she has this amazing voice. None of us could believe it. I mean, she's incredible," Lindsay said. "We're all hoping she doesn't chicken out at the last minute. She's so nervous."

Lindsay talked on and on, not seeming to need much feedback, which was good because she wasn't getting any. Nadine made a show of nodding and Dan did what he could to join in, but the visit was measured in minutes lasting hours. When a middle-aged lady wearing a puffy jacket came in to see Nadine's sleeping roommate, Dan took that as their cue and stood up. "We should probably get going," he said. "Take care of yourself, Nadine."

"No one ever comes to see me," Nadine said, with the same irritated tone she'd used earlier.

"We did, though," Lindsay said. "And we brought you candy." She gestured to the box on the table and Nadine regarded it with interest as if seeing it for the first time.

"Oh, thank you."

"Good-bye, Aunt Nadine. Take care." Lindsay leaned over to give her a hug, and Dan's heart surged with pride. All the times he and Christine had prompted Lindsay over the years: say thank you, share your toys, wait your turn, don't push. Small lessons in compassion and courtesy that they put forth again and again, never knowing if any of it was taking hold in their daughter's consciousness, and then one day, to see his daughter as a fully formed person who instinctively knew how to comfort someone else? Now that was a revelation of the finest kind.

The older woman patted her back with gentle fingers. Lindsay pulled away and said the words Dan didn't want her to say. "We'll come again sometime." There it was. A promise to return another day. Now that she'd said it, it felt like a commitment.

Dan felt a wave of resignation wash over him. He supposed it wouldn't kill him to visit again. It would be another good deed on his roster, and, on the plus side, it would be time spent with Lindsay, which was exceedingly rare nowadays and extremely precious, considering she'd be going away to college next fall. What was an hour of their time, really, in the scheme of things? Dan gave in. "We'll come back to see you another time," he said, echoing his daughter.

The visitor on the other side of the curtain murmured something to Nadine's sleeping roommate, trying to rouse her from her sleep. Dan heard the woman's voice softly encouraging the roommate to get out of bed. "Your sleep schedule is going to get all mixed up." Next came the metallic pull of curtain rings being yanked along a rod, and with it, light filling the room. Nadine's head swiveled to look.

This might be a good time to slip away. Dan beckoned to his daughter to join him and took her elbow to guide her toward the door. As they were just about to leave the room, Lindsay glanced back and saw Nadine's blank look in their direction. Lindsay said reassuringly, "We'll come back and visit soon."

And then Nadine said the words that made both of them forget they were leaving. "Maybe Anni will be here then."

A bewildered look passed between them. "Anni?" Lindsay asked.

"Your dog," Nadine said. "Your dog, Anni."

"We don't have Anni anymore," Lindsay said, and the sadness in her voice made Dan's heart break.

"I know." Nadine's tone was impatient. "She comes here sometimes."

Lindsay retraced her steps back to Nadine's bedside. "Anni? Our dog, Anni, comes here sometimes?"

Nadine's head bobbed up and down. "She goes on the elevator."

Lindsay sat down on the bed, tapped the surface of her phone, and then held out the screen to show Nadine. "This is Anni. She comes here sometimes?"

"On the elevator," Nadine said, only glancing at the phone. "No one ever comes to see me."

"Who is Anni with when she comes?" Lindsay asked.

"Going down on the elevator."

"I know. You said that. But was Anni here with someone?"

A distraught look came over Nadine's face. Lindsay's questions were getting to be too much for her.

"We should go," Dan said, tilting his head toward the door. He could tell Lindsay felt she was on to something, but he wasn't as convinced and he hated to see her get her hopes up. Nadine was confused. Clearly, she was remembering when Christine used to bring Anni to see her. "Good-bye, Nadine. Come on, honey."

When they got out in the corridor, Lindsay said, "What do you think of that?" Her eyes went wide. "What if Anni's been here? What if that's why Mom told us to visit Nadine?" She fairly vibrated with excitement.

"Your mother used to bring Anni here to visit. Nadine is confused."

"But she said it like it just happened."

"To her it did, honey. Her memory is impaired."

"No." She held up a hand. "I think it's more than that. It all fits with Mom telling us to come visit."

"Oh, Lindsay . . ."

"Don't, Dad. I know you just came to humor me, but have a little faith, would you? Just for one second, could you go along with me on this?" Her eyes flashed with defiance.

"You have to know I have faith in you," he said.

"That's random faith. That's not the same thing," she said. "Random faith in me is like—go, Lindsay, I'm proud of you and believe you'll do well on the test. This is different. This is like seeing the bigger picture."

"Okay, so what do you want from me?"

"Can we ask someone here if they've seen Anni?" she asked, putting her hands together like praying.

"Do we have time for that? I thought you had to meet Brandon." He grinned.

She said, "I'll just text him to let him know I'll be late. Not a problem." Lindsay whipped out her phone. Her fingers flew. "There," she said, putting it in her pocket. "Done." She tugged at Dan's sleeve and towed him down the hall. "We'll stop at the nurses' station."

They passed open doorways and made a wide sweep around an elderly man wearing jeans, a brown fuzzy cardigan, and bedroom slippers. "Excuse us," Dan said as Lindsay, in a rush, hurried around him.

When they got to the open counter of the nurses' station, one lone man, a bald guy in his thirties, sat behind the counter, tapping away at a keyboard. Behind him, a table held what was left of a box of cupcakes, along with a stack of napkins and some plastic silverware. A sign above the table said, "Happy Birthday, Kevin." Next to the table, an open doorway led to another room. Dan heard voices drifting from that room and spotted a half-size silver refrigerator labeled, "For Medical Use Only."

"Yes?" the man looked up. The plastic badge hanging around his neck confirmed he was Kevin, the one having a birthday. Unless there was more than one Kevin, but what were the chances?

"Hi," Lindsay said. "We've just been visiting Nadine Bruder and—"

He held up his hand. "Let me guess. She told you no one ever comes to see her?"

"Well, yes, but—"

"She does get visitors, believe me," he said. "I can tell you that her sons visit on a regular basis, so you don't need to worry about that. She just can't remember from one time to the next."

"Okay," Lindsay said in a moving-on voice. "But that's not what we were going to ask. She told us something else too. We lost our dog, Anni, and Nadine said she's seen her here." She got her phone out and pulled up a picture. It was a close-up of Anni's face, a particularly cute shot. "Have you seen our dog?"

Kevin leaned in to regard it carefully, then shook his head. "I've never seen her. I'm sorry."

Lindsay turned back to her phone, scrolling through the photos. "Here's a better picture of her whole body. You can see how big she is." She turned the screen to show him.

He took a moment. "No, I'm sorry. Still not ringing a bell."

"But sometimes people bring in dogs, right?" Oh no. Lindsay was not going to let this go.

"Oh sure, we have dogs coming in here. Therapy dogs mostly. Sometimes people will bring in a pet when they visit with a family member. I haven't seen a dog that looked like that, though."

"Is there someone else here we could ask, sir?" Lindsay asked, polite and deferential but also frowning.

Kevin glanced over his shoulder and called out, "Lisa, you have a minute?"

A gangly woman in scrubs came through the doorway holding a clipboard. "Yep?"

"Hoping you could identify a suspect," Kevin said, thrusting a finger at Lindsay's phone.

"Have you seen my dog?" Lindsay asked. "She's lost. Well, actually, someone took her." Dan watched as her eyes clouded with tears. "Nadine Bruder said she's seen her here."

Lisa took the phone from Lindsay's shaking hand and gave it a long look. "What a beautiful dog. You must be heartbroken."

Lindsay nodded.

"What's her name?"

"Anni."

"I'm so sorry, honey. I haven't seen Anni. You might want to ask down at the front desk. People with dogs have to check in."

Lindsay dabbed her eyes. "Okay, thanks. It's just that Nadine said she saw Anni on the elevator."

"The dog was by herself?" Lisa's eyebrows furrowed.

"I-I don't know," Lindsay said, stammering. "Nadine just said she comes here sometimes and that she was on the elevator."

Kevin and Lisa's eyes met, and Dan knew they were thinking that Nadine was not the most reliable of sources. Lisa held the phone out, which Lindsay took back without a word. "Maybe someone downstairs can help you." As they walked away, Lisa softly said, "Good luck."

In the elevator, Lindsay kept her eyes toward the floor, tucked her hair behind her ear, and sniffed. She silently accepted the tissue Dan pulled out of his pocket. "It'll be okay, Linds," he said. Just words, really, because none of it was okay. He put a hand on her shoulder to comfort her and she leaned against him.

They didn't get good news at the front desk either. The grand-motherly woman on duty looked at Lindsay's phone and shook her head. She said, "But just because I haven't seen her doesn't mean she wasn't here. I'm a volunteer and so is everyone else who works the front desk. I myself only come in twice a month. So you see, it's possible she was here, but unless you caught the right person at the right time, there's no way anyone could tell you for sure."

Lindsay wasn't giving up. "Upstairs they said everyone who brings an animal has to check in? Do they sign something?"

"Yes, but they only sign their name, not the name of the animal, so it wouldn't help you. I'm sorry."

"Can I see the sign-in sheet anyway?" Lindsay asked. Dan recognized the desperation in her voice.

The woman hesitated and Dan expected her to say it was against their policy or there were privacy issues, but after a moment she shrugged and said, "I don't know why not."

She shuffled through some papers in front of her until she uncovered a notebook. Flipping the cover over, she handed it to Lindsay.

Dan looked at it over his daughter's shoulder. There were dozens of names on the top sheet alone. A few had written in the date after their name; most had not. Some of the handwriting was illegible. The header at the top said, "I certify that I am bringing this animal into the Phoenix Health Care Center at my own risk. I understand that I am 100 percent responsible for the actions of my animal, and that PHCC assumes no responsibility to actions done to, or by, said animal." Clearly, this was a makeshift attempt to cover their legal liability.

Lindsay ran her finger down the list, flipped to the next page, and did the same. She turned to him and said, "None of the names seem familiar, do they?"

"No," he said, not pointing out that they probably wouldn't seem familiar, since they didn't know who had Anni. If she were even still alive.

"I'm sorry, hon," the woman said. "I lost a dog myself once, so I do understand. It's a pain like none other. When it happened to me, it was like my heart was ripped open. So I am truly sorry for your loss."

"Thank you." Lindsay stood there like she was waiting for more to happen. It wasn't until Dan made a show of returning the notebook that she turned away from the desk. The walk out to the truck was more of a trudge. Out in the parking lot she kicked up the snow in her path. "I really thought we were on to something. I really thought we might find her," she said, her voice small.

"We still might," Dan said, trying to ease her pain. "You never know."

TWENTY-FOUR

The day after visiting Gram, Andrea came home to find a box from a florist propped against the door. She carried it in to the kitchen table and opened it to find a dozen red roses wrapped in plastic. The accompanying card had a traditional valentine heart split in two with zigzagged edges. Inside he'd written: *My apologies for everything. Love, Marco.* When they were married, this kind of thing would have healed a lot of hurts. Today, not so much. She ripped the card into a dozen pieces and then took the resulting handful of confetti and flushed it down the toilet. Anni stuck her head over the toilet bowl and watched with rapt interest, not really sure what was going on, but knowing this wasn't the usual routine.

After arranging the roses in a vase, Andrea told Anni to stay, threw on her jacket, and carried them over to her neighbor Cliff's house. She rang the doorbell with her elbow and watched her breath turn to fog in the cold air. When he opened the door, she didn't wait for a greeting. "A present for you," she said, thrusting the vase his way.

His face lit up with delight. "What have I done to deserve this?" he asked, opening the screen door and taking the flowers out of her hands.

"Just a thank-you for being your wonderful self," she said. "I appreciate the times you've watched Anni and she loves you too."

Cliff stuck his nose in the bouquet. "I'd invite you in, but I have company," he said, grinning devilishly.

"That's okay. I just wanted to drop off the flowers," Andrea said.

"Cliff, who is it?" A petite gray-haired woman appeared at his side. "Oh, what beautiful flowers." She cast a sideways glance at Andrea and then at Cliff.

Andrea, who had a knack for sizing up a situation, took in the scene. The woman was older but attractive, her hair cut in a shoulder-length bob, a nautical scarf tied around her neck, dangling gold earrings on each side. Cliff, still holding the flowers, regarded this woman with pride and she looked at him the same way. Andrea saw something at the edge of that look, something that said this woman was protective of Cliff and wondered who this woman bearing flowers could be. In that second she saw what should have been obvious—red roses meant romantic love. Probably not the best choice for thanking a neighbor for dog sitting. "I'm Andrea," she said, filling the silence. "A neighbor. Just dropping off some flowers." To clarify, she said, "A gift from my ex-husband. I didn't want them around, but was thinking it would be a shame to throw them out. I thought Cliff might enjoy them." That, she realized, was probably not the right thing to say. Now she'd admitted to regifting, and to having an ex-husband who sent her roses, which was fairly unconventional, if not completely weird.

But if all of this put her in a bad light, the woman didn't acknowledge it. "What a lovely thing to do," she said with an enthusiastic shake of her head. "I'm Doreen, by the way."

"It's nice to meet you." Andrea couldn't help herself. She had to ask. "How do you two know each other?" Her finger went back and forth between the two.

"Book club," Cliff said, smiling again, his long teeth in full view. "Over at the library."

The library? Wasn't she the one who suggested the library as a place to meet people? Andrea suppressed the urge to take credit for this turn of events. Andrea flapped her hand in the direction of her place. "I should probably head for home. It was nice meeting you, Doreen."

As the screen door closed, she heard Cliff explain, "I sometimes watch Andrea's little dog when she goes out. Little Muffin. A real cutie."

TWENTY-FIVE

In the time since Anni went missing, Lindsay had seemed to adjust to life without her, but since Nadine had spoken her name, it opened up the wound and the pain was fresh again.

She and Brandon came back to their house for dinner, and afterward Dan overheard her tell Brandon the story of their visit at the nursing home. While Dan pored over graphs for work at the kitchen table, they sat on the couch in the living room watching *Donnie Darko* for the eight hundredth time. Although the space between the two teenagers and Dan was fairly open, with only a half wall dividing them, if he was quiet they tended to forget about him, similar to when he used to drive Lindsay and her friends to soccer practice when she was in middle school. As long as he didn't speak, they talked without reservation about the kinds of things they'd never normally say in front of him.

Today she turned the sound down on the movie to tell Brandon the dream in far more detail than she'd told Dan. "When my mom came into my room in this last dream, it was so real, I could smell her, you know? She smelled the same as she always did, like this soap she used to use. I was listening to music and I took the earbuds out because I could tell she had something to tell me and she had a look on her face that said it was important. Then she told me to listen up, that she didn't have much time, and I had to give my dad a message. I knew Dad was somewhere else in the house and I asked her why she didn't just tell him herself, and she said she tried, but he wasn't listening."

Dan straightened. *She tried but he wasn't listening?* No way. This had to be Lindsay's subconscious tapping into her need to communicate with her mother. To feel special, like she was the only one who could. He craned his neck to see into the other room, but could only spot the top of Lindsay's head resting against Brandon's shoulder.

She kept going, telling Brandon about how Nadine had said she saw Anni on the elevator. "She kept saying it that way—on the elevator."

"Whoa," Brandon said. "Like she's trying to give you some kind of message."

"That's what I thought!"

"Like, maybe," he said, his voice rising in excitement, "you're supposed to watch the elevator. Do they have security cameras there? Maybe they'd let you watch the footage."

Lindsay said, "I didn't see any, but you'd think so, wouldn't you? I could call and ask."

Dan heard the hope in her voice and couldn't help himself. He called out, "Remember, we're talking about a woman who is suffering from a cognitive impairment. Nadine can't remember her sons visiting from one time to the next. She's probably just thinking of when your mom used to bring Anni to visit."

Dead silence from the couch. He was the hope killer, the squasher of possibilities, the one who dared suggest that something was really nothing. He saw their heads turn to exchange a look and knew he'd blundered. "I just don't want you to get your hopes up, honey."

"I *know*, Dad." The air between them turned icy.

Right after that Brandon and Lindsay decided to go to a movie in an actual theater where Dan couldn't disturb them. They didn't put it that way, of course, but he got the message. "Enjoy the movie," he said as they left the house. "But come straight home afterward. It's a school night." From the set of Lindsay's shoulders, he could see her disdain, making it clear that of course she knew it was a school night. Did he think she was a complete idiot?

Brandon said, "We will. Good night, sir." Brandon was always polite, even when Lindsay was moody and difficult. Especially when Lindsay was moody and difficult, maybe to compensate. The door slammed behind them and Dan listened as he heard Brandon starting the engine. He went to the window and watched as he backed down the driveway, aware that his silhouette in the window probably annoyed Lindsay, but unable to look away.

Her mother did a good job handling Lindsay when she was moody like this, but he was all thumbs and missteps. Should he ignore her or take her to task? It didn't seem to matter. It wasn't really a battle per se, so there was no winning either way. After the movie, she'd be back and there would be breakfast tomorrow and other days ahead. Soon enough, though, she'd be gone for good, living an independent life, the way kids eventually do. When Dan was a child, he'd hear the adults exclaim: Where did the time go? The question had seemed foolish to him then. They'd acted as if time were a race car, speeding past, when he himself knew that time took forever to go by. Each birthday came about five years after the last one. Christmas was like the horizon, always off in the distance. A kid could grow two inches waiting for Christmas. He never understood then what he knew now. Time was as fluid as a river. Waiting for something exciting made time crawl on its knees, and working on deadline made time sprint. The good times were fleeting, the bad times excruciatingly slow.

Yes, he watched as Lindsay drove away with Brandon and knew it was only a matter of time before she'd be gone for good.

What would be left for him then? He was afraid that when Lindsay left, time would be measured in between her phone calls and visits and getting through each day would be a gargantuan task.

Morose, that's what he'd become. He'd gone from full-blown grief to numb to borrowing trouble. There was no point in anticipating a depressing future. It would come, ready or not, and there was no need to feel the pain ahead of time.

He went back to his laptop and his graphs. Once engrossed, he thought he heard Anni scrabbling by the door, and almost got up to let her out when he realized what he was doing. "I am absolutely losing my mind," he said, and realized that saying it out loud didn't do much to discount the notion.

When the phone rang, the landline they almost never used, he jumped, startled, but didn't get up to answer it. Lindsay would be in the movie by now and she'd have called his cell if there were a problem. The only calls that generally came over that number were solicitors or political calls. He wasn't in the mood to politely turn down telemarketers or volunteers. He always felt guilty cutting them off in the middle of their script, and even as he politely said good-bye, he'd hear their faint, last desperate attempts to turn things around as he was putting the phone in the cradle. No, let it ring. If it was important, they'd leave a message. If not, even better.

He crooked his neck as he heard the recording begin. Someone was leaving a message. "Hi, Dan? This is Doreen. I wanted to thank you again for brunch. That was so nice of you and I didn't invite you to brunch so you would pay, but I appreciated it. It was very gentlemanly of you." Dan got up and went over to the phone as she spoke, his hand hovering over the receiver. "I'm calling for another reason, though. I wanted to invite you over for dinner a week from Sunday at my house. I'm having a few friends over, well, two friends really, and I think you'd make a good addition to the group." This last sentence was said hurriedly, as if she were nervous. Dan kept his hand over the phone, but didn't pick up. "When you call me back, I'll tell you more. I'm thinking we won't include Lindsay this time, because she would just be bored by all our grown-up talk. So it would be the four of us. If you can make it, of course." She cleared her throat. "Okay, bye-bye. Call me when you can." Click.

He groaned. He and Christine had been to many dinners at Doreen's and he and Lindsay had been guests a few times over the last year and a half, but she'd never invited just him before. And she'd sounded so nervous too. Something was definitely wrong with this scenario. If it were closer to his birthday, he'd think it was a surprise party. But since that wasn't the case, it was probably another attempt to set him up with a woman. He'd call her back, but not today.

TWENTY-SIX

Eating lunch at the Café Mocha later that week, Andrea couldn't help but notice all the lovebird couples. Two college kids splitting an order of fries were one table over from an older couple who sat leisurely by the fireplace, sipping cappuccinos, lost in each other's eyes. On the opposite side of the room, Philip sat with a gorgeous woman Andrea presumed to be his wife, Vanessa. Vanessa had an elegant high ponytail that emphasized her fabulous cheekbones and long, swanlike neck. She and her husband were splitting a large frosted cookie and comparing notes on the flavor. Like they couldn't each have their own. Andrea sighed. First it was Cliff and Doreen, and now this. Love was definitely in the air. How nice for all of them. She reached down to drop a piece of meat to Anni, who waited underneath the table. When Anni was done eating, Andrea gave her a quick rub behind the ears. "That's my girl," she said.

When it was time to go, Andrea wrapped her scarf around her neck, and thought about putting on her knit beret, but stuffed it in her purse instead. For her, the scourge of winter had always been the cold, the slush, and the horror of hat hair. Knit hats, the kind that really kept your head warm, created static electricity and fly-away hair. Either that or dents on either side of her head. Luckily, it wasn't snowing or cold enough to require a hat, or maybe it was that she'd just gotten used to it. As they left, Joan called out goodbye, and through the door they went, Anni bounding onto the sidewalk, happy to be on the move.

They were a few blocks away from the coffee shop when Andrea heard a loud shout. "Hey!" a man yelled, sounding irate. "Hey there, you with the dog!" Alarmed, she looked up to see a dark-colored junker pausing at the stoplight on the opposite side of the street. The car looked like it had been painted with a brush, and multiple bumper stickers covered the door. The driver, a guy in his twenties, had the window down and his arm all the way out, his hand fashioned like a gun pointing straight at her. The hand shaped like a gun and a black knit hat pulled over his forehead overshadowed the rest of his appearance.

"Me?" she said, looking around, but there was no one else in the vicinity, and not very many cars either.

"Yeah, you." Now his voice was furious. "Where'd you get that dog? That's not your dog." Each word came out like machine gun fire, madder and louder. The yelling of a madman. Unpredictable and crazed.

Anni whimpered and pulled at the leash. Andrea followed her lead and kept walking, picking up the pace. Her heart pounded, as she went into defense mode, keeping her purse clutched to her side, scanning the road for other pedestrians who could help her. But no one else was around and she prayed silently that he'd just drive on and leave them alone.

"That's my dog, bitch!" The traffic light went to green and he darted a mean glare their way before driving off. Anni's body language had changed; her back hunched, tail tucked down. She trembled and pulled at the leash like she'd never done before. Already Andrea had surmised that this man was one of the frat boys, and the dog's reaction confirmed it. Anni was afraid of this man.

Andrea crossed the street and looked both ways, but the streets were ghost town empty. The businesses up ahead, a barbershop, a gas station, and a tattoo parlor, weren't necessarily the kind that would welcome dogs, but if she had to, she would dart inside for protection. She concentrated on her breathing. *Think. Think. Think.* What do people do in emergencies? Of course, they call 9-1-1. Why hadn't she thought of that right away? She paused for a second to get her phone out of her purse and Anni whined at the interruption. "Just a minute, girl." She felt better, having the phone in hand, just in case he came back.

When they went another thirty feet or so, she started to feel better. Anyone could be brave yelling out a car window. And Anni didn't look that distinctive. There had to be other dogs that looked like her. Any reasonable person would know that. She could easily make the case that Anni was her dog. She'd say she'd had her for years. Who would know any differently? And better yet, who would believe him over her?

They passed the barbershop. Through the window Andrea noticed two chairs occupied by men getting haircuts, a reassuring, everyday sort of scene. Even Anni relaxed somewhat, still pulling on the leash, but not with enough force to almost yank Andrea off her feet. As they made their way down the block, she vowed not to walk this way with Anni again. She would drive or take another route. Having pepper spray on hand wasn't a bad idea either. She'd find out where a person could get a can. Getting ID tags for Anni had been on her list, and she'd put it off for too long. This weekend she'd have the tags made and she'd look into getting a microchip implanted too. It would resolve any ownership disputes. The frat boys were not getting Anni back. It was never going to happen.

By the time they'd passed the tattoo shop and approached the gas station, her death grip on her phone had lessened a bit, and her heart rate had returned to normal, so when the man jumped out from behind the pump and onto the sidewalk, it took her by complete surprise. She gasped, the phone falling out of her hand and clattering onto the pavement.

"Where did you get that dog?" The guy's face was contorted with rage. The knit cap pulled low, combined with his unshaven face, gave him a dangerous look.

Anni cowered and tried to go back the way they'd come, nearly wrapping the leash around her legs. Andrea struggled to keep calm and pull the leash short so that she could get Anni right next to her. "I don't know what you're talking about. This is my dog," she said with determination.

"That's funny because she looks a lot like a dog I used to have. Someone reported me to the cops and they took her right out of my house." His fists clenched by his sides. "It wasn't even legal for them to go into my place. I checked. I know my rights."

While he spoke, she spotted her phone on the ground a few feet from where she stood. If she bent to get it, would he try to take Anni? "Come on, Anni," she said, clicking her tongue.

"Funny, my dog's name was Anni too. And surprise, surprise, they look exactly the same," he said, sneering. "Kind of a big coincidence." He had a wild-eyed look and was close to her now, so close she could smell the beer on his breath.

"You're scaring me. You need to back off." She let her eyes dart over to the gas pumps. A middle-aged woman dressed in a parka was running her credit card through the pay station. If Andrea screamed, she would almost certainly call for help. She spoke, trying to appear calm. "Move aside. Right now."

He hesitated, but just for a second, then took a step over and kicked her cell phone into the street. "Not until you tell me where you got the dog. Who called the cops? Tell. Me." His upper lip curled cruelly as he reached for the leash.

Andrea had a tight grip on Anni's leash, but he had his hand on it now too and was trying to yank it away from her. She tried to choke back her fear, feeling her knees go weak. At her side, Anni squirmed and whimpered, a trail of her urine steaming on the pavement. Andrea managed to spit out the word, "No," and then something unloosed and she was able to scream, just a little bit at first and then louder and louder. The kind of wail toddlers make at the mall when they don't get what they want. Earsplitting.

Time froze while she wrestled with the frat boy for control of the leash. He was in her face now, telling her to shut up. "Just tell me who called the cops!"

In those few moments she became hyper-aware of all her senses: the thin-pitched scream streaming out of her mouth in the crisp air, the pull of the leash against her gloved hand, and Anni straining to get behind her, away from him. Anni's fear rose up the leash and became her own. Steadily mounting despair overcame her while she frantically wondered if anyone at the gas station heard what was going on. She felt her stomach knot up and her throat become raw.

Andrea heard the pounding of heavy footsteps on the pavement coming up behind the frat boy's back, and then a man shouting, "Hey! Leave her alone!" The frat boy was hit from the side and caught off-balance. He let go of the leash and staggered before falling backward, landing on the sidewalk with a shocked expression on his face. Towering over him stood a man with broad shoulders.

It was Marco. Andrea had never been so glad to see him, ever, and that included all of their dating years and the day of their wedding. Marco leaned over the frat boy, who suddenly didn't seem nearly so large, and pointed at Andrea, screaming, "Did you hurt that woman? Did you? If you hurt her, I'm going to kill you." The vein in his forehead stood out, and he had both fists clenched as if ready for a fight.

"Dude," the frat boy said, still sprawled on the pavement. "Just chill."

"I'll chill," Marco said. "I'll chill your stupid mouth right up your ass." Which didn't make much sense, but when Marco got agitated, there was no telling what might come out of his mouth.

Andrea took a few steps back and soothed Anni, who still trembled and whined. The poor thing didn't like the man on the ground or all the shouting, and there was no way she could understand what was going on. Poor baby. "It's okay, girl. It's okay," Andrea said.

Marco grabbed the frat boy's coat and pulled him to his feet as easily as he would a child. "If you hurt her, you're dead," he screamed.

"I didn't hurt anyone," the frat boy said, real fear coming over his face. His eyes darted to Anni and Andrea. "We were just talking."

Andrea said, "It's okay, Marco. Just a misunderstanding."

But once Marco became angry, he couldn't shut it off just like that. He still had a grip on the guy's coat and he had the look of a man ready to punch someone.

The frat boy followed Andrea's lead. "It was just a misunderstanding."

Marco said, "It didn't look like a misunderstanding to me. I say we call the cops and get your ass charged with assault."

"That won't be necessary," Andrea said. "Really, Marco, it's okay."

"Dude," the frat boy said. "Listen to the lady. We're all good here."

"Let him go, Marco," she said gently. "He's not worth it." With Anni still at her side, she stepped into the road and picked up her cell phone, which was slick with slush. She wiped it against her coat and stuck it in her pocket, all the while listening to Marco tell the guy how lucky he was that Marco was in a forgiving mood. "Any other day I would break every bone in your body," he snarled.

"Okay, okay, I get it." The frat boy held his hands up in surrender. The sight of him afraid gave Andrea some satisfaction. Good, she thought. Now you know how it feels.

Marco wasn't done, though. "You apologize to the lady," he said, one hand on the guy's coat, the other pushing his chest. "Right now!"

The frat boy looked at Andrea and said, "I'm sorry."

"Tell her why."

He looked puzzled. "Why what?" he asked timidly.

"Tell her why you're sorry, jerkwad."

"Oh," he said. "I'm sorry I thought you had my dog . . ."

"And?" Marco prompted.

"I'm sorry I grabbed the leash and threatened you. You seem like a very nice lady and I can see now that I made a big mistake." He looked at Marco to see if his words had passed muster. "I'm really sorry. I will never bother you again." The transformation from thug to penitent was amazingly swift.

Marco gave him a shove and the frat boy staggered backward, just catching himself before he toppled over again. "Get out of here," Marco said, pointing off into the distance. "If I find out you've been anywhere near this woman again, I will hunt you down and make you pay."

The frat boy ran off, his open coat flapping in the breeze, his footsteps muffled against the snowy sidewalk. Andrea watched as he rounded the corner and went out of sight. She said, "Thank you, Marco. I really appreciate it."

"You're welcome," he said gruffly. "My car's over there. Why don't I give you a ride?"

Andrea hesitated, but only for a second. She was still shaken up from the encounter and Anni was a mess too. The idea of walking the rest of the way to the office wasn't at all appealing. "Fine," she said, nodding. "But it doesn't mean we're getting back together. I just want a ride back to the office."

She recognized his car, of course. It was a silver Jaguar, the one he'd bought used right before the divorce. Jade had called it his midlife-crisis-mobile. They could have gotten two cars for what this one had cost, but Marco had claimed it was an investment, a classic car that would only appreciate in value. Climbing into the passenger seat, Andrea pulled Anni onto her lap before fastening the seat belt. Lowering her head, Anni nervously licked her lips. "It's okay, girl. You're safe now," Andrea crooned, positioning Anni to look out the window, away from Marco, who seemed to stress her out.

"You really like that thing, don't you?" Marco said, pulling out of the gas station parking lot.

"How did you happen to be there?" she asked, ignoring his question.

"What?"

"How is it that you were there to show up at exactly the moment I needed help? Were you following me?" She glanced over. Even in profile, his grin was unmistakable.

"Sort of. I was heading to the coffee shop hoping to run into you when I saw you on the sidewalk. You looked like you could use some manly intervention."

"Don't do that."

"Don't help you? I should have driven right past?"

"No, not that. I appreciate the help, thank you," she said. "But don't go to the coffee shop trying to run into me. And don't send me flowers. I gave them away, just so you know. Whatever this is you're trying to do, it won't work. We're divorced and it took me a long time to come to peace with that. I'm in a good place. I wish you luck, but I don't want to have coffee with you or for you to send me gifts. We're done."

"Oh, don't be like that," he said, his mouth downturned. They were stopped at a traffic light, so he was able to turn and look right into her eyes. "I mean, I know I deserve it and all. My behavior was reprehensible." He grinned, both of them knowing that reprehensible wasn't a word that would normally be in his vocabulary. This apology had been scripted ahead of time. "I do love you, Andrea. I don't deserve another chance, but I'm hoping you'll give me one."

"What happened to Desiree?" Andrea asked. "Did she dump you?"

"No, um"—he cleared his throat—"it didn't work out. She wasn't right for me." The light changed and his gaze shifted to the road ahead.

"Why not? You seemed pretty certain that she was the one for you before."

He shrugged. "What can I say? It took some time to figure it all out, but I'm older and wiser now. Desiree was a mistake. A big mistake. She talked all the time and not about anything interesting. She's only concerned with how her hair looks and she fished for compliments, like, continuously. And she spent my money like I owned a damn money-printing machine. She's not you, Andrea. That was the main problem."

The amount of satisfaction Andrea got from hearing this could not be measured in earthly increments. She felt vindication times a million. "But Desiree is so pretty. And her boobs are so big."

"I guess I deserve that," he said, sighing again. "I should have listened to my mom. She said I'd regret the divorce. She said, 'Andrea is the best thing that ever happened to you.' She said someday I'd wish I could turn back time and be married to you again." He pulled into the McGuire Properties parking lot and slid into the space next to her car. "Man, was she right."

Andrea had always liked her mother-in-law, and her father-in-law too, for that matter. Hard to believe that Marco, who was such a selfish man, had such wonderful parents. Or maybe there was a direct correlation. Maybe all the years of being fussed over by his mother made him feel entitled to do whatever he wanted to other people. She unbuckled her seat belt, careful to keep it from hitting

Anni as it retracted. "Say hello to your folks from me," she said, opening the car door.

"Wait," he said, reaching over to grasp her arm. "I get where you're coming from, but could you at least think it over? We could go slow, go on a few dates, maybe. I'd like the chance to tell you where I was coming from when I acted so horribly. Not that it justifies what I did, but maybe it will help you understand. It was always more about me than you."

"That part I figured out all by myself," she said dryly. She pushed the door open a little more, and Anni, still tethered by her leash, shimmied out of her lap and out of the car.

He kept going. "The part I feel the worst about is the whole baby thing. If I had to do it over again, I'd do anything you wanted. Do the infertility tests and treatment or fill out the paperwork for adoption. Anything."

Marco was playing hardball now, hitting her in her softest, most vulnerable spot. Promising her the golden ring, the winning lottery ticket, the thing she wanted most: a baby of her own. While married, he had been on board with the idea of infertility testing when they'd initially discussed it, but as soon as he'd realized his part of it, he put a halt to all of it. Of course, he'd said it was to protect her from going through all the physical and emotional demands of the ordeal. He had stories (probably made-up) of a woman he worked with who had a breakdown after years of infertility treatments, none of which ever resulted in a baby. "All that money and all those years," he'd said with a sad shake of his head. "For nothing." When she suggested adoption, he'd said that it was a terrible idea, that the whole idea, the whole point of parenthood, was to have bits and pieces of both of them come to life in a child of their own. "I don't like the idea of raising someone else's kid," he'd said. "You never know what you're gonna get." Marco had said that he and Andrea together were enough, that they'd travel and do whatever else they wanted with the money and time a child would have devoured. He had stomped on her dream, making her feel like she was being unreasonable, selfish even, when it was he who had been selfish. And now he wanted her to forgive and forget.

She said, "This is an interesting turn of events. What made you change your mind?"

"I understand now how important a baby is to you," he said. "I didn't before, but now I do. All I want is for you to be happy."

"I am happy, thank you," she said, and pulled her arm free from his grasp. "And thank you for helping me back there. You were a real lifesaver. Good-bye, Marco."

"I'll give you some time," he said as she got out of the car. As she slammed the door, he called out, "As much time as you need. I'll call you."

Andrea waved a dismissal as she and Anni walked into the building. She felt his eyes on her back, but didn't turn around. Let him stare if it made him happy. It didn't matter to her one way or the other.

TWENTY-SEVEN

One evening after work, when Dan knew Lindsay would be working the cash register at Walgreens, he went on a mission, driving around to area businesses to take down the Anni posters. A sad task, but the time had come. Between her dreams and Nadine's mention of Anni at the nursing home, Lindsay had become obsessed with the idea that Anni was somewhere close-by and her mother was giving her clues. She looked for signs everywhere, commenting on junk mail from the SPCA and the frequency of commercials on TV raising funds for abused animals. He knew she and Brandon still went to the diner and other places that displayed the Anni posters in their windows. No doubt people asked if there'd been any developments in the case, which there weren't. Every time Lindsay called, the nice police officer said that they hadn't forgotten that Anni was still missing; that they still had their eyes open. To his daughter these were encouraging words; to Dan, they were kindnesses, a way of humoring a hopeful but unrealistic pet owner.

The hardware store had already removed the poster, which took him aback. Even though he'd given up, it seemed presumptuous for others to do so. At the barbershop, the poster had been repositioned to the lower part of the window. The florist had moved it off to the side as well. At each place, Dan went in quickly, removing them without hesitation, only explaining if someone questioned what he was doing. At the diner, though, he hesitated. Many of Lindsay's friends had written messages along the bottom: *We miss you, Anni. Sending prayers your way, Lindsay! To whoever took Anni, bring her back or else!* There were a few profanities after that one, which made Dan smile.

He had his hand on the corner, ready to peel the tape off the window, when he felt a hand on his back and heard Doreen's voice: "Dan!"

He was right near the door and hadn't seen her enter; she must have been inside already. "Hello, Doreen."

She shook her head. "Don't take that down. Lindsay stops to touch it every time she walks in. I'm not sure what the deal is, but I can see it in her eyes. It's important to her."

Dan said, "That's why I need to take it down. She's getting obsessed with Anni being gone and it's really starting to worry me." He started to explain, but Doreen stopped him.

"My soup is getting cold. Come and join me and you can tell me all about it." She gestured over to the counter where a bowl of soup and a cup of coffee were waiting. "I'll buy you dinner. I think I owe you a meal."

He shifted from foot to foot, indecisive, his eyes shooting toward the door. "Um, actually, I have to . . ."

"Don't even try to tell me you have to get home, Dan. I was just at Walgreens and I saw Lindsay there. You can't fool me. You've got nothing."

He didn't normally go anywhere after work. Like a homing pigeon, his car traveled from work to home and back again, never wavering. A habit from back in the days of returning to a wife, daughter, and faithful dog. Now there was no one waiting for him at home and Doreen knew it. The woman did have a forceful way about her. Without saying any more, she had him by the elbow and was steering him across the diner. When they got to the counter, she pointed to an empty adjacent stool. He said, "This is starting to be a habit, you shanghaiing me into joining you for a meal."

"What's getting to be a habit is you trying to avoid joining me for a meal. Which is really puzzling because most people find me to be a complete delight," she said. "Speaking of which, you never called me back the other day. Are we on for dinner a week from Sunday?" She turned her attention to the soup, blowing on the spoonful in front of her mouth.

Dinner a week from Sunday. He hadn't called back and had almost forgotten about it. "That depends," he said, taking a menu from the waitress, a young woman with spiked crimson hair. "Who's going to be there?"

"Well, aren't you the rude one." She laughed. "If you must know, it's a friend from my book club and his neighbor."

The waitress came back and stood wordlessly in front of him, holding pen to pad. "I'll have a cup of soup, a Coke, no ice, and a Reuben sandwich," he said. When the waitress walked away, he turned his attention back to Doreen. "So, tell me about these people, the book club friends."

Doreen said, "Cliff is in my book club at the library. We just finished reading the Steve Jobs biography. Fascinating read."

"And the other person?"

"Cliff's neighbor. A single woman." The waitress set the Coke down on the counter in front of them. "She's younger than us. Closer to your age."

"So Cliff is your date and you're setting this woman up with me?"

Doreen frowned. "Why must you be so suspicious, Dan? If I were trying to set you up, I would certainly tell you. People do get together to socialize and eat, you know. There doesn't have to be an agenda."

"You lost your credibility when you stuck me with Desiree." He took the wrapper off his straw. "Talk about the date from hell."

"I never deceived you. Desiree was never a date. Oh, and guess what?" Her voice rose excitedly at the end of the sentence. "Desiree and her boyfriend have worked things out and they're back together again. I have my doubts, of course, but she seems happier, so I wish them the best."

"They're back together again," Dan said incredulously. "But she said he was a sociopath. She said he told her that she was the type of woman who drove a man to drink." He didn't care about Desiree at all, but her words were fresh in his mind and he couldn't believe she'd gone back to this guy. "She made him sound heartless."

"I don't know what to tell you," Doreen said, breaking crackers into her bowl. "I never met the boyfriend, so I can't say anything about him either way. I do know that people say awful things in the heat of anger. They just worked through it, I guess." She had a thoughtful expression on her face. "I've given up trying to figure out people and relationships. Some of the ones I thought would last forever wind up getting divorced. Other couples I wouldn't bet a nickel on lasting a year are still going strong twenty years later. Like you and Christine. The two of you sure proved me wrong."

Dan's mouth dropped open and he gave Doreen a hard look. "You didn't think Christine and I would last?"

"Of course not."

"Why not?" The waitress brought his soup, but he didn't make a move for his spoon.

"He'll need crackers," Doreen said to the waitress, and then turned back to Dan. "You two were a complete mismatch from day one. And you were always arguing too. Oh, the drama." She put the back of her hand to her forehead. "I remember your mother saying she wished you two would just break up and stop torturing each other."

Dan didn't remember it being quite that dramatic. "You have to remember we were in high school then."

"And that's another thing: Who marries their high school sweetheart nowadays? No one, that's who. What if Lindsay wanted to marry Brandon?"

"Lindsay's not going to marry Brandon. She's seventeen." He took the cracker packet from the waitress's outstretched hand. "Thanks."

"You see where I'm going with this."

"When I met Christine—"

"You don't need to defend your marriage to me. Clearly, I was wrong." She pushed the empty bowl aside. "Which is my point entirely. No one can predict what the heart wants, not even the heart. Right now you feel closed off and you want to be left alone, which, frankly, young man, is no way to live. You need to get out in the world and connect with other people. You may not fall in love ever again, and that would be fine." She held up her hand, as if he were going to say something, which he wasn't. "But it would be a shame to come close to love, but keep it at arm's length, never even giving it a chance. Like if you turn down my dinner invitation, you'll never know what might have been."

"This woman, Cliff's neighbor, she doesn't think it's a blind date?"

"Of course not," Doreen said with mock indignation. She watched as Dan blew on a spoonful of his soup, and then she brought out the big guns. "If it makes a difference, I'm making your favorite breaded pork chops."

"With the stuffing and homemade applesauce?"

"Sure, if you're coming, I could do that."

He nodded. "Okay, as long as you make it clear to everyone involved that it's not a date."

"Got it," she said. "Not a date."

TWENTY-EIGHT

When Andrea and Anni walked back into the office after their harrowing encounter with the frat boy, Tommy McGuire was there, holding the door for them. "Was that Marco's car I saw out in the lot?" He'd obviously been watching through the window. When she was desk-bound, Andrea also kept an eye out to the parking lot, checking to see who was coming and going.

"What's with you guys and cars?" she said, thinking of how much attention the silver Jaguar got every time she'd driven in it with Marco. Sometimes they'd gone into a business and returned to the parking lot to find the car surrounded by men, admiring it from every angle. She never quite got it. "It's just a car. Four wheels, a bumper, an engine. Just like any other automobile."

"Spoken like a true woman," he said, grinning, and followed them in.

Andrea unsnapped Anni's leash and directed her to lie on the carpet square near her desk, then took off her coat and hung it on the rack.

"So," Tommy asked, "are you two back together now? Or just friends, or what?" He rested his butt against her desk and waited for an answer.

"We are most definitely *not* together," she said. "I ran into him. He offered me a ride back from lunch. I accepted. The end." She took her seat and turned on her computer, but Tommy didn't move. "What?"

"Nothing. That's just too bad."

"What's too bad?"

"I was hoping you two were patching things up."

"Ha!" Patching things up? Was he insane? "Why would you want that?" she asked, her eyes narrowing.

"I don't know. I always liked Marco. And you two seemed happy enough." He picked up a stack of mail and started flipping through it.

She wasn't surprised that Tommy liked Marco. Her ex-husband was a real guy's guy, the kind who was always up for a drink or the chance to talk sports. He was generous with tickets to sports events and even though he didn't enjoy golf all that much, he would fill in at a moment's notice. Other guys loved that he was a gracious loser, willing to buy drinks at the clubhouse afterward. Still, Tommy knew what a mess she'd been when they split up, so it was odd he wanted them back together. "Did Marco put you up to this? Tell you to make a case for him?"

"No, why, does he want to get back together?" When she didn't answer, he looked triumphant. "That's it, isn't it? Didn't I say he'd regret the divorce? Didn't I tell you that?"

Indeed he had, during one of the days he'd found her crying at her desk, unable to see through her bleary, tear-filled eyes. He'd said that very thing, right before he'd told her to take the day off—hell, that she should take the week off, it was fine with him. Tommy was good that way. She'd only taken the afternoon off, though. After a few hours wandering aimlessly at the mall, she was ready to go back to work and do something productive. Work was a better distraction than anything else she could think of, and having time off only reminded her that her life was falling apart. "You called it," she said. "Marco said he was sorry. He regrets the divorce and he wants us to get back together."

"That must make you feel pretty good."

"Strangely," she said, "I feel nothing." Anni yawned on her carpet square and curled up to go to sleep. "He did say he would be open to adopting or infertility treatments." Jade had found it hard to believe how much Andrea had shared with her boss, saying it was *too much information*, but it was nothing she planned. It was just the two of them, for the most part, and Tommy was such a good listener. Attentive, nonjudgmental, and discreet, a winning combination. She'd told him things she'd never share with family members, for instance, because most of them were big blabbermouths and prone to giving advice she didn't want to hear. Telling Tommy felt safe.

"Ah, poor Marco," he said.

"Poor Marco!" she exclaimed. "What about poor me? He's the one who booted me out and replaced me. He cheated on me, and lied, and broke my heart. Why would you feel sorry for him?"

"I guess I'm just looking at it from a man's perspective," he said. "His behavior was despicable, yes, but he wouldn't be the first guy to get his head turned by a flashy blonde. Men are weak, Andrea. Pathetic and weak."

"Tell me about it."

But he wasn't finished. "I never told you this, but after my divorce I woke up one day and realized I'd messed up big-time. I was sick with shame and regret, so I went back to Suzanne and begged her to forgive me. I said I'd do anything to make amends. That I wanted my family back." He looked up at the ceiling.

"And?"

He shook his head ruefully. "She wouldn't give me the time of day. Said I was a day late and a dollar short and the sight of me made her sick."

"No kidding," Andrea said, sitting back, arms folded.

"I know, I know. I deserved it." He sighed. "And I am happy now and so is Suzanne, so you could say it all worked out in the long run. But"—he held up one finger—"our family will forever be divided and it's always testy. The kids have to pick where to go on holidays and the grandkids are confused about what to call the step-grandparents. It can be messy."

"Modern families. That's the way it is nowadays."

"But see, it didn't have to be that way for us," Tommy said. "If Suzanne had taken me back, I was willing to make amends, willing to do anything it took to make it right between us. They say once a cheater, always a cheater, but I'm here to tell you that's not true, at least not for me. I would have been faithful and devoted to Suzanne until the day I died, if she'd taken me back, and I'm willing to bet Marco would do the same."

"Hmmm."

"People can change if you give them a chance."

"Maybe you're right," she said, "but he put me through hell and I don't want to go there again."

"Fair enough. It's your life," Tommy said. "I just wanted to give you another perspective. Personally, I'd go out with him just to ride in that car." He let out a long whistle. "That is one beautiful automobile."

"Why don't you just buy a Jaguar if you want one?" Andrea asked. She knew all his financials. He could certainly afford it.

"Are you kidding? The wife would never go for it," Tommy said, grinning at how the conversation had come around to make his point. "And I'm all about keeping her happy now, remember? I'm a changed man." He got up and walked into his office, turning in the doorway to say, "But if you do decide to give Marco a shot, I think you'll be pleasantly surprised."

Andrea was still thinking about this conversation that evening when she locked up the office and headed for home. Clearly, Tommy was speaking from the point of view of the one who caused the pain, not the one on the receiving end. Easy for him to say. Tommy's life had always been of his own making. He was the guy in charge, barreling into the office for a few hours here and there, checking to see that she was doing things properly, then doling out relationship advice before heading out the door again. He was free to give advice, but that didn't mean she had to take it.

Later she wondered if Tommy were somehow in cahoots with Marco, maybe psychic in some way, because right when she got home that night, Marco called, wanting to get together. Of course, he hadn't phrased it quite that way.

"Hey, Andrea," he said, purring the syllables in her name in the way she used to love. "I'm glad I caught you. I've got something really important to tell you."

That was just like Marco too, stating he was about to say something very important. He also liked to let other people know when he was about to say something funny. "You're going to die laughing," he'd say. "This is hilarious." This time, he wanted her to hang on every word. He was about to say something important or at least, it was in his own mind. She'd draw her own conclusions.

"Hi, Marco," she said wearily, leaning against the wall and pulling off her boots. Anni had raced ahead of her when she'd opened the front door, turning the corner and dashing into the kitchen. She'd probably left wet paw prints all the way to her food bowl. "What can I do for you?" she said, vowing to check the caller ID next time. "And make it quick."

"You know that ring that belonged to your grandma?"

"Yes." She shook off her jacket and hung it in the closet, no small feat with the phone wedged between her ear and shoulder. Of course she knew about her grandmother's ring. It had somehow disappeared while she was packing up to move when they'd separated. She and Marco had a big screaming match, where she'd accused him of taking it and he'd told her she was crazy. It was not her finest moment. "What about it?"

"I found it!" His voice was elated. "It was in the safe-deposit box."

She smacked her free hand against her forehead. Of course it was in the safe-deposit box; she'd put it there herself and completely forgotten. And then having forgotten, she'd torn the whole house apart looking for it. When she couldn't find it, she'd accused Marco of stealing it, either to sell or, as she had so eloquently put it, to give to his "slut girlfriend."

"Andrea, are you still there?"

"Yeah."

"Isn't that great news?"

"Yeah, it's great. Really great."

"Somehow I thought you'd be happier."

At least he wasn't mentioning her false accusations, her harpy yelling, the many ugly profanities that had streamed from her mouth over this very ring. He had the opportunity right here and now to rub her face in it, but he wasn't doing any such thing. She could give him that much at least. "I am happy. Wow, after all this time. I'm just a little shocked, is all." Anni came around the corner and Andrea reached down to pet her.

"Yeah, I was surprised to see it too," he said. "I was thinking we should meet, so I can give it to you. After it being missing for so long, I want to make sure it gets to you."

"I can stop over on the weekend. Is there a time that's good?"

"I was thinking"—there was a catch in his voice, some hesitation she couldn't quite identify—"that it would be better if we met at a neutral location. Like maybe that coffee shop you like? Noon-ish tomorrow? Would that work?" She heard the hesitation in his voice and could tell he was nervous. She'd lived with him long enough to know what that sounded like.

"Do you really have the ring?" she asked.

"Well, yeah, of course."

"And you're going to bring it tomorrow and just hand it over to me, no strings attached?" The doubt in her voice was unmistakable.

"Andrea." He said her name and let it sit there for a second. "If I say I'm bringing the ring, believe me, I'll have it with me. I don't steal women's jewelry."

He had behaved horribly during their divorce, but he was right on that count. As far as she knew, he'd divided their possessions fairly. Besides the ring, there was nothing she owned or wanted that hadn't come with her to the condo. The Jaguar was his most prized possession. In his mind, everything else could be replaced. She sighed. "Okay, I'll meet you at noon at the coffee shop," she said. Then, realizing her tone was antagonistic, added, "Thank you."

"Oh, and you might want to leave the dog at the office," he said. "For some reason she doesn't like me."

"Yeah, I noticed that." Andrea looked down at Anni's adoring upturned face, her deep-pooled eyes, smooth snout, and panting tongue. "She doesn't seem to like you at all."

Marco exhaled audibly. "Okay then, Andrea. I will see you tomorrow."

"Tomorrow," Andrea said. "At noon. Don't forget the ring."

TWENTY-NINE

When the friendly barista delivered the coffee to his table in a real mug, it struck Dan as a nice way to do business. "Here you are, sir," she said with a smile. "Enjoy!"

"Thanks," he said. What a change from Starbucks, where you stood and waited for your drink and it came in a disposable cup with writing on the side. This place was much smaller, homier. More like the coffee shops of the 1960s, where the coffee was secondary to the soups, sandwiches, and baked goods. Everyone seemed to know Joan, the woman behind the counter, and she was quick to greet them by name, rattling off their usual order. The Café Mocha. That was the name of the place. He'd have to remember it and come again, although he didn't get to this side of the city very often. He wouldn't even be here now if he weren't trying to kill time before an appointment. He'd arrived way too early, always a bad habit of his, one that could be problematic when it caught people off guard.

Today his meeting was with the head of a midwestern grocery chain that owned thirty-seven stores in Wisconsin, Ohio, Michigan, and Minnesota. If the meeting at their corporate office went well, the stores would be stocking his company's beer in the near future. He'd talked to the CEO on the phone, and it seemed like a lock, but he'd brought samples in the cooler in his truck to seal the deal.

Arriving too early would make him seem needy, so Dan had driven around for a while, weighing his options; when he saw the coffee shop, he pulled over, getting a space right in front, luckily enough. There were worse places to kill half an hour. He had his phone and could people watch. Before he knew it, the thirty minutes would be up.

It was late morning and the lunch crowd was starting to drift in. A few college kids who looked to be just a bit older than Lindsay jostled each other on their way up to the counter. Joan kidded with them about keeping the noise down or she'd fine them for being rowdy. A senior citizen couple sat stone-faced across from each other, eating chicken noodle soup, the kind with fat noodles and chunks of carrots. Another couple, a man and woman as elegant and good-looking as supermodels, finished up their drinks and vacated a table by the fireplace. One of the college girls saw the couple prepare to leave, and ran over to hold the table for the rest of her group.

There was a lot of energy here, the college kids making their way to their table, laughing as they set their backpacks at their feet. A woman walked in with a dog on a leash. The dog, a chocolate lab with his tongue hanging out, led the way to the counter. Joan called out, "Hey, Mavis and Roger, two of my favorites," and then she leaned over to give the dog a treat. Witnessing the interactions of all the people here lifted his spirits. Maybe Doreen was right and he should get out into the world a little more often.

Dan took a sip of his coffee, his eyes on the door, watching as people arrived out of the cold, stomping the snow off their boots, using their teeth to pull off their gloves. Each one following a universal pattern, all the while thinking they were unique. When a woman walked in wearing a camel-colored coat, her eyes sweeping the place in search of someone, he was hit with the impulse to stand and wave her over. The urge was so strong that he had to clamp his arms to his sides to keep from embarrassing himself. He knew her. He watched as she tucked her hair behind her ear, glanced at her phone, and then went up to the counter. "Where's your sidekick?" Joan asked the woman, and Dan strained to hear the answer.

"Back at the office today," the woman said, and then rattled off her order, which he didn't quite hear.

His view was of her backside, brown hair falling past her shoulders, a belted coat, a trim purse held at her side. Her voice was familiar and a picture formed in his head of her standing next to a car. The woman from the parking lot at Bodecker's on Main, the one he'd talked to after leaving Desiree at the table.

When Joan said, "I'll have that out for you in a minute, Andrea," it clinched the matter. Andrea was her name. He tried to remember everything he knew about her. She had a dog, which she had to go home to feed. In the restaurant she'd been sitting with the redhead who knew Desiree. The connection to Desiree, however tenuous, didn't speak well of her, but in the redhead's defense, she didn't seem to like Desiree, which probably was true for Andrea as well. Poor Desiree. Obnoxious and unlikeable. Not having to see her anymore had made Dan think more charitably of her.

All of the tables were occupied. When Andrea walked through, searching for a spot, Dan couldn't suppress it any longer. As she came past, he said, "I'm leaving soon, if you want this table." He'd gotten her attention. She glanced down and saw the empty chair on the other side of the table. "Just give me a few minutes," he said, holding up his cup of coffee. "And I'll be gone."

She pulled out the chair and sat, her coat still on, the purse swinging off her shoulder. The recognition came a second later when her brown eyes widened in amazement. "Dan?"

"You remember me?" He was oddly thrilled to hear her say his name.

"Well, of course." She grinned. She'd said it as if he were very memorable. "You're Dan, Dan, the parking lot man. The one who had lunch at Bodecker's on Main."

"Yeah." He found himself grinning back, his head bobbing in agreement. "That's exactly right. You have a good memory."

She tilted her head toward the window at the front of the shop. "So that's your truck out there using up two spaces?" Dan glanced at the window and started to apologize, when she gently said, "I'm only kidding. It is a *really* big truck, though."

"I'm not compensating for anything," he said hurriedly.

"I didn't say you were."

They grinned at each other, the easy camaraderie of two people who clicked on some unseen level. The silence was fine, until it wasn't. Dan cleared his throat and said, "I definitely remember you. Even before I saw you in the parking lot, I noticed you eating lunch with your friend at the restaurant. The red-haired woman."

"And you were having lunch with Desiree. But it wasn't a date." She set her purse under the table by her feet.

She knew Desiree too, then, and her tone implied a definite dislike. He explained, "Definitely not a date. My aunt thought we should meet. She sort of set the whole thing up. I'm not even sure why, really."

"Wow." Andrea shook her head, an amused look coming over her face. "Does your aunt like you?" She loosened the belt on her coat and began to unbutton the front.

He chuckled. "I thought she did, but after that lunch I did wonder. How is it that you know Desiree?"

Andrea sighed, a heavy exhale as if the thought of answering the question made her weary. "It's a long story and it's not that interesting. She's not a friend, if that's what you wanted to know."

"Yeah, I got that." Dan remembered the red-haired woman dipping down to give Desiree a hard stare and then asking if she was enjoying her lunch date, like she'd caught her in the act. But what exactly that could be, he had not a clue. He took a sip of his coffee and realized he'd downed the last of it. Soon enough he would have to go to his appointment. But he wanted to talk to this woman a little longer. For the first time he'd met a woman who intrigued him, someone who was easy to talk to and definitely easy on the eyes. He knew what Doreen would say. She'd say he should ask her out for coffee or lunch. That it didn't have to be a date but that he should be out in the world, meeting people, doing things, socializing. But the thing was, they barely knew each other, and he didn't want to scare this woman off. He cleared his throat again and asked, "Do you work around here?"

"About a mile away," she said. "I'm the office manager for McGuire Properties. My boss owns more than a hundred rental properties, most of them residential, and I take care of, well, everything, really. He's not in the office much."

"He's lucky to have you," Dan said. There was a long pause where they just sat, quietly looking at each other, both trying to decide what to say next. He was sorely aware of the time limit and was about to ask if she'd want to meet for lunch some other time, because he really had to go, but he was stopped before he even started, because the friendly woman from the front register now stood in front of them, holding a tray of food. She ceremoniously placed a salad and silverware in front of Andrea, as well as a large glass of lemonade.

"There you go, Andrea," she said, turning so Dan could see the name tag identifying her as Joan. She set a dog treat next to the plate. "And here's something for you to take back to your little—"

"Andrea!" A man's voice rang out. Behind Joan towered a dark-haired guy, as bulky and wide as a linebacker. "What's going on? I thought you were meeting me," he said, giving Dan a hard look. Joan, seeming to sense an awkward situation, scooted around this interloper and made her way back up to the front, allowing herself one last curious glance back as she went.

Andrea raised her chin. "You're late."

The string of tension between Andrea and this guy was so strong, Dan felt like he could reach out and pluck it. He scrambled to his feet and said, "I was just going." He grabbed the empty mug so that his side of the table was clear, and gestured. "All yours." He was referring to the chair, but even as he said it, it occurred to him that it sounded like he meant Andrea.

"See you later, Dan," Andrea said, looking up at him almost regretfully. Her lips stayed parted a split second longer like she was going to say something else, but Marco slid into the vacant seat and started blathering about the drive over and getting stopped by a train, so Dan just nodded, took his mug up to the counter, and left for his appointment.

THIRTY

Marco always did have terrible timing, Andrea thought, when she spotted him looming over their table, giving poor Dan a death-ray glare. Joan had just delivered Andrea's lunch and was in the process of presenting her with a dog treat to take back to Anni, which was so like her. Joan had a kind heart and was extremely thoughtful. This would have been the perfect opportunity to talk about Anni and see how Dan felt about dogs, which would be really telling. If he was a dog person, that would have elevated him in her mind. But she never got the chance because Marco had to come lumbering in, the Neanderthal that he was, trapping Joan in front of the table. She'd had to maneuver to extricate herself.

"What's going on? I thought you were meeting me," Marco had said, his tone practically accusatory, like, what was Dan doing with his woman? Which was weird, because the divorce had been his idea, and he'd never been that way, even when they were married.

Dan didn't waste any time getting out of there. Who could blame him? She'd only managed to sputter something about talking to him later. And then he was gone. If he was interested, maybe he'd come to the coffee shop some other time. Unlikely, though, given the way Marco had acted. Dan's backside as he walked out the door was probably the last she'd ever see of him.

Her attention went back across the table to Marco, who was talking about the difficult drive over. She supposed it was a backhanded apology for being late without having to actually apologize. The story was that he'd had to stop for a train, and then had trouble on the expressway. "They have I-94 down to two eastbound lanes for about three miles. Good Lord, the traffic was unbelievable. I was at a complete stop for fifteen minutes. And then they had the ramp closed. Really inconvenient for me." He shook his head.

"Just for you?" Andrea asked, joking.

"What do you mean?" His face was blank.

"I mean, it was convenient for everyone else?" He still wasn't getting it. She tried again. "It was a joke. I was trying to point out that everyone going that way had to deal with it."

"Well, yeah, but I don't care about them. I don't even know them."

"Right." Andrea didn't even try to hide her smile. He never understood when she was kidding. This lack of communication had been a hurdle when she was legally bound to Marco. Now it was just ridiculous.

"So who was that guy you were talking to when I got here?" Marco asked, folding his hands on the table in front of him.

"Dan," she said nonchalantly.

"Dan who?"

"My friend, Dan. That's all you need to know," Andrea said. Knowing Marco, he'd friend Dan on Facebook or figure out they had a mutual friend. Next thing she knew, they'd be golfing or meeting for darts. No, even if she never saw Dan again, there was no way she'd want that asteroid hitting the planet.

"Okay, have it your way." He glanced around the coffee shop. "What does a guy have to do to get a cup of coffee around here? She was just here a second ago. Jeez."

"You have to go to the counter and order," Andrea said. "But before you do that, where's my ring?" She held her hand out, palm up, and raised her eyebrows.

"I'll get to that." Marco gave her a wry smile. "Impatient, much?"

"Seriously, I want my grandmother's ring, Marco." Was he jerking her around? A lump of fury rose in her throat. She shouldn't have to jump through hoops to get something that belonged to her in the first place. And it wasn't just any possession; it was a family heirloom.

"You'll get it, you'll get it. I've got it right here." He patted the outside of his jacket. "Just let me get my coffee first." And off he went, sauntering up to the front like he had all the time in the world. Deliberately infuriating as only Marco could be.

Andrea watched him up at the counter, laying his charm on Joan. They were both looking in her direction now. Marco smiled and gave her a little wave. He was probably giving Joan the inside scoop on their failed marriage. Meeting him here was a bad idea, but then again, she couldn't have anticipated running into Dan, and she'd honestly thought Marco would hand over the ring and leave. She should have known it wouldn't be that simple. Sighing, she picked up her fork and took a stab at her salad. Her other hand rested on her thigh, fiddling with nothing where a leash should have been. It was odd to be here without Anni at her feet. Having the dog nearby always calmed her. Plus, Anni might have growled at Marco, and he'd have given her the ring right then and there. Funny that the only time she showed her teeth was with Marco. She was usually such a gentle, sweet dog.

When Marco returned to the table, he was all smiles. "That Joan is super nice!" She'd forgotten his habit of using the word "super" as an adjective for everything. "I told her we used to be married and she thought it was great we were still on good terms." He took a sip of his coffee. He'd gotten a ceramic mug instead of a disposable to-go cup. Obviously, Marco thought they would be visiting for a while. It occurred to her to argue that they weren't on good terms, but she was tired of playing verbal tug-of-war. She'd only agreed to meet him for one reason.

"The ring?" She held out her hand again. This time, though, he nodded and pulled the box out of his inside jacket pocket.

"See, I told you I'd give it to you."

She flipped open the lid and saw the ring pillowed in the middle, exactly as she'd remembered it. What a relief. She'd been planning on going to see her grandmother soon, maybe tomorrow night after work. Would seeing the ring prompt her memory? Unlikely, she knew, but she wanted to try. Andrea reached out and touched the stone, reassuring herself that it was secure in the setting.

"Put it on," he urged. "You always did like that thing."

Bossy, that's what Marco was. Always having to manage every situation. Still, she was pleased to finally have the ring in her possession, and it would be easier to keep track of if she were wearing it. Andrea took the ring and slipped it onto her finger. She and her grandmother had the same size hands, petite with slim fingers.

Marco must have been thinking the same thing, because he said, admiringly, "You always did have skinny fingers. Not too many women could even get it past their knuckle. That's a really tiny ring."

Not too many women could even get it past their knuckle. Andrea had a sudden realization, one she didn't like. She blurted out the accusation, somehow knowing it was true. "Oh my God, you let Desiree try on the ring."

He tilted his head. "What? What are you talking about?" He said it like an actor in a play who'd been unjustly accused. A really bad actor, who wasn't all that convincing. She'd been married to him long enough to know when he was lying, or trying to deflect, anyway.

She snapped the case shut. "I can't believe you let her wear my grandmother's ring. Have you no sense of decency?"

"It's not like she wore it," Marco said. "I mean, she really couldn't. It's like child-size," he added hastily. "She saw it when I brought it home, and before I could stop her, she picked it up and tried it on. Right away I told her to put it back. She only had it for a second."

"I thought the two of you weren't even together anymore," Andrea said. "You said that it didn't work out, that she was a mistake." He'd also said he wanted to get back together with Andrea, but she didn't even want to say the words out loud because it might be taken the wrong way and she didn't want to encourage him. He had no idea who he was dealing with now. She and Marco? Not happening.

"We aren't together," Marco said, enunciating each word like Andrea was a preschooler with a listening problem. "It's over with me and Desiree. It was a mistake. A big mistake. The only good thing that came of the whole mess is that I realized how much I miss you."

"Okay, let me get this straight. You and Desiree are no longer together."

"Right," he said, looking prematurely happy. "That's it."

"And it's also true that you just found the ring in the safe-deposit box recently."

"Yes."

"So how was it that Desiree was at the house to try the ring on? I mean, if you're not together anymore and you just found the ring, how did that timing work out?"

His smile faded. "You don't understand."

"So you've had my ring for a while and didn't return it to me? *Or*, you just found it and Desiree tried it on recently, which means she's still in your life? Which is it?"

"Neither one." He held up a hand to explain and Andrea had an image of him running in place trying to catch up to his lies. "I *did* just find the ring. Desiree came back to the house for some of her stuff, and she saw it on the table. I told her to leave it alone, but that woman is a bubblehead. Doesn't listen for crap. Not like you, Andrea." He kept talking, reminiscing about a vacation they'd once taken to the Florida Keys. It had been a fairly idyllic trip and he was trying to suck her into the emotional vortex of their shared good times. Nothing like traveling with Desiree, he said, and went on to list all the ways she annoyed him.

Wanting to flee, Andrea felt her hand tighten around the leash that wasn't there. Her stomach clenched the way it did during every dispute she'd ever had with Marco. He would never admit when he was wrong. Ever. Never said he was sorry. He never admitted to forgetting or misunderstanding or doing any of the things that human beings do. Marco was always right, and he would just keep on talking until the dizziness of his words made her head ache. Before, she had always given in. Good grief, most of the time she wound up apologizing for things he had done.

His other strategy, which he was employing now, was to change the subject to one that made him look good, and then get her to agree with him. Most of the time she'd walked away feeling lucky to have him. Out of all the women in the world, Marco had chosen her. That's how she used to think, anyway.

She looked at him across the table, still talking, his hands gesturing, completely in love with his own words, and suddenly the obvious hit her. She had no ties to him anymore. Marco was not her problem. She had a car, a good job, a nice condo, friends and family, and a dog. And now she had her grandmother's ring. Andrea did not need him. If she never saw him again, her life would go on and all would be fine. She grabbed her purse and pushed back from the table. "I have to go, Marco," she said. "Don't call me again."

She rushed out of the place, her coat draped over her arm. As she passed the front window, she spotted him inside, still looking at the doorway she'd just walked through. The expression on his face said he couldn't believe it. Stunned, that's how he looked. Andrea, who'd always been as malleable as a marshmallow, had finally stood up to him. She felt a sense of pride, but on a more practical level, she also felt cold. Once she'd gotten past the window, she stopped to put on her coat and gloves. Part of her thought Marco might rush out and try to change her mind, but he didn't. That wouldn't have been his way. He liked to be in charge and chasing her would have reeked of desperation.

When Andrea got back to the office, she called Jade. They never talked on the phone during work hours, but Andrea couldn't wait and she knew Jade would understand. She told her the whole story, ending with, "And then I told him, 'Don't call me again.'"

"Whoa," Jade said. "Very ballsy of you. It's about time. I heartily approve." Jade had been telling Andrea to grow a backbone the entire time she was married. Back then, she thought Jade couldn't possibly understand how much compromise was required in a marriage, how much of a trade-off was necessary to keep things running smoothly. She'd been deluded back then.

"I can't believe he let Desiree try on my ring. I hate thinking of her touching it," Andrea said, tilting her hand to see the light catch the gem. With the ring still on, she'd washed her hands with liquid soap and water as soon as she'd gotten back to the office, trying to scrub away all traces of Marco and Desiree. It smelled like antibacterial soap now, which wasn't the most appealing odor, but it gave her the satisfaction of knowing she'd wiped it clean and it was all hers again.

"Yeah, that was sick. But you know, she's pretty much touched everything else you used to cherish."

"She's welcome to it now," Andrea said. "I don't want anything to do with Marco anymore."

"So tell me about this Dan."

"Ah, Dan." Andrea leaned back in her chair and took a deep breath, looking up at the ceiling. "What can I say about Dan?" She tapped her fingers on the desk. "He's just really great."

"Oh my God, you're totally in love with him," Jade exclaimed.

Andrea sat up. "No, don't be ridiculous. I barely know him, how could I be totally in love with him?" In fact, she thought, they'd hardly begun to talk when Marco had arrived. It wasn't anything Dan said, or did, it was just something she sensed about him. Something really appealing that was hard to put into words. A quiet strength. A decency. Warmth. He didn't seem like the type of guy who had anything to prove. "I just really liked him. You know how sometimes you meet someone and you just hit it off? I don't know how to describe it, really. I just felt like we clicked." She thought Dan felt the click as well, but it was possible she was projecting her own hopes onto the situation.

"So what's your strategy for seeing him again?" Jade asked.

"Strategy? I don't have one, really. I have lunch at the coffee shop a few times a week. Maybe I'll run into him again."

"Well, that's pretty lame." Andrea heard a crunch on the other end of the line, the sound of Jade taking a bite out of something, probably a carrot stick.

Andrea said, "That's all I've got. I don't know his last name or anything else about him."

"You have to think a little harder than that. What else do you know about him?" said Jade, who prided herself on always thinking creatively.

"I'm not calling Desiree, if that's where you're going with this."

Jade said, "No, my dear Andrea, that's not where I'm going at all. You know more about this guy than you realize. He drives a large red pickup truck, right? Did you catch the license plate number?"

"No."

"Okay, what I'd do next is tell Joan he left his gloves or something behind and you don't know his last name. She might know his name or maybe he paid with a credit card and she can look it up."

"Not doing it."

"Why not?"

"Because it's manipulative and underhanded and immature. Plus, Joan would just tell me to give the gloves to her, that she'd hold onto them until he came in again."

Jade was undeterred. "Well, how about this? You call Bodecker's on Main and ask if Desiree and Dan had a reservation for lunch the day we saw them there. If it's in his name, then voilà! You've got him."

"Jade, are you even listening to yourself? That's creepy. Besides, they aren't going to give out that kind of information."

"They will if you come up with a good reason."

"And what would that be?"

"I don't know. This is your thing, not mine. Help me out here. I can't be brainstorming all by myself."

Andrea said, "I think I'll just see if I run into him again at the coffee shop. If it doesn't happen, it wasn't meant to be."

"It wasn't meant to be," Jade said, lightly mimicking. "Don't tell me you're leaving it up to the universe to decide. The universe has better things to do. You have to take charge. Make it happen. Do like Martina Dearhart says and open your arms wide and say 'hello, love!'"

This was Jade at her most exuberant. Andrea could picture her on the other end of the line with arms outstretched and chin lifted heavenward, doing jazz hands. She could be very convincing when she wanted to be. "That's all well and good," Andrea said. "But I think I'm going to stick to my plan."

"Your plan is no plan."

"And yet," Andrea said with finality, "it is mine."

"Well," Jade said, not even trying to hide the fact she was chewing, "good luck with that."

THIRTY-ONE

Outside the wind howled under the eaves, keeping Dan awake. Even with Christine gone all this time, he tended to stay on his side of the bed, or at least that's how he started out when he first settled in for the night. Sometimes he'd wake up in the morning in the middle, covers askew, his arm flung over her pillow as if he had been holding her in a dream.

Other times, like tonight, he felt her presence so strongly it was as if he could reach out and touch her. The energy and warmth emanating from her side was exactly as it had been when she was alive. Once, half-asleep, he actually slipped his hand under the covers and let it drift over, half expecting to feel her there, to be able to caress her palm the way he used to, but she wasn't there, of course. He never made that mistake again, but when he got the sense she was there in those moments between wakefulness and sleep, he found himself talking to her, whispering the way they always had. He felt better afterward, talking about his troubles, foolishly hoping Christine had actually heard him.

Sometimes he talked about work, but most of the time it was about Lindsay. Nothing major, just basic parenting issues like the fact that she wanted to stay out all night after the prom. All of her friends were going to a party at one of her girlfriends' houses, and then the whole group planned to go out for breakfast in the morning. Lindsay had argued she'd be going off to college in the fall and then he'd have no idea how late she stayed out. When Lindsay presented it that way, it sounded reasonable. Was one night now so different from the freedom she'd have next September? He didn't think so, but he wished he could run it past his wife. She always had such a good take on things.

Sometimes, after having one of these one-sided discussions, Dan woke up knowing the answer to his questions. Did Christine have a hand in that, or was it his subconscious at work? He wished there was a way to know for sure.

That night, listening to the soft moan of the wind, something different was on his mind. It troubled him that he'd felt a connection to Andrea, the woman he'd run into in the coffee shop. He liked her. And while they had sat across from each other at the table, everything around them fell away. The background noise, the other people—none of it mattered. It was just them and there was nowhere else he wanted to be. Surreal, in a way.

He couldn't put his finger on what it was about her that affected him this way. True, she was pretty without being flashy, easy to talk to, and had a ready smile. But it was more than that. Andrea seemed familiar, and not just from seeing her in the parking lot at Bodecker's on Main. There was an immediate comfort level with her. He knew from past experience this was not a common thing. It wasn't just that he was lonely (which, in fact, he was, although he'd deny it if anyone brought up the subject), because he didn't feel this way about everyone. That Desiree, for example. He'd have to be the last man on the planet to welcome her presence in his life and even then he'd want to live in separate houses. And not in the same neighborhood even. No, it was more than simply being lonely. There was something about Andrea, something he couldn't put into words.

Dan had even felt a surge of jealousy when that other guy showed up, the loudmouth Jethro who'd barged in like he owned the place. The only thing that made him feel better was Andrea's reaction. She wasn't all that happy to see the guy and she looked somewhat wistful that Dan was leaving. He felt that way too.

And that was the problem, the conflict that raged inside of him. He couldn't be attracted to another woman because he still felt married to Christine. It was so odd that she was no longer his wife, because they hadn't gotten divorced, never even talked about separating. Ever. They'd been happily married, rarely argued, still enjoyed each other's company right to the end. She never once got on his nerves to the point where he wished her gone. The fact that she was ripped out of his life was a tragedy. He was not single by choice, and yet he was indeed single, because he was alone. He'd been left behind.

He whispered, "Christine?" His voice melted into the darkness, and he went on. "Christine, I miss you." Outside the howling had subsided to a low moan. It would be a bad night to be stuck outdoors. "Lindsay will be gone in a few months, and I'll be alone in this house. I don't know how I'm going to deal with that. How am I supposed to go on without you?" He waited, taking a deep breath. "Would you mind so much if I had someone else in my life? No one could be like you, I know . . ." A lump formed in his throat. This was insane, he thought, this talking to himself. He was getting all worked up, and for what?

A sign, he'd give anything for a sign, but he knew life didn't work that way. He was on his own. He sighed and the wind outside echoed the sound. Dan lay there for a long time, thinking about how he would live his life going forward. Drowsiness washed over him and he felt himself sinking comfortably into the mattress until at last he was asleep.

THIRTY-TWO

The next day after work, Andrea found herself singing along to the radio as she drove to visit her grandmother. Anni sat comfortably on the passenger seat, her nose pointed at Andrea instead of the view out the window. Andrea found herself talking to Anni in a high-pitched, silly voice. She had no idea where this voice came from. One day it was just there.

She reached over and gave Anni a pat. "Are we going to see Gram? Oh yes we are, oh yes we are." Anni's ears perked up, responding to the inflection in Andrea's voice. "She's going to love seeing you again, my beautiful baby."

After pulling into the parking lot at the nursing home, Andrea snapped the leash onto Anni's collar and led her across the parking lot. Anni had developed a distaste for wet, slushy snow and walked carefully, pulling her feet up in an exaggerated way, like she was walking on hot coals. "I don't like it any more than you do," Andrea said, coaxing her along. Of course, people didn't have to actually walk barefoot in the snow, so it wasn't the same thing at all. Anni's feet had to be freezing and wet. Maybe, she thought, it was time to get some of those little doggie boots she'd always thought were so ridiculous. Funny how different the view looked from the other side of the fence.

Once past the glass doors, Andrea recognized the older lady with the silver bouffant hair who sat behind the counter. She'd been the one who'd made a big fuss over Anni the last time they'd visited. Today she had a phone against her ear, and one finger held up to indicate she'd be right with the older gentleman who stood waiting in front of her. Her face showed a flash of recognition upon spotting Anni and Andrea, and she smiled and waved them through without making them sign in.

Everywhere they went, they got star treatment, Andrea thought. Who knew having a dog elevated a person's status to that extent? In the elevator, Anni stood facing the door, like she knew how this was going to go. When the doors slid open, she scampered out, immediately evoking comments from people in the hallway.

"Hey there, little doggie!"

"Look at that cute puppy."

"Aww."

A white-haired woman parked in a wheelchair outside her doorway stopped Andrea to ask, "Can I pet her?" and when given permission, reached down to tentatively touch the top of Anni's head. "Oh so soft," she said. "So sweet." Andrea, who had planned to go right to Gram's room, felt the urgency fall away and stayed rooted to the spot. She crouched down next to the woman's chair. "She likes you," she offered. "You seem to have a knack for petting her in just the right spot." The woman's hands were gnarled, the veins evident through papery skin, and her movements were shaky, but she managed to pet Anni's head with short strokes. For her part, Anni sat still, as if she knew.

After a few minutes, Andrea got up and patted the woman's hand. "We have to go, but I'm glad we got a chance to visit with you." The woman nodded, not saying anything, but when Andrea glanced back, she was waving to them with trembling fingers.

This was a good thing, sharing the joy of having a pet. And such a simple thing to do. When Andrea got to Gram's room, the door was open. Still, she knocked on the doorframe before coming in. "Gram?" she said.

A young woman in scrubs sat on the bed facing her grandmother, who was sitting in the recliner with her arms raised toward the ceiling like she was surrendering. Both of them turned to look when Andrea walked in.

"Did I come at a bad time?" Andrea asked.

The young woman shook her head, making her dreadlocks shiver. "Just finishing up her PT. I was putting Mrs. Keller through her exercises. We've got to stay limber, you know." She stood up and gently guided Gram's hands down to her lap. "We can wrap up early, Mrs. Keller, since you've got a visitor."

As she walked past Andrea, the physical therapist reached down to give Anni a pat. "What a sweetie," she said.

"She seems to have a fan club here," Andrea said.

"Just keep bringing her back." She stood up and Andrea saw that her name badge had "Alicia Banks" printed under her photo. "The residents really seem to respond to animals, especially calm dogs like this one."

After the woman left the room, Andrea brought Anni around to the other side of Gram's bed. "Hey, Gram."

Her grandmother blinked before smiling. "Hi, honey."

"I brought my dog Anni again to see you. Remember, I brought her with me last time?"

"Sure I remember."

That was the frustrating thing about conversations with Gram. She was so agreeable that it was hard to tell if she actually remembered or was just playing along. At least she wasn't argumentative like so many people with impaired memories. It was a small consolation.

Gram reached down to touch Anni's head, patting her awkwardly. "Aren't you a sweet doggie."

Andrea glanced over to see that the bed on the other side of the room was no longer there. "Your roommate's not here. Did she get transferred?"

Gram followed Andrea's eyes and looked over for a second, but didn't say anything. The woman had either died or had been moved to the hospice wing. Gram didn't know or didn't want to say.

"Can I carry her?" Gram said, crooking a finger at Anni. Carry her? Andrea was sure this was one of those times when words got muddled in her head.

"You want to hold her? On your lap?" She asked. When Gram nodded, she went to pull the crank so that the chair would lean back, then lifted Anni up onto her grandmother's lap. At just over thirty pounds Anni was no lightweight, but she didn't struggle when Andrea picked her up, which made it easier.

Gram closed her eyes and rested her hand on Anni's back. Today, Gram looked tidy, with her hair neatly combed, wearing knit pants and a matching button-down top. Not too different from how she always looked, aside from her hair color. It made Andrea miss the old Gram, the one who used to give her advice, the grandmother with whom she could have a lively conversation. Gram always loved a good laugh, but this new grandmother, the one with holes in her memory, was a different version of the original. Still a sweet woman, but she'd lost her sparkle. Gram opened her eyes, looking surprised to have a dog on her lap. "Will you look at that!" she said. "Such a sweet little thing."

"That's my dog, Anni."

Gram nodded. "I haven't had a little one like this in a long time."

"Yeah, it's been awhile." Being agreeable was key.

When Gram seemed to lose interest, Andrea lifted the dog off her lap and set Anni back on the floor. Anni snuffled over to the corner, her nose to the ground. Whatever scent trail she was on, it kept her happily occupied. Andrea suddenly remembered how she had planned to prompt her grandmother's memory. "Gram, remember when you gave me your ring? The one Grandpa gave you?"

She was quiet for a long time, processing the words. Finally she said, "My ring," twisting her finger like she was just now noticing that she no longer wore it.

"Yes, the ring Grandpa Fred gave you? Do you remember?"

"Of course I remember."

Did she remember Grandpa Fred or did she remember the ring, or both? Or was it none of the above, and she was just being agreeable? Andrea didn't know, would probably never know, but she plowed forward. "You gave me your ring for safekeeping, and for a while it was at my old house, but now I have it again." Andrea snapped open her purse and pulled out the jeweler's box. "See?" She got out the ring and held it out for her grandmother.

"My ring!" she said happily, taking it from Andrea.

"It's beautiful, isn't it? I had it cleaned and it's as beautiful as the day Grandpa gave it to you."

"The night," Grandma said, her head bobbing up and down.

"Excuse me?"

"Fred gave it to me at night." She smiled. "The moon was out."

"You remember when Grandpa Fred gave you the ring?" Andrea asked cautiously.

Her grandmother clutched the ring in her hand. "We went dancing. We danced and danced like the only people in the world. And we went outside and then he took a box out of his pocket."

"This box?" Andrea held it up.

Gram continued as if Andrea hadn't spoken. "He said, 'I want you to be my wife and I promise I will love you forever.'"

Andrea found herself holding her breath. Sometimes it happened like this, but you never could predict the timing. It was as if there were a tear in the fabric holding back Gram's memories and she was able to unexpectedly access them on occasion. "And he did love you forever," Andrea said.

"Oh, I miss him." She put her clenched fist up to her heart. "I miss him so badly."

"I know. I do too."

Anni returned from her exploring and, as if sensing she was needed, rested her head by Gram's feet. Andrea sighed and leaned over to rub her knuckles over the dog's back. "Grandpa Fred was a good man. You were lucky. I hope I find someone who will love me forever."

Gram said, "You did."

"What?"

"You did find him to love you."

Andrea's heart sunk. She sat up to meet her grandmother's eyes. "Oh no, Gram, I'm not with Marco anymore. I'm sorry to say we got divorced." Gram had been at Andrea and Marco's wedding, looking smart in a lovely lavender dress with a matching hat. This had been after Grandpa had died, but before her slip into dementia. Her grandmother had danced all night and had been one of the last ones to leave the reception. Was it possible Gram actually remembered Andrea and Marco's wedding day and all that came with it—the vows, the celebration? What had once been the happiest day of a young bride's life? Now Andrea couldn't bear to even look at the pictures. Marco's betrayal had turned it into a sham.

"No." Gram shook her head. "Not Marco."

Andrea looked down at Anni and wondered if her grandmother was referring to the dog. Certainly Anni's love was guaranteed, but that wasn't what they'd been talking about. "Do you mean Anni? That she'll love me forever?"

But her grandmother was gone now, having receded back into herself. The old woman settled against the chair's headrest and closed her eyes. Her thin lips mouthed words Andrea couldn't hear and then stopped, staying slightly parted. In a few seconds' time, she'd dozed off. The memory of her proposal had worn her out, or maybe it was the physical therapy. Andrea gently unfolded her grandmother's hand from around the ring and kissed her cheek. "I'm going to just put this somewhere safe for you," she said. "Okay?" Even as she snapped the jewelry box shut, her grandmother didn't stir. "Good-bye, Gram," she said. "Sweet dreams."

Andrea tiptoed out of the room, but Anni was not quite so considerate. The only sound as they left the room was the clicking of Anni's toenails on the linoleum.

THIRTY-THREE

When Dan woke up the next morning, his first thought was that he should stop at the Phoenix Health Care Center after work. A few days earlier, Lindsay had made copies of a photo of Anni with their contact information, which she'd e-mailed to the nursing home. The administrator had e-mailed back saying they'd have to bring in physical copies if they wanted them posted on each floor, something his daughter found infuriating. Her biggest search strategies for finding Anni so far had involved trying to get the dog's photo to go viral on Facebook. She didn't understand that not everyone was as tech savvy. "How lame is this?" Lindsay had said, holding her phone out so that he could read the woman's response.

He couldn't see it without his reading glasses, but he wasn't going to tell her that. "Just tell me what she said."

After Lindsay explained, she said, "Like they couldn't just print them off at their end. Jeez!" The last word was said as if she alone carried the weight of the world, and had to do *everything*. "How lazy can you be?"

"It might not be laziness," Dan said, feeling empathy for the poor woman. "It's probably just company policy." He knew a thing or two about that. Sometimes in business, things got so convoluted.

"What kind of policy doesn't let people find a lost dog? I mean, please, people, have a heart."

After that she'd printed the notice on regular printer paper, and left a stack on the kitchen table with a Post-it note asking him to drop them off as soon as he could. Every morning he looked at the fliers, sighing over the photo of Anni's little face, and every day he had a good reason why that particular day wouldn't work out. He'd been working longer days lately, trying to get the new lager line up and running, and hadn't been getting home before seven as it was, but today he woke up with the thought in his head that dropping off those sheets was a priority. He'd let it wait for far too long. He'd make a point to leave at five thirty at the latest, drive straight to the Phoenix Health Care Center, and get the chore done.

That would give Lindsay peace of mind. She still had it in her head that Anni was out there, just waiting for them to find her and bring her home. He appreciated her faith, even as he didn't share it. Anni had been gone too long. With every passing day his hope was being chipped away, and now the thought of ever finding Anni seemed remote at best.

He stuffed the printouts in his briefcase right before he left the house, and when he left work at night, he double-checked to make sure they were still there before heading out to his truck. His day had gone well, no big problems at work, and not too many small ones either.

Dan slid behind the wheel, noting that he didn't even have to brush snow off his windshield. He pulled out of the parking lot without having to wait for oncoming traffic, and hit all the green lights on the way to the expressway. This is how it always went, it seemed to him. On good days everything lined up perfectly, like the universe was trying to help you along. And on bad days? Well, on bad days, you better watch out because if something bad was going to happen, it would, and there'd be no stopping it. Today, though, was a good day. He'd had that feeling from the moment he'd awoken.

He got a good space in the nursing home parking lot too, watching as a car vacated a space in the front row around the side of the building, and grabbing the spot immediately after it pulled out. If the woman at the front desk wasn't busy, he could dash in and out and be on his way home in minutes. He was feeling so charitable that it occurred to him he could stop in and see Nadine while he was here, but then he rationalized that dinnertime might not be ideal for a visit. Soon, though, some weekend day very soon.

He went through the glass doors, relieved to see that the woman at the front desk didn't look busy. She had a friendly-looking older woman look, big smile, gray hair done up in some kind of beehive thing teased up five inches from the top of her head. "What can I help you with, hon?" she asked in a high-pitched, Minnie Mouse voice.

Dan set his briefcase on the floor and told her about their previous visit, about how Nadine, a family friend, claimed she had seen their stolen dog visiting at the Phoenix Health Care Center. That was as far as he'd gotten, when the woman interrupted. "You said your friend is up on the third floor?" When he nodded, she said, "You know that's our cognitive impairment floor."

"I understand that—"

"Many of our residents up on the third floor are so easily confused." When she shook her head, her hair didn't move, not one iota. "I'm sorry to be the one to tell you this."

Dan gritted his teeth. "I realize this, really I do. But you have to understand that my daughter is heartbroken over this." He was too, if the truth be told. "And I promised her I'd drop these off and make sure they got distributed on every floor in your facility. If there's any chance at all that this would help us find our dog . . . well, we've looked everywhere else."

"I see."

"We e-mailed ahead of time, and Ms. Kasbaum said it would be fine."

"Oh," she said, brightening. "If Ms. Kasbaum said it's okay, then it's fine by me."

"Great." He set his briefcase on the counter, snapped open both sides, and grabbed the stack of papers, conveniently paper clipped by Lindsay. Closing it up again, he grabbed the handle and, at the same time, handed her the printouts. "Our contact information is at the bottom," he said, stating the obvious. "My daughter and I thank you. We really appreciate it."

Dan was almost to the glass doors when he heard the woman cry out, "Wait, wait just a minute." He turned to see her waving the sheet over her head. "I've seen your dog."

His heart picked up, matching the pace of his footsteps as he made his way back to the counter. "You've seen her? When?" For a split second he allowed himself to hope.

She stood up and he understood the reason for the tall hair. She wasn't much taller on her feet than she had been sitting. Her words came out in an excited, breathy stream. "I mean I just saw her, today. At least it looks like the same dog. I mean, could there be two that look the same? I guess there could be, but boy, she looks just like the photo. Exactly like this photo."

Dan swallowed. "Okay, let's back up for a minute. The dog that looks like Anni was here today? Who brought her?"

"A young woman. Late twenties, or maybe thirty, it's hard to tell. Kind of long brown hair, well, not real long, just past her shoulders, I guess. Pale skin, very pretty. That's all I know." She held out one empty hand apologetically. "She had a nice smile."

"She was a visitor, or what?"

"Visiting a resident, I guess. She'd been here before, so I just waved her through . . ." Her face grew stricken as she spoke and Dan knew why.

"So she didn't sign in," he said. It was only a guess, but her face already told him the answer.

"No, she didn't sign in," she said. "I'm sorry. I always follow the rules, but I was on the phone and someone was waiting to ask me a question, and she was such a good little dog. She'd been here before and everything was fine. I thought it would be okay. I'm just a volunteer." Her face crumpled like she was about to cry.

"It's okay," Dan said. "If she's been here twice, chances are she'll come back, right?"

"Right." The woman pulled a tissue out of the box next to her phone, put it up to her nose, and blew.

If she started crying, Dan didn't know what he was going to do. He said, "Maybe some of the staff will be able to identify the woman and the dog. And it might not even be my dog. Please don't be too hard on yourself. Everyone makes mistakes."

"Thank you for being so understanding." She pulled out a fresh tissue and dabbed at her eyes. "When I think of your little girl missing her puppy, I could just cry."

"So," Dan pressed on, "when did all this happen? Can you remember what time she arrived and left? Approximately?"

"Well," the lady said, sniffing. "She got here not too long ago. It's hard to remember." Her mouth pulled from side to side as she thought. "And she left . . ." She glanced up at him, puzzled. "I don't actually remember seeing her go. I mean, sometimes I miss things, but you'd think I'd notice that little dog . . ."

Dan gulped. "So there's a chance she's still here?"

"I guess." She leaned over the counter and twisted her head to see the two side-by-side elevators. Her forehead furrowed, as she tried to remember. "I mean, I don't know for sure."

Dan reached down to grab a copy of the sheet with Anni's picture. "I'm going to go up to the third floor and see if I can find them. I'll leave my briefcase here." He set it down on the floor in front of the counter.

"And I'll make some phone calls," she said excitedly. "I'll call the other floors in the building and ask if they've seen a lady with a dog."

As Dan rode up the elevator, he wondered if the place had a PA system. Making an announcement seemed like the most expedient way to handle this. The woman hadn't offered, though, and maybe they had specified requirements for using the system. He'd ask after he was done checking the third floor.

The elevator car stopped on the second floor and when the door opened, he saw a woman about his age leaning on a walker. She wore what he was starting to believe was standard fare for the place, comfortably stretchy clothing, in her case yoga pants and a hooded sweatshirt. Pushing the walker slowly in front of her, she was halfway into the elevator, when she said, "Going down?"

"No, up."

"Oh shoot," she said, backing up one baby step at a time. "Sorry to be a bother."

"No trouble at all," Dan said, stepping forward to hold the doors for her. He shot looks in both directions, but there was no sign of a lady with Anni on the second floor. At least not that he could see from the elevator. "Have you seen a woman with a small dog? Sometime in the last hour or so?"

"Nope, can't say that I have." She nodded and kept inching backward.

"Okay, thanks." The door closed and the elevator shuddered before continuing its rise to the third floor. After getting buzzed through the locked door, he wandered down the hall until he came to the nurses' station. The last time he and Lindsay had been here, a sign on the back wall had said, "Happy Birthday, Kevin." Since then, a new sign had replaced it. This one said, "Congratulations, Cleo." Someone either had a baby or was retiring. A sheet cake underneath the sign sat partially eaten, and some empty punch cups were scattered nearby. No one sat at the desk, but voices drifted from the room beyond. Down the hall Dan heard someone say loudly, "I'm not going to tell you again," and then the sound of a door slamming, muffling what came after. He stood at the counter for a second before calling out, "Excuse me?"

A woman in scrubs, a blood pressure cuff in one hand, walked through the doorway. A pair of glasses dangled off a chain onto the front of her scrub top. "Yes? Can I help you?" She had a weary look about her, like it had been a long shift.

"I hope so," Dan said, holding up the sheet. "A few months ago, someone stole my dog. Her name is Anni."

"Uh-huh." The woman glanced down at the blood pressure cuff as if thinking about her next task, the one she'd been about to do before Dan's interruption.

"A patient here reported seeing my dog, and the woman at the front desk thinks she was here today, with a woman with brown hair, visiting one of your residents. I wonder if you've seen her?"

From a room off to the right, a television came on, volume full blast, followed by someone yelling for it to be turned down.

The nurse sighed. "Just a minute." She turned around and yelled, "Tim! It's happening with that TV again." Facing Dan once more, she said, "What size dog we talking about, sir?"

"Small to medium, I guess. About thirty pounds."

The woman struggled to put her reading glasses on with one hand, then leaned in to take a good look. "Today, you say?"

"Yes, with a woman in her late twenties or maybe early thirties, pale skin, brown hair. Did you see them?" Down the hall someone reduced the volume on the offending TV and now it was just a murmur in the distance. "She had a nice smile?" Now he was reaching, but that's all he had to go on.

"No, but let me ask someone in back—" She turned around. "Tim? Tim!"

Tim came out, a cup of punch in his hand.

"Have you seen this dog?"

He glanced at the sheet. "Yeah, like two minutes ago, with a really cute girl."

"Two minutes ago?" Dan looked up and down the hall. "Is she still on this floor?"

"Nope, she was leaving. You just missed them."

"Just missed them—like how long ago?"

He shrugged. "A few minutes, maybe. I just buzzed her through the door."

Dan silently cursed his poor timing. She had to be going down one elevator as he was going up the other. He didn't wait to hear any more but nodded and took off in the direction of the stairwell, having remembered it from his previous visit. His footsteps pounded out her name. Anni. Anni. Anni. She'd been here, he was sure of it. It had to be her. Only seconds later, he reached the door to the stairwell, but his sense of urgency had caused time to slow. He reached for the knob and couldn't turn it, tried again, and then once more, but it was no good—it was locked. Dan slammed a fist against the door. Anni was so close. All he needed to do was get down two flights of stairs. Why was the universe conspiring against him?

The nurse came huffing down the hall toward him, a ring of keys on the end of her outstretched hand, like a baton in a relay race.

"It's locked," he said miserably, stating the obvious.

"That's because we don't want the residents to fall down the stairs," she said, stopping in front of him and fumbling with the keys. "With their confusion and physical problems, it could be a huge problem." She added, "It's just for the third floor, though."

When she got the door unlocked and pushed it open, he said, "Thanks," and darted through the opening and down the metallic stairs. He heard her voice behind him call out, "Good luck!"

His footsteps echoed off the concrete walls as he clattered down the stairs, down and down to the next landing, and around the corner. One more flight and he'd be on the first floor. Just one more flight. With any luck, he'd catch them in the lobby.

Bursting through the door to the first floor, he was disoriented for a second trying to get his bearings. A staff member, a young man in blue scrubs, came around the corner and Dan asked, "Which way to the lobby?"

The guy gestured to the hall in front of him, and he was off, jogging the short distance to the open area, past the vacant desk that should have been occupied by the beehived woman. Dan's head swiveled from side to side, his mind calculating the time frame between the elevator door closing and now. The woman could well be in the parking lot by now. Unless the receptionist had stopped her and they were waiting somewhere else and looking for him?

His gut told him to keep going, so he left the building and went out to the parking lot. It had become pitch-black in the short time since he'd been inside. The lights on each end of the lot were on, as well as the lights along the walkways. He stepped out and the wind hit his face, making him blink. And then he saw it, the flash of a brake light as a car left the lot and turned onto the roadway. He ran in the direction of the car, knowing he'd never catch up, but hoping he'd spot a license plate number or at least get a better look, but halfway to the road he realized it was no use. Damn. Well, he wasn't entirely sure that car held Anni anyway. Maybe she was still in the building.

He trudged back in, feeling disheartened, hoping against hope that somehow he'd still find her. The woman with the tall gray hair was back at her station now, and his briefcase was on the floor in front of her counter, right where he'd left it. "Did you see them go by?" he asked.

Her worried look confirmed his fear. "No, did you see them?"

When Lindsay was a little girl and things weren't going her way, she'd fall to the floor like she'd been struck, curl up into a ball, and wail. That's what he felt like doing right at that moment. And here he'd always thought she was being overly dramatic. "I think they just left," he said. "Why weren't you here?" He tried not to sound accusatory, but it still crept into his voice. Where the hell did she go? How hard was it to sit at a desk for ten minutes?

"I was just in the bathroom for a minute." Her Minnie Mouse voice was at a super high pitch now and her face crumpled like she was about to cry. "I take this water pill, and I had to go right away. It was just for a minute. I'm so sorry."

"They must have walked right past here." He felt his jaw clench in frustration.

"I already called the first and second floor, and I knew you were going up to the third, so I figured it was covered. I was only gone a minute."

Only one minute. One crucial minute. He ran his fingers through his hair and said, "Don't worry about it. Things happen." Unfortunately the things that kept happening to him were not good. One disaster after another, it seemed.

She held up the printed sheet with Anni's photo on it and shook it. "I'm going to make sure everyone who works here sees this. Someone has to know something. I promise you, this will make the rounds."

Dan sighed. It wasn't her fault someone stole his dog and it wasn't her responsibility to find her either. Her feeling guilty wouldn't bring Anni back to him. "It's not your fault," he said. "You've been very kind. Thank you."

"I mean it," she squeaked. "I will personally make sure everyone here sees this."

"I'd appreciate it," he said. "Tell them if they see Anni, they can call day or night. Anytime. We just want her back."

THIRTY-FOUR

On the way home from her visit with Gram, Andrea stopped at PetShop to buy more dog food. There was probably enough in the bag to last several days, but the uncertainty of winter weather always motivated her to stock up on essential items.

The inside of the store was brightly lit and well organized. If anything had changed since her last visit, she couldn't tell. She grabbed a cart and pulled it behind her, letting Anni walk alongside, and went straight to the food section, where Andrea grabbed a medium-size blue bag. Up at the front of the store, the teenage girl at the cash register put down her phone when they approached. "Did you find everything all right?" she asked in a monotone, flicking her hair over her shoulder.

"Yes, thanks." Andrea fished out some money, and after the girl gave her change, another thought came to mind. "Is Bruno working tonight? I was hoping to talk to him."

The girl gave her a blank look. "Who?"

"Bruno," Andrea said. "Old guy, bald, not much taller than me." She held a hand up to indicate height. "He helped me pick out some dog food the last time I was here."

"There's no Bruno working here."

Could she have gotten the name wrong? She'd been so certain he'd said Bruno. "Is there someone else who looks like that?"

The girl shook her head. "Not that I know of."

"How long have you worked here?"

"About a year."

"Okay, thanks. I guess I got it confused," Andrea said, still puzzled, but also disappointed. She'd been looking forward to telling Bruno that he'd been right, Anni was a life changer for her. And also that the dog food had been approved by the vet. All around, his advice had been spot-on.

Driving home, it struck her. Bruno didn't work at PetShop. He was another customer who was just being helpful. Just a nice man offering some advice. No wonder the girl had no idea who she was talking about. She felt a little foolish, but how was she supposed to know? Anyone would have assumed the same thing.

At home she lugged the bag from the car into the house and set it in the corner of the closet. As she did it, she found herself narrating her actions to Anni who followed right behind. Anyone listening would think she was insane, or else that she was one of those dog nuts who think their pet is a person. Oddly enough, Anni was taking on human qualities. There were moments she swore Anni understood what she was saying. She definitely picked up on Andrea's moods, which was more than she could say for a lot of people.

Between work and stopping at the Phoenix Health Care Center and PetShop, it had been a long day. With the sun going down so early in the winter, the evening had a finality to it, like a deadline had come and gone. It was only seven o'clock, but it felt like bedtime. To complicate matters, she was hungry, but didn't feel like cooking. It looked like she'd be having soup for dinner again.

Andrea was eating at the coffee table in the living room, the TV on, Anni resting with her head on Andrea's stocking feet, when the doorbell rang. Anni lifted her head and gave her a look that said, what gives? Andrea shut off the sound and got up to look out the peephole, surprised to see her neighbor, Cliff, standing on her front stoop, his knit hat in hand like a gentleman caller. She opened the door. "Cliff? What brings you here?"

She envisioned a problem—he'd locked himself out of his place, or his pipes had burst—but he looked fairly calm for an elderly man standing out on her stoop in the cold and dark on a weeknight, like he just wandered over and wanted to make conversation. "I'm sorry to trouble you, but I have an invitation."

"An invitation?" Anni was right by her side now, her body leaning against Andrea's leg, her nose halfway out the door. Normally Andrea would reactively reach for her collar, but Anni had shown a decided dislike to the cold weather and wouldn't be bolting outside anytime soon.

"Yes," Cliff said, shuffling his feet like he was trying to recall what to say. "From my lady friend, Doreen. You met her the other day? From the book club?" His voice trailed away and his eyes darted down, noticing Anni for the first time. "Well, there's my little Muffin," he said, reaching down to give her an enthusiastic rub behind the ears.

Andrea wasn't sure what all of this was about, but it seemed to be taking more time than it should. By now the open door had allowed a wind tunnel to pass through her condo, probably lowering the overall temperature of the place by several degrees. "You want to come in?" Andrea fervently hoped not, so she was relieved when he shook his head.

"Nope, just dropping off the invitation." He pulled a white envelope out from behind his hat and presented it to her with a flourish. "It's for dinner at Doreen's. She would be very pleased if you could make it."

Andrea noted her name, *Andrea Keller*, written in lovely script across the front. It was the kind of cursive handwriting not taught in schools anymore. "Thanks."

"One of the reasons it would be great if you can make it," Cliff said, "is that I don't usually drive at night anymore and if you're coming, we could drive together, you see." He was smiling uncertainly, like he wasn't sure how she'd take it.

"Yeah, okay," Andrea said. "I'll have to check my calendar, of course, to make sure I don't have anything else going on that evening. I'll let you know later. I was just eating dinner."

"Oh, I'm sorry," he said, looking horrified. "I thought this would be a good time."

"It's fine," she assured him. The cold air kept coming and Anni, bored by the lack of action, had wandered off. Still, he hadn't moved. "I don't want to be rude, Cliff, but I think you're going to have to either come inside or else go, because I'm freezing here."

"Oh, I can't come in," he said, shaking his head. "I just wanted to drop off the invitation."

They exchanged good-nights and after the door was shut, she watched him through the window to make sure he got to his unit safely. *What was that all about?* she wondered. Once Cliff was indoors, she settled back on the couch and opened the envelope. It was a card, not the flimsy kind from the dollar store, but one that had been custom printed on heavy card stock. The front was linen-colored and glossy with a monogram at its center, the initials DKR intertwined with what looked like pansies. Inside at the top was today's date. Underneath was a short note written in gorgeous, precise handwriting.

> *Dear Andrea,*
> *I hope you will forgive the impropriety of an invitation from someone you've only met once. Cliff speaks so highly of you that I knew you'd be an excellent addition to a small dinner party I'm*

hosting on Sunday at five p.m. Casual attire is fine. Cliff seems to feel that you could drive together, but if that's not convenient, it's not a requirement, so do not feel obligated. I really hope you can make it. I'm looking forward to getting to know you better.
Fondly,
Doreen
P.S. Feel free to bring your little Muffin. I love dogs!

Doreen's phone number was printed neatly at the bottom next to "Regrets Only."

Well, this was certainly awkward. How was she going to get out of this? She imagined having to make small talk with strangers, and on a Sunday night too, when she was mentally getting ready for another workweek. When the weather was cold like this, she tended to stay home after dark, burrowing into her home in a way she never would during warmer temperatures. And then there was the possibility that this would start something; that she'd have to reciprocate and have them over for dinner. She barely made dinner for herself anymore. The idea of hosting a dinner party was daunting.

She knew what Jade would say. One word: go. Jade loved meeting new people. She would tell Andrea she was being antisocial, that the universe was interconnected and you never knew who you might meet. That wasting away at home was not doing her any good. All of which was true. Every time Andrea had dreaded going to a social event where she might not know anyone, it had worked out fine. Most of the time she was glad she went. She tucked the card back into the envelope. She would go. She would go, and she would drive Cliff, and she would talk to strangers, and it would be fine. Fun, even. Jade would be proud. If the universe was sending her an opportunity, she was saying hello to it. She had nothing better to do. And at least she'd have a better meal than canned soup from the microwave.

Putting the empty bowl into the sink, she decided she'd tell Cliff tomorrow. He'd be so happy.

It wasn't until later that she dug her phone out of her purse to recharge it on the kitchen counter overnight and noticed she had a message. Nonchalantly she touched the screen to listen, flinching when she heard Marco's voice. "Andrea?" he said. "Andrea, I have made a terrible mistake." There was a long pause and Andrea thought that might be it, but he started up again. "I don't expect you to understand. I don't understand it myself. It was like I lost my mind. I wasn't myself. I was unhappy with myself and I convinced myself I was unhappy with you, but I was wrong. So, so wrong. If I could have one wish, it would be to go back and have things the way they were before when we were together. I miss you. I miss being your husband. I need you. Please call me." His voice broke up at the end, as if he were about to break into sobs. "Please. It would make me so happy to talk to you. Just give me a chance. I'm dying here. I love you."

This was one of those times Andrea wished she didn't live alone. She'd love to have had someone else there to call over and say, "Check this out. Can you believe him?" This was a side of Marco seldom seen. He either was a good actor or he was truly heartbroken. A few months ago she may have felt sorry for him. It would have given her poor ego a boost anyway, knowing she was missed.

She played the message back again, and then twice more. The last time she noted all the times he used the word "I." Typical. All of it was about him, and how he felt. Even his apology was more about him than about her. He didn't claim responsibility for how he'd savaged their marriage, how he'd nearly caused her to have a breakdown. For the longest time she'd felt like she was hanging on by a thread and now, more than a year later, he'd changed his mind, realized his mistake? Too little, too late. Life didn't work like that. You couldn't just tear someone down and throw them out like garbage, then come back more than a year later saying never mind, let's go back to the way things were. At least that's not how it worked with her. She deleted the message, plugged the phone in, and went to bed.

THIRTY-FIVE

Dan drove home with a heavy heart. Out of habit, he pulled up to the mailbox to get the mail before parking in the garage and trudging into the house. He'd come so close to finding Anni. She'd been right there in the adjacent elevator. If he'd been a few minutes earlier or later, they would have crossed paths. Or if the door to the stairwell hadn't been locked, he might have caught them in the lobby.

The woman at the front desk, the one who'd fallen down on her duty, seemed to think that the visitor and the dog would be back, and when that happened, every staff member in the place would know. But what good would that do? If it was Anni, and he was certain now it was (just a feeling, but a strong one), whoever had her would just say it was her dog. If he weren't there to challenge her, the person, this mystery woman, would take Anni home, never to return. And then they'd be back to square one.

Lindsay wasn't at Walgreens tonight; she was home, Brandon-less. He found her sprawled on the couch, TV on, laptop open on the coffee table, talking to someone on her cell, which was set on speakerphone. When he walked in, she said, "Say hi to my dad," and a girl's voice yelled, "Hi, Lindsay's dad." He heard a scrap of melody in the background. Every teenage life had its own soundtrack.

He shook his head and grinned. Teenagers were mercurial; their pendulum swung from aggravating to delightful and back again. The in-between was rare. "Hi, Lindsay's friend," he said back, leaning over the phone.

"You don't need to get close like that, Dad," Lindsay said, laughing, and then told her friend, "My dad thinks he has to get his mouth right over the phone, like it's a walkie-talkie."

Dan had learned not to be insulted by this kind of thing. Christine had told him long ago it was important for Lindsay to feel like she had the upper hand in some areas, and, as it turned out, technology was definitely one of those areas. Someday, Christine had said, Lindsay would realize their wisdom and then she'd be turning to them for advice. So much of life was about timing.

Dan set the mail on the kitchen counter, hung up his coat and put away his gloves and hat, then heated up some leftover meatloaf and green beans. He finished his meal around the same time Lindsay wrapped up her conversation. Before she could move on to the next thing, he called out, "Linds? Do you have a minute? I want to talk to you."

"Sure." When she came into the kitchen, she pulled up a chair and eased into it, her phone in her hand like it was part of her. At least her eyes were on him. "What's up?"

"You were right about Anni and the nursing home."

"What do you mean?" She set the phone down on the table. Now he had her complete attention.

"She was there. A nurse identified her. She was with a woman and they'd just left right before I got there." He told her the whole story, how he'd been so close, but hadn't been able to beat the elevator down to the first floor. Lindsay was silent during the telling, hanging on every word, nodding like he was giving her instructions. He'd felt like a failure and had been afraid she'd feel let down, so her reaction surprised him.

"Oh, poor Dad," she said, uncharacteristically reaching out to squeeze his hand. "How awful. I'm sorry I wasn't there to help." Empathy shone through her eyes and she gave him an understanding smile. In an instant he had a flash of Lindsay as a sixth grader, all arms and legs and flyaway hair, and in another instant she'd morphed to how she looked now, a vision of young womanhood, soon old enough to live on her own. And after that it could be anything—traveling the world, buying a house, getting married. She'd grown up before his eyes. How had this happened? "But the good news is," she said, brightening, "that we know she's okay. She's not dead. And now I feel like we're going to get her back for sure. Didn't I tell you?" A smile spread wide across her face. "I think Mom is working on this for us."

"I hope you're right." It was the best he could manage.

Later, after Lindsay had gone to her room to do homework, he shuffled through the stack of envelopes on the counter. Sorting the mail had always been Christine's job. After she passed away, he acquired a habit of letting it pile up. Most of it was junk, but there were always a few key pieces that needed actual attention: bills to be paid, notices from the DMV to renew license plates, birthday and Christmas cards. He'd learned to weed through the pile pretty quickly and tonight he sorted expediently, tossing aside two catalogs and a postcard from a Realtor who'd sold a house down the road, before setting aside the cable and the energy bill. At the bottom of the stack, he came across a handwritten envelope addressed to him. He pulled out a beige-colored card with the initials DKR on the front and opened it to find a note from Doreen reminding him of her dinner invitation on Sunday. *A place at the table will be reserved for you,* she said.

He almost laughed at her certainty. She'd also written: *I will expect you at five o'clock.* Doreen was a sly one. Here he'd been living his life, minding his own business, thinking he was safe, and now he'd been snared by a senior citizen determined to pull him out of his comfort zone. Well, there were worse ways to pass a Sunday evening, and the food was sure to be good. Five o'clock? He'd be there.

THIRTY-SIX

Marco couldn't just leave it at one message. He called her every day, several times a day. At first the messages were more of the same: pathetic, begging ramblings asking for forgiveness and saying how much he missed her. As the week went on, his voice began to have an edge to it. He demanded to know why she didn't return his calls, insisted she was rude for not getting back to him. The last message, on Thursday, said he was getting worried about her, that something terrible must have happened to her, that the Andrea he knew would never ignore a phone call. And that's all he wanted, he reiterated, a chance to talk to her, to explain where he was at right now. It wasn't too much to ask, he thought. His voice sounded strained and frantic at the same time.

Andrea played the messages over the phone to Jade. "That is one scary, egotistical dude," Jade said. "You want my advice?" If history served, the question was rhetorical; Jade was going to offer her take on the situation regardless. "Call him when you know he won't pick up and leave a message saying that you got his messages, you aren't interested in talking to him, and if he persists you'll take legal action, because this is harassment."

"What kind of legal action would I take?" Andrea wondered aloud.

"I don't know," Jade said. Andrea could picture her waving her concerns away with the flick of her manicured fingers. "But it's not important, because you're just trying to make a point here. You have rights. This is bordering on stalking. Tell him to knock it off."

So she did. The next morning, when she knew Marco would be in the shower (he was predictable in his grooming), she left a brief message. "Hi, Marco, this is Andrea. I did receive your messages, but I'm not interested in talking to you or meeting with you. I wish you well and I don't want to have to take legal action, but I will if you continue these phone calls." She'd been reading off a piece of paper, and kind of trailed off at the end, losing her resolve. "Okay, that's all I have to say. Take care." She improvised that last bit and thought she came off pretty well overall. Message sent, and she'd soft-pedaled it too. Saying it Jade's way would have pissed him off and she didn't need more drama. She did wish him well and hoped he'd take care. Despite what he'd done to her, she didn't lie in bed at night imagining scenarios where his car would careen off an overpass into a river or that Desiree would turn out to be a serial killer, the kind who'd thrust a knife into Marco's heart in the middle of sex. No, she'd evolved beyond that. Marco could go off and live his life and she'd live hers, and with any luck the two would never meet again.

After that, the only message she got was from Cliff, telling her they didn't have to drive together to Doreen's for Sunday dinner, since he was going over early to help her get everything ready. He said he'd meet her there. His tone was apologetic, as if he were the one who'd reneged on the favor. Oh well, it didn't matter all that much, although having Cliff with her would have made walking into Doreen's house that much easier. But of course, he'd be there when she and Anni arrived.

By the weekend, Marco and his messages had nearly slipped Andrea's mind. On Sunday afternoon, she dressed for her big dinner at Doreen's. The invitation had said casual attire was fine, but she wasn't falling for that. Over the years she'd found it was better to be the best-dressed woman in the room than the worst. The word "fine," too, was nebulous in her view. Did it mean it would be fine to show up in jeans, as in, you wouldn't be turned away, but everyone would think a little bit less of you? No, better safe than sorry. She had to find middle ground. Not dressed up like going to a wedding, but more than going to the office.

Andrea tried on several outfits before settling on a knit dress with a colorful scarf, hoop earrings, and black dress boots. Once it was all assembled, she stood in front of the mirror checking her reflection from every angle. She nodded approvingly; the outfit would do. Andrea puffed up her cheeks and exhaled, then said to Anni (who was also looking in the mirror), "Now I look almost as pretty as you."

Getting ready took more time than she'd anticipated and they still had to pick up a bottle of wine on the way. Andrea attached the leash to Anni's collar, put her in the car, and they headed out. It was dark already, and the air was chilly, but she found it tolerable, which was what happened when she got used to winter's bite. She kept her gloves in her pockets and her coat unbuttoned, as if spring might come around the corner any minute. When they arrived at the store (it was called "Spirits," but it clearly specialized in wine, based on the display in the big front window), she pulled into a space on the street in front, noticing that they closed at five. She would be cutting it close.

Anni whined when she turned off the engine, anticipating being left behind. Uncanny how she knew when Andrea was making a stop herself versus when both of them would be leaving the car. This time, the whine was particularly heartbreaking, making her hesitate. "It's only going to be a minute. All I'm doing is buying a bottle of wine." Once again, she was talking to a dog, this time expecting her to understand the concept of a minute. Anni whined again, and she begrudgingly said, "Okay, let's go." She grabbed the leash and got out, letting Anni out as well. As the dog trotted after her, she tied the leash to a signpost in front of the car. "I'll be right back. Be good," she said, and then hesitated. Was it okay to leave her? She debated for a second, glancing up and down the empty sidewalks and taking note of the store's big front window before deciding it would be fine. She was running late as it was and would only be in the store for a minute. Glancing back, she watched as Anni squatted and did her business.

A bell jangled as she entered the store, and a young man standing behind a counter off to one side said, "Welcome to Spirits. My name is Carter. If you need any help, just let me know." He had a magazine open in front of him and turned a page as he spoke. "We close at five, just so you know." He patted the register, as if to make a point.

"Got it. Thanks." Andrea fast-walked through the store, aware of Anni waiting out in the cold. The bottles were lit from behind, glowing amber, red, and clear, a certain beauty to them. She walked past the whiskey and the bourbon, past the brandy and vodka and all the other liquor, to the wine section, which turned out to be bewilderingly expansive. She was in a hurry, so she narrowed down the wine by type, then by price, and grabbed two bottles chosen solely for their appealing labels. Hopefully the store had gift bags. She didn't notice any on the way in, but they had to have them. It only made sense. Up at the register, she plunked both bottles on the counter, labels facing Carter. "If you were going to be a guest at a dinner party for senior citizens, which wine would you pick?"

"I would bring both," he said, with a merchant's grin.

"Yeah, maybe you would, but I'm not going to." She grinned right back at him. "Nice try, but if you won't pick, I will."

"This one, then," he said, taking the one costing five dollars more. An incredibly mercenary move. He had to be the owner of the store.

She asked about a bag and he added it to the purchase, making a show of sliding it into the bag. As she was signing her credit card receipt, Carter said, "Wasn't that your dog?" She glanced up to see his head turned and followed his gaze to the front window. The signpost now stood empty, no dog attached. Before she could say anything, Carter said, "That guy that took him; is he with you?"

Her breath caught in her throat, and she ran to the front, her purse banging against her side, the wine still on the counter. The bell jangled when she threw open the door, and she slipped through the opening, hearing Carter call out, "Hey! You forgot your—" before the door slammed shut. Cars were parked up and down the street and vehicles drove past, but there was no sign that a dog had ever been attached to that signpost. No sign of Anni anywhere. Andrea looked up and down the street, her insides hollow. Frantic, she screamed, "Anni!" over and over again, until she heard a faint barking carried on the wind.

Her head whipped in the direction it came from until she saw Marco pop up from behind a parked car on the other side of the street, holding Anni, who was straining at the leash and really barking now that she spotted Andrea in the distance. Andrea ran toward them, her arms and legs pumping, the slush in the street spitting every time her foot hit the pavement. "How dare you!" she managed to yell. "How dare you." When she approached, her hands flew out, hitting him in the chest and trying to get the leash away from him. "You stole my dog."

Marco held the loop of the leash over his head, keeping Anni close. "Slow down there, Andrea. Just calm down." Anni strained at the leash and alternated a low-grade growl with a weird yipping, completely overwrought. "I'll. Give. You. The. Dog." He spoke slowly, still holding the leash out of her reach. "If you'll just hear me out."

"I will kill you," she said, in a voice she didn't even know she had, and she meant every word. "You are a vile, horrible human being."

Anni stopped barking and just looked at her, worried. "See," Marco said. "Even the dog thinks you should give me a minute."

"I'll give you ten seconds." Her hand grasped the section of leash near the collar. "And then so help me God I'm going to start screaming for help."

"It didn't have to come to this," he said. "All you had to do was answer one of my messages."

"Nine."

"Okay, okay. I wasn't planning on taking your dog. I just needed to tell you something important and then I saw you going somewhere all dressed up, stopping to buy liquor, and I just, I don't know, lost it. Jealous I guess. Old habits die hard. In my heart, you're still mine."

She felt a wave of disgust. There was no important thing he had to tell her. This was more Marco being a bully while pretending he cared. Cars slowed as they went past, and Andrea felt helpless. He'd put her on display. After all this time, he still felt he had power over her. "Eight," she said with granite fierceness.

His face contorted in anger, two vertical forehead ridges forming above his nose. "Stop it," he said, yanking on the leash with such force that it jerked Andrea's hand, causing Anni to yelp in pain.

Anni's cry shot like an electrical jolt up Andrea's spine. "That's enough. We're done," she screamed, and went to disconnect the collar from the leash, but Marco was pulling on it at the same time, making it difficult. Andrea stamped on his foot with the heel of her boot, and he jumped back, pulling so hard that he lifted Anni off her front paws. "Stop it!" she said. With fumbling hands, she finally disengaged the catch from the leash, but she didn't grab the collar quickly enough and Anni took off in a panic, darting down the sidewalk and between two parked cars.

Andrea heard the horror before she saw it, the thump of what had to be Anni being struck by the car, and the awful screech of brakes, and then a horrible silence. Andrea ran down the block into the street, and knelt in the slush next to Anni's small body, as perfect looking as she was motionless. Just the way she would sleep at home, sprawled out on the bed, flat on her side, except she now was in the road, alongside a car, which had stopped. A car door slammed and an older man's voice from above said, "I'm sorry. I'm so sorry. I didn't see her, honest. She just came out of nowhere."

THIRTY-SEVEN

Dan felt shy about attending the dinner party at Doreen's. She'd sent an actual written invitation, which made it seem formal, so he dressed accordingly in dress pants and a button-down shirt. He debated wearing a tie and even laid three on the bed, but ultimately decided against it. Better to be slightly underdressed than look like a pretentious jerk. He also debated wearing a V-neck sweater over his shirt before remembering how Doreen kept her house overheated in the winter months. Between getting dressed and stopping at the store on the way over, his timing was thrown off, so instead of being really early he arrived exactly at five. Surprisingly, he didn't notice any other cars in front of Doreen's house. He wondered if he'd gotten the date wrong.

"Welcome, welcome. Come right in!" said Doreen, opening the door in her usual sprightly manner. Dan stepped over the threshold, handing her a box of candy. He'd spent a lot of time wandering the aisles at the grocery store debating what to bring. He seemed to remember Christine saying that flowers, although gorgeous, sometimes put the hostess on edge if things weren't going well in the kitchen. *They have to stop what they're doing, unwrap the bouquet, hunt for a vase, cut them down, and arrange them. And then if they already have a centerpiece, it's awkward. Do they switch it out with your flowers or not? The idea is to bring a present, not to give them more work.* Funny, sometimes he had trouble remembering Christine's voice, while other times a whole Christine monologue came to him unbidden, as if she were right at his elbow giving directions. He'd finally opted for the candy. If Doreen didn't want it, she could send it home with Cliff. The important thing, the way he understood it, was to not show up empty-handed.

Doreen accepted the box and said, "Oh, how thoughtful. Thank you, Dan."

"I'm sorry I'm late."

"Oh, don't be ridiculous. You're right on time!" He leaned over for her hug, and she pressed her cheek against his, giving him a whiff of floral perfume. Now he saw, partially hidden behind her, an older gentleman wringing his hands uncertainly, like he wasn't sure what his role was in all this. Doreen turned to Dan. "Meet Cliff Johnson, a friend from book club."

Cliff Johnson cleared his throat and said, "Pleased to meet you, Dan." When Dan offered his hand, Cliff enthusiastically took hold, pumping it up and down.

Doreen ushered them into the living room, where she directed Dan's attention to the fire in the fireplace. "I think it's dying. Dan, would you mind adding a log?" She and Cliff exchanged pleased looks, which made Dan think this whole thing was somehow orchestrated to make him feel useful. Or else something about the fire was a private joke between them. But Dan had no problem doing fire duty either way. Doreen's fireplace was a traditional wood burner, with a red-brick facade discolored from years of soot. Dan chose a good-size log from the metal box on the floor and used the poker to insert it among the burning logs, making sure they had some space between. With the right exposure to air, the flames shot up with a satisfying whoosh. Cinders shot out of the assemblage of wood, reminding him to close the mesh curtains. When he was done, he stood back to admire it and was nudged by

Doreen, who handed him a glass of white wine she seemed to have pulled out of nowhere.

"Thanks," he said, taking an approving sip.

"I know you're usually a beer guy, but at my house it's wine," she said, motioning for all of them to sit.

Because of his business, people always assumed he was a die-hard beer guy, the kind who had a mug with every meal. The truth was he enjoyed beer, but sometimes went days or weeks without it, despite having access to it at work. He'd seen the guys who gave in to temptation on a daily basis, the ones who didn't think they were alcohol dependent because it was only beer. It was a slippery slide down to the bottom and he'd made up his mind a long time ago not to approach the edge. "No, I like wine. This is good." He sat in a wing chair and glanced around the room while taking another sip. "When is your third guest arriving?"

"She should be here any minute," Doreen said. She and Cliff sat so close together on the couch, there was only an inch between them. Awfully chummy for two book club friends. "Her name is Andrea. A lovely young woman."

Cliff jumped in and said, "Andrea is my neighbor. Nice, nice girl, went through kind of a rough divorce, but she's not one of those sad-sack bitter types. Just a great gal, I tell you. She and her little dog just bring a smile to my face." He reached over and patted Doreen's hand. Doreen grinned, pleased. "Sometimes I watch her dog for her. Little Muffin, I call her. Looks just like a dog I used to have years ago."

"Did you say her name is Andrea?" Dan asked, remembering what he'd now thought of as his Andrea, the woman from the coffee shop. It had to be a coincidence. It wasn't that uncommon a name.

"Andrea Keller!" Cliff said. "You're going to really like her. You can't *not* like her." He had a chuckly, confident quality to his voice.

"What does she look like?" Dan asked.

Doreen gave Cliff's thigh a gentle slap. "See and you were so worried. I told you he'd be open to meeting Andrea."

"No really, what does she look like?" The fire flared up, momentarily distracting him. When he looked back at them, they seemed to be eyeing him with satisfaction. He explained, "I met an Andrea recently, but didn't catch her last name. I'm wondering if it's the same person."

"Well, *my* Andrea," Cliff said, "is real pretty. She's a little more than thirty, and has these big doe eyes. Brown hair, but not a flat brown, more like the shampoo commercials when the light hits the girl's hair. She's not real tall." He tilted his head, considering. "Not too short either, kind of medium. Has a nice smile and a fine figure."

"Trust a man to notice that particular detail," Doreen said with a smirk.

"The man asked what she looked like."

"He didn't ask for her measurements."

"Well, I was trying to be accurate." They were sparring like an old married couple now. Dan might as well not be in the room.

"Oh!" Cliff said, holding up one finger. "And she has a great job too. Runs a property management company. She's like the owner's right-hand man. Or I guess you'd say"—and now he and Doreen spoke in unison—"right-hand woman."

Dan spoke cautiously, "Do you know the name of the company?"

"Oh, sure. McGuire Properties. The guy owns like a third of the city."

"He's exaggerating, of course," Doreen told him.

Dan gripped the arm of the chair. What were the chances it would be the same woman? And yet it was. Everything matched: her name, her description, the place of employment. What an amazing coincidence. If this were in a book or movie, people would say it was too much, that it was contrived and way too convenient, but truly life could be this way sometimes. One day you're talking about a kid you knew in grade school, someone you hadn't seen for thirty years, and a week later you run into the guy, and find out you've been a customer at the same gas station for years. Synchronicity, that's what it was. He nodded emphatically. "It's the same woman. I'm sure she said she works for McGuire Properties."

"How did you meet her?" Doreen asked.

"At a coffee shop. All the tables were full, so we wound up sitting together and talked for a while." He left out the part about their first fleeting encounter in the Bodecker's on Main parking lot. He could still envision her standing next to her car, snowflakes drifting all around like they were in a snow globe. That time, the few moments in the parking lot, had been the start of something. Something almost imperceptible, but definitely there. The coffee shop was where the attraction took hold.

"Did you like her?" Doreen asked, clearly pleased at this turn of events.

"We only spoke briefly, but yes, she was very pleasant."

Doreen glanced at her watch. "Pleasant, but not prompt," she said.

"She'll be here," Cliff assured her. "Andrea is very reliable."

"Did you give her directions?"

"I tried to, but she didn't want them," Cliff said. "She has one of those thingies in her car." He snapped his fingers. "The satellite locator thing."

"A GPS," Dan said.

"That's it." Cliff nodded. "And on her phone too. Trust me, she'll be here. Probably just delayed by traffic."

Knowing that Andrea was the woman from the coffee shop made the passing minutes even longer. He wanted to see her again, and Doreen's house was a safe place to get acquainted. Doreen had an easy way with people and if the smell of the pork chops wafting from the kitchen was any indication, they were in for a real treat. Wine tended to loosen up people too. Yes, this might be a good way to learn more about her. But then again, it all felt so orchestrated. He hoped she wouldn't think he had a hand in this—first the accidental meeting in the parking lot, then the coffee shop, now a dinner party they both were invited to. (Although dinner party was a bit of a misnomer. Could four people be a party? He thought so, but if so, it wasn't much of one.) No, he didn't want to seem like a stalker. Though come to think of it, the same could be said for her. Twice now she happened to show up where he was. Maybe she had planned this? The uncanny coincidences made him paranoid.

Doreen made small talk, filling in the quiet with details about their book club. He got a clear vision of the other members, most of them retirees, only two of them men—Cliff being the smarter of the two, she said. They alternated non-fiction—thick biographies and histories—with novels, some light reads, others heavy literary tomes. "As soon as I hear a book has lush prose, I know I'm going to hate it," Cliff said. "That's when it's time to skim."

"Those are my favorites," Doreen said, laughing. "They take a little patience, but it pays off. You learn to savor those kinds of books."

Cliff wasn't buying it. "I'm too old to savor. Just tell me a story, that's what I want." He rubbed his temples as if the thought of reading something complex made his head ache.

Dan watched the back and forth between the two and saw it all unfolding in front of him. Even if they weren't in love now, they would be soon enough, and Cliff and Doreen would wind up married. They'd do this dance for a while, the book club, the dinners, the late-night conversations, and eventually they'd do the math and figure it made no sense to keep two separate places when they were always back and forth. They would have a late act chance of happiness. It was possible for some people.

Finally, after twenty minutes of polite conversation, Doreen said to Cliff, "You better call her and see if she's still coming. Those pork chops can't wait much longer."

Cliff fumbled a phone out of his shirt pocket, and took a long time scrolling through his contacts looking for Andrea's number. Dan could imagine Lindsay having a field day with that one, doing an impersonation for her friends, showing them the way Cliff squinted at the screen. They weren't mean kids; they just didn't understand. They grew up with technology all around them and had no way of knowing how it snuck up on the older generation, how Dan and everyone else who was older would just get the hang of something when it morphed into something else, something more complex. They wanted to keep up, they really did, it just required three times more effort than it did for the young people.

Cliff finally found her number and pushed "Call," then listened, his ear right up against it even though it was on speakerphone. It rang once, twice, three times. Just when Dan thought it would go to voice mail, a woman answered, "Hello." One word, but it was clipped and ragged, like they'd caught her in the middle of a good cry.

"Andrea? Honey? This is Cliff. I'm over at Doreen's. Where are you?" He scratched his head, a look of intense concentration on his face. Off to one side, the fireplace hissed and crackled.

Dan heard a stifled sob coming from the other end of the phone. "Cliff, I'm sorry, I can't talk."

"What's wrong?"

"It's Anni. Marco tried to take her and she ran into the street and got hit by a car."

"Oh no," Cliff said, his hand flying to his chest. "Oh Andrea, I'm so sorry. That's terrible."

"We're going to the vet now." She sniffed. In the background a man asked her a question they couldn't make out. She said, "I have to go. Tell Doreen I'm sorry." An audible click ended the call.

"Who's Anni?" Doreen asked.

"It's her little dog, the one I was telling you about," Cliff said. "Cutest little thing, smart too. Poor Anni, hit by a car." His eyes glinted with tears. "I can't stand thinking about her being hurt." He swiped his eyes awkwardly with his knuckles.

"I thought her name was Muffin," Doreen said.

"No, no." He waved his hand like wiping away the misunderstanding. "That's just what I call her. Her name is really Anni."

A shiver ran through Dan. He asked, "What does Anni look like?"

Doreen saw where this was going and rushed in to explain, "It's just that Dan and Lindsay lost a dog and her name—" but Dan had already gotten his phone out and found a photo. He thrust the phone in front of Cliff's face. "Does she look like this?"

Cliff leaned in to look, his eyebrows furrowed. "Now how did you get a picture of Andrea's dog?"

"That's not Andrea's dog. She's my dog," Dan said. "She was stolen from us."

Cliff raised his eyebrows. "She sure looks like the same dog. But Andrea wouldn't have stolen your dog. She's a good person."

Dan felt all the blood leave his face. "Call her back. Right now. Call her and ask where she got the dog." A frantic feeling came over him, a knot in his stomach that said Anni might be dead or dying and he had to know. He had to know if it was her.

Cliff didn't want to, judging by the way he stalled, saying first that he didn't think this was the right time because Andrea was clearly devastated and then that he was sure it was just a coincidence, but Dan was persistent, so he tried again. It didn't matter, though. Andrea didn't answer the phone, which gave Dan the sinking feeling that once again Anni had been right within his reach, but pulled cruelly away before they could connect.

Doreen tried to smooth things over. "No point in getting all upset until we know the facts, Dan. I'm sure we'll get this settled in the next day or so. Until then, I wouldn't jump to any conclusions."

Dan knew he should let it go, but he just couldn't. He heard himself going on about it, showing Cliff more pictures, telling them about the incident at the nursing home, and Lindsay's dream of Christine saying they'd get Anni back. Cliff was already upset and all of Dan's rambling wasn't helping, but he just couldn't seem to stop. He saw a look pass between the two that said he'd gone off the deep end. At least that's how he interpreted it. Doreen had them sit down to eat, and still Dan talked, going on about how smart Anni was and speculating about all the ways she could have wound up in Andrea's possession. "Maybe she's a friend of the people who took her?" he mused. "Or bought her from them?"

"You're making yourself sick over this," Doreen said in a motherly way. "Why not just wait and see?"

Cliff shook his head. "Andrea wouldn't be friends with people like that. She's a classy gal." His mouth came together in a thin line and he glanced off to one side, like he was trying to remember. "I think she said one of the tenants had her and they weren't supposed to have dogs, so she wound up with her."

"And it may not even be your Anni, but an incredible coincidence," Doreen said lightly, passing Dan her homemade applesauce. He dutifully spooned some on to his plate. She could have been serving anything, none of the flavors registered, his mind stuck on the idea that Andrea, someone he'd actually met, might have his dog. And somehow let Anni get hit by a car. It took all he had to keep from looking up every vet emergency place in the tri-county area, getting in his car, and systematically checking each one for Anni. Calling would be faster, but he knew sometimes that was no good. You got the answering service, who paged the doctor, who called you back. If you were lucky. Most of the services were being replaced by voice mail nowadays.

This inner turmoil reminded him of a time when he was a kid, about ten or eleven, and his dad was late coming home from a hunting trip. The weather was bad, snow turned to sleet that then froze, turning all the roadways into skating rinks. The local news coverage showed accidents up and down the interstate, and Dan's mother had paced the floor, determined that her husband had been in an accident. By the time he walked through the door, two hours past due, but safe and sound, she'd worked herself into a frenzy, and threw herself into his arms sobbing with relief that he was still alive. At the time, Dan had thought she was being ridiculous. Overly dramatic. But now, he understood.

After dinner he helped Doreen and Cliff clear the table, then said, "I don't want to be rude, but I really think I should head for home."

Doreen nodded like she had been expecting this. Cliff said, "Would you mind giving me a lift home?" Of course Dan said it was no problem. He'd spoiled the evening; driving Cliff home was the least he could do.

In the car, he tried to get Cliff to give him Andrea's phone number, without success. "I just wouldn't feel comfortable giving it out without her permission," Cliff said. "But I'll give you my number and you give me yours, and I'll let you know the minute I hear anything. Promise."

When they got to Cliff's place, Dan pulled up in front of his condo and stopped to program the numbers into each of their phones. "Thanks," Cliff said, taking the phone from his hand. "Well, good night, then."

He opened the door, but before he could get out, Dan asked, "Which one is Andrea's place?" In the dark, all the condos looked the same, each section connected like a strip mall and set up in rows like the streets of a small village.

"It's that one over there." Cliff pointed. "The one with the blinds down."

Dan followed the line of his finger to the end unit across the street. "She's right on the end?"

"Yes, indeed." Cliff shook his head. "So horrible about what happened to her little dog. I'll be praying for her, that's for sure."

Dan wasn't sure if he meant Anni or Andrea, but the sentiment was nice either way. He sat in the car with the engine idling and waited until the old guy went into the house. Then he turned the car around, and parked on the side of Andrea's unit, out of Cliff's sight. If it took all night, he was going to wait for Andrea to come home.

THIRTY-EIGHT

The old man who hit Anni felt terrible, apologizing over and over again, but Andrea couldn't even acknowledge him, much less console him. She looked at Anni lying there in the street and for an excruciatingly long minute was sure she was dead. *Please, please, please,* ran through her head, a prayer and a plea combined, and when she reached out to stroke Anni, and Anni moved just slightly, a tremor more than anything else, she felt like her prayer had been answered. Andrea lifted her head and screamed, "Someone call for help!"

She took in the scene all at once: the older gentleman, nattily dressed in a navy peacoat and newsboy cap, wringing his hands, tears streaming down his face; Carter, the cashier from Spirits, running toward them from across the street; a random middle-aged couple who'd stopped their car and were walking over to see what had happened; and Marco, who lingered around the fringes like a malevolent spirit. Carter said, "I just called 9-1-1. The cops are on their way."

Anni whined and Andrea turned her attention back to her, making soothing noises. "It's okay, baby. It's okay."

"What happened?" the female half of the couple asked. She and her husband were a matched set with dark leather jackets and plaid scarves. She wore a black beret, set off jauntily to one side. "Did she get loose?"

"She just ran out between two parked cars," the elderly gentleman said, his voice cracking. "I didn't see her, honest."

"I have to go lock up the store," Carter said to no one in particular. Andrea heard his footsteps recede as he trotted back across the street.

A few minutes passed and although Andrea's attention was completely on Anni, she was aware of the activity around her. The old man went back into his car to turn his flashers on, Carter came back once the store was securely locked, and the middle-aged couple, who really hadn't seen anything, left after telling Andrea they were truly sorry and hoped her puppy would be okay. Marco said nothing, but she saw his feet out of the corner of her eye. He'd caused this, and she wanted him gone, but she couldn't muster the necessary emotion to lash out at him just now. All her energy was directed toward Anni.

A squad car pulled up and two officers came out. Just knowing they were there made Andrea feel better. One of them, an impossibly young-looking cop with a buzz cut, crouched down next to her and asked, "Is this your dog?" His manner was kindly. When she nodded yes, he said, "We called ahead and the emergency vet is on standby waiting for you to bring her in. Is that what you want?" She gulped and nodded again. Somehow she'd lost her voice, but that turned out to be okay, because Carter from Spirits said, "I saw the whole thing," and suddenly their focus was on him, the star witness, taking notes of everything he said. Carter gave them her name (he'd gotten it off her charge card) and told the story from the beginning. When Carter said Marco had taken Anni from the signpost, Marco, who'd been quiet the entire time, spoke up, irate. "This is my wife's dog. I didn't steal it."

Andrea found her voice then, although it sounded strange even to her, forced and guttural. "I'm not his wife. We're divorced and I didn't give him permission to take my dog. He was following me. I didn't even know he was here."

Anni lifted her head at the sound of Andrea's voice, stress and fear in her eyes. Andrea stroked her head, afraid to touch her anywhere else in case she had internal injuries. "It's okay, hang in there, Anni." She looked up at the police. "Can we take her in now?"

"Are you going to want to press charges?" The cop motioned to Marco, who looked like he wanted to punch a wall.

"No, I just want to get Anni to a hospital," Andrea said.

The officer leaned over and quietly said, "Even if you don't press charges, you might want to think about taking out a restraining order." He handed her a card. "Call me if you have any questions or any more problems."

The old man brought a blanket from his car, and they wrapped Anni up like a baby. He'd stopped crying, although his face was puffy and red. "I'll drive you," he offered, pointing to his car, a black BMW, and Andrea, not able to think straight much less drive, nodded mutely. He opened the door for her and she arranged Anni on her lap. Through the windshield she saw Marco talking to the cops, laying on his Marco charm. At one point, he waved and smiled sympathetically in her direction; she cast her eyes downward, refusing to acknowledge him. The old man got behind the wheel, telling her, "I got the directions from the police officer. They said to tell you they'll get your statement later."

A knock on the window on her side of the car, just before they pulled away, caught her attention. It was Carter, holding out the gift bag with her bottle of wine. "You left this on the counter," he said through the glass.

She didn't want it anymore, but he'd been so kind, calling the police and giving his statement, that she rolled down the window and accepted the bag. "Thank you."

"I hope Anni is okay," he said. "I'm sorry."

Andrea was overwhelmed by the kindness coming from all sides. As the old guy drove, she found herself choking back tears. "We'll be there soon," he said, in a voice so sweet that it made her cry even more.

"I'm sorry," she said, wiping her eyes with the back of her hands.

"Don't be. You're entitled. My name is Guy, by the way."

"I'm Andrea." Her phone rang then and she fumbled it out of her purse, intending to turn it off, but then saw it was Cliff. She'd completely forgotten about the dinner party. She answered, but kept it brief, telling him what had happened and apologizing for her absence. When the conversation was over, she turned off her phone so that it couldn't happen again.

Guy drove expertly, maneuvering around slow drivers while still staying within a safe margin of the speed limit. "I can't believe this happened," he said. "My whole life I've never even been in an accident. I'm so careful. I saw her come out between the cars and the next thing I know, I heard a big thump, so of course I stopped. I just couldn't believe it. I feel terrible."

"It wasn't your fault. She just ran out. It happened so fast. I couldn't stop her." Andrea stroked Anni's head and she let out a slight whimper. "There's no blood. That's a good sign, right?"

"You'd think so, but there could be internal injuries." They turned right onto a wide street lined with businesses, office buildings, and strip malls, most of them closed. A gas station's lighted sign shone off in the distance. "Can I ask you something?" Guy said, glancing over to get her reaction.

"Sure." Andrea kept her hand lightly on Anni's side.

"That fellow, your ex-husband, is it true that he took Anni, and you were struggling to get her back and that's what led to her running into the street? I mean, that's what the guy from the liquor store said he saw."

"Yes, that's how it happened."

"So why aren't you mad at him? Your ex-husband, I mean."

"Mad? I'm furious," Andrea said.

"You don't seem mad."

"Trust me, I'm mad. I just don't have time to show it right now."

Guy shook his head. "If I live to be one hundred, I'll never understand women." A lit sign just up ahead said "Emergency Animal Clinic." He pulled the car into a space by the door. Andrea already had the door open and her feet on the ground before he'd even turned off the engine. She carried Anni snug against her chest and opened the door with crooked fingers. A red-haired woman met her in the entryway. "Is this from the car accident the police called in?"

"Yes."

"I'm Dr. Fischer. Come this way."

Andrea followed her to an examination room and gingerly set Anni down on the table. Another woman appeared through an open doorway and took over, unwrapping the blanket from around Anni's middle and running her fingers over the dog's midsection. Dr. Fischer beckoned to Andrea to join her in the hallway. "Let's let Dr. Bauer take a look, shall we? Just tell me exactly what happened."

Once Andrea started, she couldn't seem to stop from babbling. All of her anxieties and guilt rushed out at once. "I shouldn't have left her alone, but it was only for a minute while I ran in to the store. I was on my way to a dinner party and I didn't want to come empty-handed." Dr. Fischer didn't rush her; in fact, she looked like she wanted to give her a hug. Andrea went on telling every detail and ended by saying, "I didn't see any blood. That's a good sign, right?"

"Possibly. We'll know more after we examine her and take some X-rays." Without even realizing it, Dr. Fischer had been steering her to the waiting room where Guy sat waiting. "Just take a seat. We'll come and get you in a little bit."

Andrea sank into a chair and gave Guy a weak smile. "They seem very capable." She ran her hand over her hair and twisted it nervously. "It's my own fault. I shouldn't have left her tied to that signpost. You know how even as you're doing something, you think it's probably a bad idea, but you do it anyway? I just told myself it was only for a minute. I was in such a hurry. So stupid." She pulled a tissue from her coat pocket and used it to blow her nose. "I was so stupid. I can't help but think I'll never see her again. Alive, I mean." A lump rose up from her throat, making her gulp. Her eyes filled with tears.

"Hey, hey," Guy said, alarmed. "No need to think the worst." He patted her back. "I've been thinking while I've been sitting here, and you know, I don't think I hit her after all."

Andrea stopped. "What do you mean?"

"I think she hit me. I mean, I think she ran into the side of the car and knocked the wind out of herself. Think about it—a dog Anni's size hit by a car would be pancake batter right from the get-go."

She nodded. It made sense. "I hope you're right."

Guy didn't make a move to leave, and Andrea found his presence comforting, so she didn't tell him he could go. He'd brought the wine bag in with him and made her smile when he held it up and said, "I'd give anything for a corkscrew right about now."

After about an hour Dr. Fischer came out holding a clipboard and said, "I have good news. No major injuries, just an abrasion on one side of her head and a concussion from the impact. We'd like to keep her overnight just to keep an eye on her. She'll probably be sore for a few days too."

Gratitude flooded every cell of Andrea's body. "Thank you, thank you!" She got up and hugged the doctor and didn't even care that it wasn't appropriate.

"My pleasure. That's what we do here. I'm just glad we have a happy ending for you and Anni." She had paperwork for Andrea to sign and then there was nothing left to do but go home.

THIRTY-NINE

Dan spent about an hour inside the parked truck outside Andrea's apartment. He let the engine run until he saw the fuel needle dipping dangerously close to empty, at which point he shut it off. Which meant he no longer had heat. He really hadn't thought this through. At least he wasn't sitting in the dark. The condo units were like a Disney World village with old-fashioned light posts along the sides of the streets and similar but smaller lampposts next to the walkway leading up to each unit. Between that and the Christmas lights on the eaves, trees, and bushes, it was bright. A person could read a book out here even during the darkest night.

When he started getting sleepy, he got out of the truck and walked up and down the short row of houses. It occurred to him that if he didn't pay attention, Andrea could come home, pull into her garage, and lower the door behind her without him even realizing she'd returned. He didn't want to miss her and leaving wasn't an option. He wasn't going to wait even one more day. If she did have Anni, that meant Anni had been hit by a car. The not knowing was killing him.

When a car pulled into Andrea's driveway, Dan watched from around the corner. The car idled while the garage door rose, and he hurried to catch her before she went into the house. When the car stopped and he heard the engine shut off, he walked up the drive-way, calling out, "Andrea?" as she got out of the car. The garage door was still up and the overhead light was on, so he could see her perfectly: her slightly windblown dark-brown hair, purse over her shoulder, keys in her hand.

He hadn't counted on her reaction, how she immediately stiff-ened defensively, gripping her keys between her fingers so that they pointed outward. "Who is it?" she said sharply.

"It's me, Dan. We met at the coffee shop?" He held his arms up to show he had nothing to hide. "I was at my aunt Doreen's tonight for dinner. You were invited too, I hear." He jerked a thumb in the direction of Cliff's house. "I guess Doreen and Cliff know each other from book club."

Her shoulders relaxed, although her expression was puzzled. "Huh," she said, pausing. "Small world. Why are you here?"

He got right to the point. "I think you have my dog, Anni. She was stolen from my house two months ago. I'm desperate to find her." Andrea took a step backward, like she wanted to be able to bolt into the house if he tried something funny. He continued, talking rapidly. "I showed Cliff a picture on my phone and he said it looks like the same dog. Can you tell me where you got your dog?"

"You think Anni is your dog?"

"I do," he said. "I know it's kind of creepy springing it on you like this, but I have to know. Where is she? Is she okay? Cliff said she was hit by a car."

"No, she's, um, going to be okay." Andrea put her hand up to her forehead. "I'm sorry, I just need a minute here." She blinked a few times and cleared her throat. "This is unbelievable."

"I'm sorry for just showing up like this. But if you do have my dog, it's the answer to my prayers."

"I'm just . . . I can't think straight." She shook her head. "It's been the night from hell. Anni's spending the night at the clinic, just for observation. She ran into the car, we think, so it's not as bad as it seemed at first, but still it was traumatic. For her and for me. But the vet says her injuries are minor. It was a miracle, really. If she'd run out in the road one second earlier, she would have been killed."

"Can I come over there?" He pointed. "Or would that weird you out? I just want to show you pictures of Anni. My Anni."

She nodded and he came into the garage and handed her the phone. He could tell by the look on her face that she recognized her Anni as being his dog, and for a moment he felt sorry for her.

"I'm pretty sure it's her," she said, letting out a sigh.

"Can you tell me where you got her?"

Andrea said, "Why don't you come in and I'll make some coffee and tell you all about it." She gestured to the door; her keys dangled from her pointer finger, not a weapon anymore.

Andrea had been lost in thought when Dan walked up her driveway. His voice calling her name had scared the hell out of her and her fear turned to absolute astonishment when she realized all the connections: Dan, the man she'd struck up a conversation with in the coffee shop, was related to Doreen, who was in a book club with Cliff, who happened to be her neighbor. Very small world all around. As if that weren't enough, he now might be laying claim to Anni. It was a bit mind-blowing.

Andrea knew inviting a strange man into her house was risky, but she didn't feel at risk. If anything, he seemed a little scared, standing on her rug and not moving off it until she invited him to follow her into the kitchen. It felt like the middle of the night, but it was only just past seven. Winter nights played tricks that way. She put coffee on to brew and then started telling him about how she found Anni chained up on the frat boys' balcony.

"That was them. I'm sure of it," Dan said. "My daughter, Lindsay, saw the guys who took Anni, but she couldn't get to the car fast enough. Punks. She thought they were drunk."

"You have a daughter?"

"Yes, she's seventeen. She'll be going off to college next year."

"You and your wife will miss her, I bet."

"No wife. It's just me." Dan said, matter-of-factly. "I'm a widower."

"Oh, I'm sorry." She was relieved he was single, but she was sincere in saying she was sorry for him. The poor man lost his wife and now his dog, but why did it have to be Anni? Anni was her dog. She continued, "So I've had Anni ever since. I took her to the vet and got her checked out and there was no microchip."

"We didn't get her microchipped, but she had an ID tag."

She shook her head. "Her collar had her name on it, and that was it. I took her home and it just felt right, you know? I take her to work with me. I love her. Everybody loves her." Already she was making a case for keeping Anni. Andrea got up to get mugs out of the cabinet, then poured coffee out of the pot. "Cream or sugar?" she asked, like this was a normal social event.

"Black is fine," he said. When she placed the mug in front of him, he slid his fingers through the handle. She realized then that he hadn't taken his jacket off. They were both on guard.

She continued, telling him about the stop for a bottle of wine on the way to Doreen's and everything that happened right up until she came home to find him waiting outside her condo. "You must think I'm negligent for letting her get hurt, but I would have traded places with her if I could have. I feel really guilty."

"It's not your fault."

"Yeah, well, it feels that way," she said. "I was so happy when the vet said she's going to be fine." She cast her eyes downward and took a sip of coffee.

"I know this is a tough situation," he said. "If it is Anni, then we both want her."

"And we can't both have her," Andrea said, which is what they'd both been thinking.

"Is there any way . . ."

"Yes?"

He looked straight into her eyes and what she saw was pleading. "Is there any way I could go with you tomorrow when you pick her up? We don't have to decide how to handle this just yet. I just want to see her, and make sure it's really her."

Andrea tilted her head to one side, considering. "I'm not trying to be difficult, but this is a lot for me to process. Can I take the night to think about it and get back to you?"

He nodded. "Fair enough."

FORTY

When his cell phone rang the next morning and Dan saw it was Andrea, he breathed a big sigh of relief. "The emergency clinic called just now," she said, sounding happy. "They said we can pick Anni up this afternoon. She's doing really well."

It was the word "we" that did it for him. Just the sound of it made the day several shades lighter and filled him with a kind of buoyant hope. Maybe life could get better after all. He spoke cautiously, "How did you want to handle this?"

"Why don't you come out to my place around one?" she said. "We can drive together."

"You didn't go to work today?"

"No, I took the day off."

Coincidentally, so had he. The previous night's events had emotionally sucked him dry; he knew he wouldn't be able to bear a normal workday with Anni on his mind. When the alarm went off, he rolled over to turn it off, and then picked up the phone to leave a voice mail for his boss saying he'd had a family emergency the night before and needed the day to take care of some details. Now he was glad he had the day free. "Okay," he said to Andrea. "I'll be there at one."

He tried to time it so that he'd arrive right at one, but once again he'd miscalculated and arrived twenty minutes early, making him look overeager. He was, in fact, overeager, but he hadn't wanted to let it show. Sitting in the truck outside her front door, he didn't pick up the phone to call her or get out to knock on the door, just waited for one o'clock to come. But at five minutes to the hour, Andrea came out and knocked on his window. He lowered it to hear what she had to say.

She held up her car keys and said, "I'm going to be driving. You're welcome to ride along with me if you'd like."

He left his truck at the condo and became her passenger, watching her profile as she drove. Unlike most people, she didn't feel the need to fill the space with empty chatter, but she did say a few things, all of them heartfelt and sincere. "You know," she said. "I didn't get much sleep last night, which is why I look so horrendous." (He actually thought she looked really pretty.) "You should know that I debated going to get Anni from the clinic, putting her in the car, and relocating to Canada, but you seem like a really good guy, and I just couldn't do it." She glanced over and he could see now that her eyes did look tired, but, in all fairness, the rest of her looked great.

"I've heard that Canada won't enforce dog extradition, so that would have been a good choice," he said.

She laughed, a throaty, startled laugh. "That was really funny, but can you give me some credit here for doing the right thing? I'm telling you that I'm not going to cause a fuss about giving Anni back. I realize that you're her legal owner."

"I appreciate that."

They were at a stoplight now and she gave him her full attention. "But I want you to know that this is breaking my heart. I haven't even had her that long and I feel like she's part of me." She blinked away what might have been the start of tears. "That's why I'm giving her back. If I feel this way after this short a time, I can only imagine how you feel. And I don't want to be the cause of someone else's misery."

He was touched by her kindheartedness. The rest of the ride was quiet, somber even.

They arrived at the clinic, and when the lady tech brought Anni out to the waiting area, Andrea burst into tears, so happy and relieved to see the little dog. Almost reflexively, she threw her arms around Dan, and he found her joy contagious. Emotions flooded through him, like she had awakened something inside him he hadn't even noticed was missing.

Both of them knelt down next to Anni, who raced back and forth between them, as overjoyed as a child who thought she'd never see her parents again. She jumped on them and licked their faces, her tail thumping wildly. "Now that's one happy dog," the vet tech said, handing the leash over to Andrea.

Dan let Andrea act as the dog owner, only stepping forward to offer to pay, but she brushed him aside and got out a credit card. "It's my fault she was injured. I should pay," she said. Dan let it go, thinking they'd work it out later.

In the car, Anni settled on Dan's lap as Andrea drove. He stroked her head and noticed Andrea had become very quiet. "My daughter, Lindsay, is going to be overjoyed when she sees Anni," he said. "She never gave up hope."

"Did you tell her about the accident?" Andrea asked, looking stricken.

"No." He shook his head. "She's had her heart broken too many times. I didn't want her to know anything until it was definite."

"Well, it's definite now," Andrea said sadly.

Dan felt her pain and said, "Would you like to go with me when Lindsay sees Anni for the first time?" He made the offer, not thinking she'd go for it, but to his surprise she nodded and said, "I'd like that very much."

He called ahead to the high school to get Lindsay excused early, and was told they'd have his daughter wait in the office, that he could just come in to sign her out. Andrea followed his directions to the school and he again admired her profile, the lift of her chin as she checked for cross traffic before pulling out into intersections, the way her hair fell over her shoulders, framing her face. She was exceptionally pretty. He could have looked at her all day.

When they arrived half an hour later, he directed her to pull up to the curb in front of the entrance, while he went to get his daughter. Opening the glass door, he glanced back to see Anni's face at the car window, watching with rapt attention. Behind her, Andrea gave him a small wave, urging him to keep going. It occurred to him that Andrea could just drive off, taking Anni with her. She could cut off all contact after that, forcing him to take legal action to get his dog back. Andrea wouldn't do that, though. He was certain.

In the office, Lindsay stood there with her coat on, her backpack resting at her feet. When she caught sight of her father, her face crumpled in relief. "What's wrong?" she said, and he realized she'd expected the worst: a death in the family, a house fire, a cancer diagnosis. Something so horrible that he would inexplicably pull her out of school without warning.

"Nothing's wrong," he said, going over to the counter to take a clipboard from the outstretched hands of the school secretary. "I just needed you to leave early today."

Lindsay put her hand on her hip. "Dad, you pulled me out of a test. I'm going to have to make it up now." Her attitude had switched from worried to annoyed in the time it took him to sign his name.

"This is important," he said, beckoning for her to follow him. "You'll be glad." They left the office with him in the lead and Lindsay grumbling that this better be important. When he reached the door, he saw Andrea leaning against the side of her car with

Anni at her feet. Lindsay, behind him, still clueless, kept asking what was going on. He opened the door for her and she walked through. At the same time, Anni caught sight of Lindsay and let out an excited bark, and Andrea let go of the leash.

The moment Lindsay recognized what was happening, she dropped to her knees with arms outstretched, and cried, "Anni, oh Anni," over and over again in between ragged sobs. Joyfully the dog bounded into her arms, barking and letting Lindsay bury her face in her fur.

Dan met Andrea's eyes and saw the sacrifice on her end. He mouthed the words, *thank you*, and she nodded. It was everything, but not enough.

FORTY-ONE

"Anni, Andrea, and Dan," Joan said, delivering their lemonade and sandwiches. "My favorite trio. The ones to beat." On the floor next to Andrea's chair, Anni's tail thumped happily as if she understood every word. Joan flipped her a dog treat, and with ladylike precision Anni snapped it between her jaws. "Enjoy your lunch, you two."

"We always do, thanks, Joan," Dan said, flashing a grin. He and Andrea had started thinking of the Café Mocha as their lunch place around the same time as they started thinking of Anni as belonging to both of them. In the last year, Anni had spent most workdays with Andrea at the office, and between the two of them, and Cliff and Doreen, they drove her back and forth. Anni adjusted fairly readily; it was Lindsay who'd had the meltdown. "Exactly why are we sharing our dog with this person?" she'd asked, hands on hips when she heard the plan.

Dan had explained that it was payback for Andrea saving Anni, and that Andrea loved Anni as much as they did, something Lindsay found hard to believe. He added, "And you know, Lindsay, when I work late and you're busy, Anni is sometimes here all by herself for eight or ten hours. It's better for her to be with Andrea than stuck inside our house." He'd also made it sound like it would only be for a few weeks. A transition period, he'd called it.

After that, Lindsay had begrudgingly accepted it, calling Andrea the doggy day-care lady. Not really a compliment, but their paths didn't cross much, so it wasn't really a problem. Yet.

Dan had several good reasons for sharing his dog, but the real reason was something he couldn't quite put into words. He admired the way Andrea set aside her own desires to return Anni to her rightful owners. He saw the pain in her eyes when Anni leaped into Lindsay's arms, but there was happiness too. Happiness for them. It was clear she was a woman of great empathy.

That was when he suggested what they'd come to call "the arrangement." The dating had started as an offshoot of driving Anni back and forth. First it was lunch at the Café Mocha, and then it was the occasional dinner when Lindsay was working or out with friends. And then one day, she mentioned a movie she wanted to see and it turned out he wanted to see it too. It only made sense to go together. Finally, one day something funny happened at work and he thought, *wait until I tell Andrea about this*, and it occurred to him that they had somehow gotten into the habit of calling each other every single day. Still, it wasn't until Lindsay asked, "So are you *dating* this Andrea person?" that he realized what had happened.

"Yeah, I guess I am," he answered. Lindsay didn't say anything, but she wasn't jumping for joy. "Is that okay with you?"

"I guess it's fine," she said, exhaling dramatically, "as long as you don't, like, marry her or anything."

"Actually, I am planning on asking her to marry me. Not now, but sometime in the future." Until that moment, he hadn't planned anything of the sort, but now he knew it had been in the back of his mind for some time. Hearing Lindsay voice an objection had brought it to the forefront. "I don't know if she'll say yes, but I hope she does. And I know it will be a difficult adjustment for you, but I hope you'll be okay with it."

"I don't know about this," Lindsay had said, her mouth downturned.

"I know," he said. "Change is hard, and we've both been through a lot, losing your mom and then with Anni getting stolen. If Andrea and I do get married, she won't replace your mom. One person can never replace another. But I think if you give her a chance, you'll really like her. And I think I deserve some happiness too. I'm only forty. I could live a few more decades." Almost the exact words Doreen had said to him. It had taken this long for the truth of it to sink in.

That had been months ago and he hadn't brought it up again, but Lindsay did, periodically saying things like, "If you and Andrea get married, I hope she won't want to change all the furniture," and "You guys wouldn't have another kid, would you? I mean, you're kind of old to have a baby, right?"

"We're going to have triplets," he had said. "And you'll be babysitting them every Saturday night."

"Ha-ha," she'd answered. At least he got her to smile.

Dan had worried that Marco would crop up again, but Andrea had filed for a temporary restraining order for harassment and, between that and the police questioning him, he'd backed off completely. A few months later, Doreen heard that Desiree now sported a very large diamond ring; she and Marco were engaged. When Dan relayed the news, Andrea said, "Now he's her problem."

Andrea visited her grandmother every week and always took Anni, who'd become a celebrity at the nursing home. Dan often joined them and they made a point to stop in and see Nadine as well. He wasn't sure if Nadine really appreciated it. In fact, she'd once snapped, "Why are people always bothering me?" but the sight of Anni softened her and they'd even managed to get her to smile, which was no small thing. Dan thought of it as a good deed done in Christine's memory. Gram was another matter. She was always happy to see them, and usually knew Andrea, but never quite got the knack of who Dan could be. Still, her face lit up at the sight of the dog and she loved petting Anni. Their visits made a difference.

As the months went by, Andrea spent more time at Dan's house. He cooked meals for her and she helped him plant tomatoes and green beans in his garden. They took Anni for long walks in the fields around his house, and once, when Anni raced off after a squirrel and they were momentarily alone, he impulsively pulled Andrea into an embrace and found himself saying, "I love you."

"I was starting to think I'd never hear you say that," she said, which was odd because he felt like this was sudden. Like he'd rushed things. She smiled. "I love you too, Dan."

That fall, Andrea had come over to help pack Lindsay up for the dorms and the two of them seemed friendly-ish, which might be as good as it was going to get. By the time he'd decided the timing was right to propose, his daughter had accepted the idea. She was at college and immersed in her new life there. One weekend when Lindsay was home, he took her along to the jewelers to help pick out the ring. He'd narrowed it down to two different styles, and let her choose between them. "If she says no, can I have it?" she asked, an evil glint in her eye.

"Not a chance," he answered.

Dan wasn't a romantic guy by nature, but he wanted to do this right. He'd thought of a dozen different scenarios for a proposal, but only came up with one that was a good fit for the two of them. The Café Mocha, the place where they officially met, seemed apropos, and Anni needed to play a part as well. When they were done eating, he casually said, "Did you notice Anni's new ID tag?"

"New ID tag?" Andrea said, puzzled. She reached down to Anni's collar and found the heart-shaped tag. "When did you put this on?"

"When you left to go to the bathroom," he said, trying to hold back his grin. "Read it."

She squinted and read, "Anni. If found please return to Andrea Keller . . ." She looked up, confused. "My name and your address?"

He got out of the chair and down on one knee, pulling the box out of his pocket. He flipped open the lid to show her the ring. "Andrea Keller, will you marry me?" He took it all in at once, the way her hand flew up to her mouth, Anni jumping on him, licking his cheek, and the hush that fell over the surrounding tables. He silently prayed he wasn't making a fool of himself. Everything hinged on her answer.

"Yes, I will," she said, tears spilling from her eyes. She leaned down and put a hand on either side of his face and planted a kiss on his lips. A smattering of applause came from around the coffee shop, accompanied by the sound of someone whooping in the background.

"I promise I'll make you very happy," he said.

She whispered into his ear, "You already have."

ACKNOWLEDGMENTS

My gratitude to those who helped get *Hello Love* out into the world is endless.

Terry Goodman, Jessica Poore, and the rest of the team at Amazon are simply the best of the best. Terry, thanks for listening and for making me laugh. Jessica, you're a valuable ally. I hope I stay on your good side.

Many thanks to Kay Bratt, Kate Danley, Kay Ehlers, Khris Erickson, Geri Erickson, "Eagle Eye" Alice L. Kent, Rachel Leamond, and Michelle San Juan, all of whom took the time to offer advice and suggestions.

To Michelle and Ivan San Juan, who would never leave their precious Anni tied up to a signpost outside of a business, thank you for lending me her name and likeness. I'm sorry the fictional Anni had to endure such trials.

Kay Bratt, Chapter Forty is dedicated to you. You know why.

My family—Greg, Charlie, Maria, and Jack McQuestion—are my reasons for living and writing, and I love them all.

Last, and most importantly, I thank the readers who enable me to write novels for a living. You matter more than I can say.

If you have enjoyed this book, and it's not too much trouble, a short review posted on Amazon or Goodreads would be very much appreciated. And if you'd like notification of my upcoming book releases, visit www.karenmcquestion.com and sign up for my newsletter.

ABOUT THE AUTHOR

 Karen McQuestion has written books for kids, teens, and adults, and is published in print, e-book, and audio through Amazon Publishing, Houghton Mifflin Harcourt, and Brilliance Audio. Many of her titles have spent time on the top 100 Kindle list. Her publishing story has been covered by the *Wall Street Journal*, *Entertainment Weekly*, and the national NPR show, *The Story with Dick Gordon*. She has also appeared on ABC's *World News Now* and *America This Morning*. She lives with her husband and kids in Hartland, Wisconsin.